The
WOLF
and
his KING

The WOLF and his KING

FINN LONGMAN

A retelling of 'Bisclavret', from the *Lais* of Marie de France

First published in Great Britain in 2025 by Gollancz
an imprint of The Orion Publishing Group Ltd
Carmelite House, 50 Victoria Embankment
London EC4Y 0DZ

An Hachette UK Company

The authorised representative in the EEA is Hachette Ireland,
8 Castlecourt Centre, Castleknock Road, Castleknock, Dublin 15, D15 XTP3,
Republic of Ireland (email: info@hbgi.ie)

1 3 5 7 9 10 8 6 4 2

A CIP catalogue record for this book
is available from the British Library.

ISBN (Hardback) 978 1 399 62099 4
ISBN (Export Trade Paperback) 978 1 399 62100 7
ISBN (eBook) 978 1 399 62102 1
ISBN (Audio) 978 1 399 62103 8

Typeset by Deltatype Ltd, Birkenhead, Merseyside

Printed in Great Britain by Clays Ltd, Elcograf S.p.A.

MIX
Paper | Supporting
responsible forestry
FSC® C104740

www.gollancz.co.uk

For Emmet, who knows which parts of this book are true.

Historical Note

This novel aims to evoke the world of medieval literature more than it strictly conforms to the facts of medieval history. My source material is, after all, deeply unhistoric in its approach: Marie de France's *Bisclavret* seems to be set in Brittany, amidst a chivalric culture that resembles her own twelfth-century context, and yet features a king, though Brittany was a duchy in this period. (The presence of a werewolf, I find, doesn't trouble historians in the same way.) Marie is pinning Anglo-Norman tails on a fantastical and vaguely 'Celtic' donkey, as is often the case with the so-called Matter of Britain, and her setting must best be understood as 'a place that is familiar to us, but also strange enough that these stories may exist'. For modern readers, this setting is less familiar, with its barons and knights, but it remains a world of story more than history, ideals rather than realities. As such, the novel you are about to read cannot easily be pinned to a particular year, its geography mapped with any great specificity, or its politics compared against records of real wars and dynastic struggles.

Still, if you wanted to place this story in a historical context, you would likely find the second half of the twelfth century to be the best fit; if you seek geography, we are in Brittany, in this universe an independent kingdom. The royal court is most likely to be found in the east of the kingdom and the all-important forest is, perhaps, an echo of Paimpont Forest, the Brocéliande of so many Arthurian tales. I have tried to ensure the material and intellectual culture suits this setting, and to draw as much as I can on contemporary sources when seeking metaphors and imagery. But if I have occasionally indulged in anachronisms (or flights of imagination) for the sake of plot or aesthetics, I have done so safe in the knowledge that medieval authors would never have hesitated to do the same.

Jadis le poeit hum oïr
E sovent suleit avenir,
Hume plusur garval devindrent
E es boscages meisun tindrent.
Garvalf, ceo est beste salvage
Tant cum il est en cele rage,
Hummes devure, grant mal fait,
Es granz forez converse e vait.
Cest afere les ore ester:
Del Bisclavret vus voil cunter.

In the old days, people used to say—
and it often actually happened—
that some men turned into werewolves
and lived in the woods.
A werewolf is a savage beast;
while his fury is on him
he eats men, does much harm,
goes deep in the forest to live.
But that's enough of this now:
I want to tell you about the Bisclavret.

- Marie de France, 'Bisclavret'
(trans. Hanning & Ferrante)

hominis tibi membra sequestro,
generosa et fragmina credo.

Body of a man I bring thee,
Noble even in its ruin.

—Prudentius, 'Hymnus X: Ad Exequias Defuncti'
trans. Helen Waddell

I

Him

He isn't a knight.

He's not even a man, these days – not always, not in the ways that matter. The wolf comes often enough to rob him of a future, but not so often as to rob him of his name. Yet. It tugs at the frayed edges of his mind, pulling loose the threads, and one day, he's sure, the gnawing insanity of his animal skin will win. He'll lose himself, become fully beast: this he knows the way he knows the ache of change when it settles into his bones.

Part of him fears it. Part of him welcomes it. It would hurt less, he thinks sometimes, to lose everything than to bloody his fingers trying to hold onto something already shattering.

For now, he knows himself. Knows when the fragile wonders that are his fingers warp into claws. Knows when his spine shatters, his neck breaks, and his body remakes itself into something unholy. He's grown to recognise the signs – the swelling soreness of his joints, the bite of his teeth against his lips, the taste of his own blood like salt in his mouth – but he still slips out of his skin suddenly enough to be caught off guard and slowly enough to hurt.

It has always been this way.

Bisclavret is used to it.

He lives his life in exile. Quarantine, almost, keeping the

wolf-sickness away from the markets and the towns and most of all the court, where once his father performed great deeds as baron and knight of the king. So his mother told him, anyway, when he was a child and there was still hope of a cure. Not forever, she promised, would they live here on her meagre estate in the shadow of the hills and on the edge of the woods, as far from the salt of the sea as any could be in a land shaken and pummelled by waves. One day, he would receive his father's sword and the gift of his lands, and all would be restored: he to knighthood, she to joy, the wolf to memory and nightmares and half-forgotten tears.

But now she is dead, and the sickness has not left him, the possession not yet undone.

Once, when he was young, there was a priest who saw the damnation that thrust itself into his skin, but did not flee. Nor did he try to exorcise him with rituals and candles, scourge and invective and pain. Instead, he took the bruised, childish hands of the boy in his own and prayed, earnest and terrified. And after a few weeks in his own body, the boy thought, perhaps, that it had worked.

But the wolf came back. It always comes back.

The same priest warned him not to speak of it, as though he needed warning. 'If they know what you are,' he said – clutching his prayer beads, white-knuckled, his mercy only just outweighing his fear – 'they will never let you be anything else.'

He is not sure, in truth, whether he *is* anything else.

Just a wolf-sick boy, exiled and unwanted.

Bisclavret cannot remember a time before the plunging agony of transformation, but as a child it came infrequently, once a month at most. He'd have weeks to forget how it feels to wake with blood under his nails and fogged memories of how the night was spent and a growing fear: *don't let me have hurt anyone.* Now, though, now he loses himself a day each week, sometimes more; he's afraid to keep too close a count of it, for fear he'll find himself calculating how many more years he'll have with a voice before he's robbed of it entirely.

So, no, he's not a man. Just enough-man, enough-human, to know what he's missing. Enough to remember his mother's tales of adventure and feel a hollow grief for something that never was. Enough to know that the secrets written into his skeleton have shaped him into something that can never see the light.

Enough to long for knighthood: a glittering, unattainable dream.

Once, as a child, he saw the knights passing by, the king in their midst and his son at his side and laughter in the air. They hardly seemed like men themselves – they were some new creature, shimmering silver skin like fish scales, as Other as himself, but entirely unlike him. Their eyes were bright; their joy, their brotherhood, was an ache to witness.

Childhood is a distant memory now. And the fair beardless youth amongst those knights, seeking the first thrills of chivalry, is long grown into a man. A man and half an exile himself – even here, Bisclavret has heard tell of the king sending his son and heir to foreign courts to learn better the violence of ruling, the art of war, fearing the quiet prince might be more naturally inclined to the monastery than the battlefield. If he has yet returned, word of it has not reached this place.

But even if the prince is ill-suited to war, he is better suited to the crown than a wolf-man to knighthood.

Bisclavret cannot fathom why the Almighty formed him in this body; he wonders, sometimes, if his nature is a test and a trial, the Adversary at work to torment his mother like Job. If so, she did not live long enough to receive her reward on earth, for she died believing him possessed and his future bleak. Perhaps

3

she was right. It is not for him to pretend to be something blessed. It would be presumptuous – blasphemous, even – for such a creature to shrive himself in the chapel and let them paint the cross on his forehead before raising him to sword and horse and brotherhood.

And even if it were not a sin and a lie, the risk is too great. One day he may lose his mind along with his body, and then what? Would he kill, or only maul? Without human reason to restrain his actions, would he reveal himself to be the monster he's always feared, secretly, that he is?

No. Bisclavret knows his place, and he is not a knight. He will never be a knight.

But he will dream of them, all the same.

✳ ✴ ✳

'He'll be crowned in a week, and there'll be a hunt to celebrate.'

His cousin. Resplendent in court garb, all bright colour over gleaming mail, the finest armour his lord can bestow upon him. When, as children, they played at knighthood together, it was not to a landless life of service to another lord that either aspired – but his cousin is a younger son, an inconvenience, sent here to this estate as a companion to his infirm kinsman and only later to court. By then there was no money to equip him, but he's found a lord, and a part to play, which is more than can be said of Bisclavret.

His cousin is still travel-stained from his long journey, but his eyes gleam with possibilities. Two days' hard riding to bring word: the king is dead, the prince recalled from distant courts, the kingdom altered. An accident, a terrible shock, of course, but amidst the mourning many perceive the jewel of opportunity. The young prince – now king – has been gone long enough that none at court may yet claim his favour, and it is a rich fruit to be plucked.

'I cannot see what this has to do with me,' says Bisclavret, folding his arms. He has lost weight this summer. The wolf takes it from him, punishing him for keeping it from hunting the way it craves.

'You owe him oaths,' his cousin reminds him. 'Your mother's land is yours. You are a noble, however pitiful your estates. You will be expected at the coronation to swear your fealty.'

Bisclavret's heart sinks. He inherited his land some four years past, and ought by rights to have sworn to the old king, but the man was cantankerous and disinterested in the doings of minor gentry, so long as they held back from poaching in his forests and parks. His cousin is right, though: he will be expected at the coronation. Three days' journey, at the least, if he doesn't want to torment his horse the way his cousin has done these past two days; a night or several in the king's hall; the same journey in return.

Too much entirely for a man with a wolf in his skin.

'It's not possible,' he tells his cousin. 'I will have to send my apologies. Meet him when next he takes a circuit. Tell him I am infirm, or injured, or—'

'But this is your chance,' his cousin interjects. 'Did your mother not always plan to present you at court and reclaim your inheritance? The new king will be seeking loyal barons. No doubt he will be more than ready to restore your land, in exchange for your gratitude and good favour …'

'A nice idea,' says Bisclavret drily. 'You have forgotten the wolf.'

'I have forgotten nothing,' says his cousin. He was all of twelve summers old when he learned the true nature of Bisclavret's infirmity and has kept faith with him in the years since, when most would have turned their back. 'But you can't mean to spend the rest of your life here. Your father was a knight. A baron. His place should have been yours.'

And if his father had waited just a month or two longer to die in the old king's service, it would have been. As it was, he died without sons, Bisclavret still in his mother's womb, and his land reverted to the crown.

'Then perhaps the king will grant me lands on his next circuit, but I cannot travel that long. The wolf—'

'Surely you can manage a week,' says his cousin, but he must read the answer in Bisclavret's expression, because concern crosses his face for the first time. 'Does it truly come so often, now?'

Bisclavret looks away. He has done his best to create the impression of the wolf as an infrequent visitor – an occasional lapse, not a constant haunting. All men, after all, have moments of weakness. But weekly ... weekly starts to look like a habit.

'Sometimes,' he says. 'Especially in the winter. I think the cold ...'

His cousin doesn't care for technicalities. 'You can transform on the road. There will be no one to see you. Once at court, if you slip away, I can make some excuse for you, and they'll be none the wiser. No one will be surprised by a little eccentricity, in any case, after so long in exile.'

Nobody expects you to be more than a rustic fool, he means; it's funny how he intends this as encouragement. As though the people of the court will overlook Bisclavret's appearance, too: the way the wolf leaves him lean and hungry, burns a sharpness into his bones that no amount of hearty food can fill out; his hair, always overlong; his skin, disfigured by small scars, souvenirs of another life. Now and again, he runs his fingers over the marks and tries to remember how they got there, but

6

a wolf's memories map uneasily onto a man's body. How can he remember hurting his hand, when hours ago he didn't have hands at all?

And his clothes – he only needs to glance at his cousin to know that his own clothes are hopelessly old-fashioned, the cheap blue and brown dyes faded with age. Fine clothes would be quickly ruined by being shrugged from a changing body and abandoned somewhere out among the trees, but he cannot appear before the king looking like he works his own fields.

'You assume I choose the time and place of my changing,' he tells his cousin. 'I do not. The wolf comes when it wills, and this is too great a risk. You will take my apologies to the court.' And he will never regain his inheritance, and he will never be a knight, and he will pretend to forget the youthful games he played, sparring with his cousin as though he could ever be anything other than this: a monster poorly disguised in human skin.

'Bisclavret,' says his cousin sharply. 'Do you intend to do nothing but waste away here? How long will you hide yourself from the world?'

How *long*? He has never been granted the reprieve of an end-date for his condition. It is a fact of him, more certain than the shape of his teeth or the rhythm of his heart, they that are as changeable as all his mutable flesh. There will never come a time when it is safe for him to step out of his seclusion.

His cousin again reads the answer in his face, and for a moment his frustration is tinged with grief, as though Bisclavret's concerns are tragic rather than rational. 'Your mother would have wanted you to seek your birthright,' he says. 'Your inheritance is yours to claim.'

'My mother kept me here and died in exile rather than risk

the danger you are suggesting,' Bisclavret points out. 'I cannot be my father. I wouldn't know how to begin.'

'I would help you,' says his cousin, and now he is almost begging. 'I would be your man, if you would will it.'

So he thinks to exchange his lord for Bisclavret. That explains his pleading; to serve his own family would be an easier yoke than service to another man in exchange for his arms. But he is asking for the impossible.

'I cannot make this journey. I cannot sleep in the king's hall. Imagine if the change—'

'I would help you,' says his cousin again. 'Find you a place to sleep – the stables, if you insist, somewhere secluded. And you will swear your oaths to the king and speak to him of your father and he will restore you, and then you will have your own land, enough of it to roam in your wolfing, in place of this patch of fields. Wouldn't that be a fair exchange?'

He makes it sound tempting. Tempting, and dangerous, and just enough like their childish dreams of glory to burrow deep into his heart and tug on the buried, secret desires he hid away once he grew too old to play at knighthood and too wolf-sick to pretend humanity. But his father's lands – the lands that were promised to him, a home where he could live safely rather than in exile …

Wouldn't that be worth it? A few days of struggle, for the years of safety that might follow? Perhaps, if he is careful, the wolf might be kept at bay long enough to make it possible.

'I cannot stay for the hunt,' he warns his cousin. 'I'll have to leave after the coronation. The risk increases with every day I spend at the castle.'

A smile casts its light on his cousin's face. 'So you will come.'

'I will come,' he says, heavily. 'And swear my oaths, and see what results of it. But if the king grants me nothing then let that be the end. I will not beg him.'

'You think it so likely that you'll fail to impress him?'

Bisclavret remembers the king as a boy, scarcely more than a child, fair-haired and wondering as he rode out amongst his father's knights. He can't imagine that head bearing a crown, that mouth speaking oaths. He can't imagine how it will feel to kneel before him, to swear fealty, to kiss him.

'A king with good judgment would see the truth of me,' he says finally. 'And will know what to do with that truth.'

His cousin reaches out and tucks a strand of Bisclavret's hair behind his ear. 'He will see you as your father's son,' he says, and it is the kindest thing anybody has said to him in longer than he cares to acknowledge. 'But first we must find you some better clothes, or he will see you as a peasant. Come. There's no time to be wasted.'

2

You

✦ ✵ ✦

The feast has hardly begun and already you are weary of it. It has been a long day of oaths and promises, the new weight of your father's crown heavy on your brow. You suppose you'll grow accustomed to it, just as you'll grow used to being at the centre of festivities, the object of everybody's eye. For now it remains strange, unfamiliar after three years as an unwanted prince at another's table, and the castle feels less like the home of your childhood and more like a gaol of cold stone closing around you.

A month ago it was summer, and your father was alive. Then a fall from his horse, a festered wound, and he was gone; the messenger sent to fetch you said little more than that, and didn't need to. You thought you had longer. But now the trees have dropped their leaves and the winter is fast approaching, the many hearths of the castle unable to chase the chill from the air or beat back the encroaching blackness.

And you are king, and this feast is in your honour. If only you wanted it.

Your mood is at odds with the festivities, your father's knights and retainers deep in their cups, every loyal man from across the kingdom dressed in his finery and seeking joy and good company. You received their oaths today, and their kisses, and it should warm your heart to know that they love you, but they loved your father too, and do not know you, and only owe you their swords.

The noise of the hall drowns the senses. Half-shouted conversations obscure each other, a mess of sound by the time they reach you; voices compete with the minstrels for volume. You squash the futile urge to flee. They have scarcely let you outside the castle walls since your return, and you ache with the need to walk down to the lake and see if it still reflects the stars of the clear autumn night in its inky depths, the way it did before you were sent away. To let the darkness dance your feet to somewhere you hardly know; to follow the tracks of the deer deep into the forest; to remember the land you were kept from.

Instead you sit here, on this dais, away from the mass of faces you half recall. They have left space on either side of you for the wife you don't have and the favoured ones you wouldn't know to invite to your side. A little way down the table sit your barons and advisors, deep in conversation with each other and ignoring you; at the other end sit the ladies of the household. One is the daughter of your father's most favoured knight, lately deceased; she will remain under your protection until she marries, halfway to a sister or a niece. She is accompanied by a kinswoman of hers, you think, and two maids, but while she offers you a fleeting smile when she catches your gaze, it cannot diminish the space between you and make this seat a less lonely one.

They might have thought to choose company for you, you think resentfully; they must have known you had nobody to summon to your side. You haven't so much as a squire to serve you at table. Your only true friend in the castle is the scribe you brought back with you from your exile, and he would never be permitted to sit beside you, if he were invited to a feast like this at all. Even your knights are strangers these days, though you see among them the faces of those you knew as a youth. It will take time to earn their companionship again, whatever oaths they've sworn.

'Sire?' Someone wants your attention. You thought you'd done your duty, the rituals of the day over; you'd resent the petition, except that it interrupts your loneliness. 'Sire, I beg a moment of your time on behalf of my cousin.'

You look up. The voice belongs to a knight you recognise but don't know well, though you could hardly be said to know any of them well, now. He's a lesser knight, sworn to one of your men, arrayed in his livery; you can't remember where he hails from, but you have a vague sense that it's somewhere quaint and rustic, and that he has rather more brothers than any man hopes to have in the line of inheritance ahead of him.

He is also, to your surprise, spattered with mud, his once-bright clothes soiled by bad weather and a hard ride. It's unlike him to appear dishevelled, nor were you aware that he had any cousins with whom you might concern yourself.

'Your cousin?' you say, half-engaged despite your exhaustion.

'He would have been here this afternoon, sire, to swear to you as was proper, but the elements turned against us and our horses were lamed some thirty miles from here.'

And by the looks of him they'd been travelling some time before that happened. Most likely he's one of these very minor nobles with scarcely enough land to raise his taxes – a coastal backwater, perhaps, or something out in the hills to the west. His absence this afternoon would have been noted by your sen-eschal and the record-keepers, but you hadn't marked it.

'I daresay I can find it in me not to see disloyalty in his absence,' you say, dredging up a smile, and the knight returns it, nervously. 'Bring him forward, then. A feast is as good a place as any to take a man's oath.'

No doubt your seneschal would feel differently. But the knight looks relieved. He turns and gestures, and a man begins moving across the hall towards you. He has a loping stride, easy as a huntsman over rough ground and just as unsuited to a feasting-hall; he covers the distance in moments, and then he is standing before you.

He's near enough your own age, give or take a year or two – slightly younger than his cousin, you'd guess, and even more rustic in his dress. He has no armour and no surcoat: he's clad in red wool over a blue undertunic, his sleeves cropped and practical, and he wears no hood or cap, so that his damp hair falls unfashionably loose and long past his shoulders. But he has a rough-hewn beauty, unpolished, all cheekbones and sharp eyes and eyebrows like sword-slashes.

He bows his head. 'Sire,' he says, taking your hand and kissing it. 'I must humbly beg your forbearance for my absence at the oath-taking. It was not disrespect that kept me, but poor weather and a difficult road.' His voice is hoarse, low – strained, perhaps, by the ravages of his journey. The cold weather has flushed pink his cheeks and nose, and there is something unsophisticated yet lovely about it, juxtaposed as it is with the coal-black of his eyes and his dark hair.

'Indeed, it's clear you've had no easy journey,' you remark, raking your eyes over his muddied clothes; whichever servant took his cloak did a poor job of brushing the dirt from his chausses and boots before they let him into the hall. 'What is your name?'

The young man glances up and meets your eyes. 'Bisclavret,' he says.

Bisclavret.

You mouth the name to yourself, tasting it, trying to place it. You can't; you don't think you've ever heard it before. No

chance, then, that this man is a long-forgotten childhood play-
mate, here to rekindle an acquaintance. A relief, in truth, for
after years away you have enough difficulty matching names to
faces without attempting to recall the friendship of another age.

But you would know more of this man – understand him
better before you take his oath. 'Where is it you have travelled
from, Bisclavret?' you ask, taking no small thrill from the shape
of the name on your tongue as you voice it.

He names a place you have never been, and adds, 'Some way
to the west, before the mountains proper, with woodland on
one side.' It is the description one gives when expecting no
familiarity with an estate; it must be very small, for you never to
have heard of it. 'The land was my mother's dower, and passed
to me now four years ago.'

So his mother is dead. 'And what befell your father?'

'He was killed in your father's service a little more than a
quarter-century ago, a month before my birth.' He hesitates,
glancing sideways at his cousin for help, but the knight only
nods encouragement. Bisclavret continues: 'He was a baron of
the old king, and when he died without issue, his lands reverted
to the crown. I ... I did not inherit. Sire,' he adds, a little hastily.

For a wild moment, you're struck by the absurd desire to
ask him to call you by your name. Nobody has done so since
you returned from your exile, as though the syllables have been
forgotten in your absence and you are nothing to them now but
your crown.

But you refrain. 'You have been as much an exile as I have,
then, and for far longer. Your mother didn't think to bring you
to court, and ask for the return of your inheritance?' Your father
might have granted it, if he liked the old baron enough; he was
not an especially loving man, but he could be generous to those
who pleased him.

Now he does falter, looking to his cousin again. The knight steps in: 'Motherhood suited my mother's sister ill, and she was often unwell. I was fostered on her estate for some years in my youth, to give company to Bisclavret and ease the burden on her. She would not have felt able to come to court. It is, as we have found, no easy journey to make.'

And it is the cousin who has prompted him to make it, you suspect, for Bisclavret looks as uneasy here as you feel, his discomfort greater than can be attributed to his wet clothes. But those must be unpleasant enough.

'Come,' you say, and gesture to the bench beside you, close as it is to the warmth of the hearth. 'Sit by me, and tell me of your father, and I will take your oath when you are dry and fed as any of the king's men should be. Both of you,' you add hastily. 'You have both suffered on your travels, and have need of the fire.'

The knight's eyes widen, for few of his status would be offered a place beside a king at a feast. But he must recognise the invitation as the hollow courtesy that it is, for he bows and says, 'You have my gratitude, sire, but I must to my lord. I will leave my cousin in your hands.'

'But—' Bisclavret begins, as though about to object to his abandonment, but his cousin nudges him forward with an encouraging look and then is gone, off to find his own lord and the comforts of his proper place.

You are not sorry for his absence, for it leaves you alone with Bisclavret, unpolished and lovely as he is. For the first time all evening, you have stopped counting the moments until you can leave.

'Sit,' you say again, gesturing to the seat beside you.

With that same bestial grace, Bisclavret circumnavigates the table and sits beside you.

'Are you hungry?' you ask him. There is enough food in front of you for a dozen close companions to dine at your side, and you have only been picking at it, but it is clear he is unsure whether he is allowed to accept the offer. You take pity on his unease and push a dish towards him, so that politeness demands he take a portion. He's slender, even gaunt – not starving, for he lacks that hollow-eyed look, but still he is thin in the way of a man who burns more fuel than he can replace. And after such a journey as the one he has had, he will be in need of sustenance.

The hearth is warm, and you see the tension in his body begin to ease as that warmth reaches him, tempering the chill of his damp clothes.

'Tell me,' you say, when you deem that he has settled enough to answer, 'are you here to beg me for your father's lands? Do you come seeking your fortune and advancement?'

There is a moment's pause while he chews and swallows his mouthful of food, and then he says, in a steady tone, 'I am here to swear fealty to you, sire. The capacity in which I do so is for you to decide.'

A smile tugs at your lips. 'You mean if I were to make you a knight and lord of your father's lands, you would swear to me as such and forget that you had come here with only your mother's estate to your name.'

He inclines his head in acknowledgment of the remark, both the possibility and the humour in it. 'I would not forget my exile, for it is all I have known. I think perhaps you are a man who knows what it is like to become yourself away from the lands that should have been your home.'

Is that what you have been doing, these last few years: becoming yourself? Perhaps. You have practised the arts of the chase and the kill enough to satisfy even your father, and if you have also gained an education in the discourses of the scholars and clerics while you were about it, well, he is too dead to know of it. Mostly, you've been learning what it's like to be alone in the world, away at a court that bears little love for your kingdom and its stubborn refusal to be annexed into a greater empire.

'Forgive me,' he says, worried by your silence. 'I spoke out of turn.'

'No,' you say. 'Perhaps you are right. Perhaps I have learned myself in my exile, and I will not readily forget it.' You regard him for a long moment – so long that he flushes scarlet, as intriguing as it is becoming. He has the sinewy physique of a man not built for inactivity, and you would sooner see him amidst the woodlands of his home than here in this hall, hazy with smoke and drowning in voices and the strumming of minstrels.

You imagine it is beautiful there, this lonely estate of his in the shadow of the hills and the trees. You have long been enchanted by woodlands as more than a home for game and a place of hunting: by the way the spring blossoms and the pale green of new leaves defy the lingering remnants of the winter chill; by the bluebells gathering along the borders to herald the coming of summer; by the rich colours of the autumn, all bronze and brass and candlelight. Bisclavret would look well there.

Impulse stirs your tongue to action. 'Ride out with us tomorrow,' you say, before you can think better of it. 'The hunt.'

He blushes so easily, this interesting young man. 'I could not,' he says. 'I am not ... prepared.'

Of course – his horse is lame, his clothes filthy from travel, and he will have no hounds or weapons to contribute. But no matter. 'I will have you outfitted,' you say. 'I have many a fine courser for you to ride, and no shortage of equipment.'

'That is ... very kind, sire, but—'

You want him on that hunt. You want to know what he is capable of; you want an excuse to ride with him; you have the sense that if you do not press him now, he will slip between your fingers and disappear, back to his home, for another quarter-century of quiet absence, and you will never see him again.

'Your father must have ridden out with mine,' you say, carefully calculating. 'It would have been a way for him to prove his skill. His fitness for war, should it be needed.'

Do you want your father's lands? you might have said to him. *This is how you prove yourself to me. This is how you earn them.*

Bisclavret hears it, and you see his desire warring with something you can't identify – some fear, some inner conflict. Perhaps a lingering remnant of his exile, a shyness amidst the unfamiliar court.

'Ride out with us,' you say again, leaning towards him. 'Let me see what manner of man you are.'

He bites his lip, and your gaze is caught by it. You cannot look away from his mouth. If he had a courtier's manners, he would not feel able to refuse you. He would do whatever his king asked of him.

You asked him, in part, because he doesn't.

'If you wish, sire,' he says at last, and some forgotten part of your heart howls in triumph.

3

Other

✦ ✴ ✦

the forest is rain on moss and rotting leaves,
bright fresh scents away from the smoke
and the heady human smell of wine and rich food
that nags at memory – *where was I?* – a snare
the shape of borrowed clothes on lost skin
and music in a mind that has no word for song.

discordant with itself, lost in a castle –
the king – the song twists – *when I was me*
when I was whole I was at the castle
and the king – becomes forest-sharp,
becomes a hunger like being unmade,
pulling apart a body newly created.
it begs to run from a place unknowable,
and the hunger is a gnawing thing,
a beast in itself, guiltless and bloodied.

small deaths, sheep deaths, swift and simple
as the scent of iron. tomorrow the debt,
tonight the loss and the hunger and the blood.
walking a wolf's track leaves a wolf's prints,
sure as winter – *this is not me this is not*

what I am meant to be – sure as hunger,
no way around it but to run and running
is a kind of death with all that falls behind.

but sometimes there's nothing, no choice
but movement, no whisper but teeth,
and every heartbeat murmurs run

               and run

                  and run

     will I ever stop?

4

You

Ride out with us.

You've hardly slept, remembering his hesitation, that fear and desire tangled up in each other. What is it that Bisclavret is afraid of – and what is it that he wants?

You rise early, before the huntsmen have set off. Dawn is uneasy and grey, but there's a fresh scent in the air: the rain has passed, and if your luck holds, the sun will shine later.

Impatience hums beneath your skin as a servant stitches tight your sleeves, such that eventually, with the uncertainty of one still adjusting to your edict to *speak to me, in the name of God, I cannot abide this silence*, he asks, 'Are you excited for the hunt, my lord?'

That's a sound enough excuse for your twitching, you suppose. Though excitement doesn't come close to touching this tangle of feelings: the relief at leaving the castle and breathing fresher air; the thrill and the fear of a boar hunt with all its dangers; the ever-present awareness that this is a test. Your people no longer know you, and they wish to. Today will demonstrate your strength and skill in arms and your father's canniness in sending you away to learn, or it will mark you the unmanly failure of a son he thought you were when last you saw each other. It's a heavy burden to place on a spear and a dagger.

'Yes,' you say absently, when you realise that the servant is waiting for an answer. 'Yes, it will be welcome to hunt here again. I have been gone too long.'

When you are dressed – and oh, how welcome these more practical clothes, free of the trailing sleeves of your coronation bliaut; you are already tired of being decorative – you descend to the hall, where your lords are waking, their eagerness for the hunt tempered by the heavy remnants of last night's festivities weighing down their heads. You scan their ranks for Bisclavret, but there is no sign of him.

But there, by the door, far from the hearth, is his cousin. You cross to him. 'Is Bisclavret here? I had thought to take him to be equipped for the hunt. I'm aware he did not travel prepared.'

His cousin blinks, and swallows. 'He is ... that is to say, he was taken ill after the feast, and left to seek relief. I believe the air in here was too close for him, and the wine too strong.'

'Ill?' You choke back your dismay. It will be nothing serious. 'Wine-sickness, I assume? He would not be alone in that.'

'Something of the sort,' admits the cousin, but he looks uneasy, and his fingers twist in the fabric of his surcoat. 'He intended to sleep in the stables, I think. He cares a great deal for his horse, and after the journey ...'

A kind man to care so much for his lamed horse that he would give up his place by the fire to spend the night with her. 'Then I will seek him there. Thank you.'

The knight looks startled by your thanks. 'Sire,' he begins. 'I must ask ...'

'Speak freely.' You are not surprised that those who knew your father are hesitant to offer opinions or indulge their curiosity, but it's tiresome nonetheless, when you have no intention of punishing them for it. It will be far easier to rule if you are loved and understood than if you are not.

'How did you convince him?' He cannot look at you as he speaks. 'He is reclusive, shy; it took some cajoling to convince him to travel for the coronation itself, and he was determined that he could not stay, but would leave when he was pledged to you. But now he has agreed to ride out with the hunt.'

'He is not yet pledged to me,' you say, as if that explains it, and perhaps it does, desire and obligation keeping Bisclavret here, his father's lands held to ransom. But still he hesitated when you asked him to stay – you saw that. You saw how he almost refused you, and it charmed you, that he considered saying no to a king.

'Then you have promised him something more?' asks his cousin. 'His inheritance?'

Oh, he is clever, this landless knight, engineering this situation to bring his cousin back into the court's favour and restore a family impoverished by the old baron's death and the past quarter-century away from the court. Perhaps, if Bisclavret rises, he stands to gain a knight's fee of his own, and that, for a man with too many brothers, would be heady enough temptation to risk retrieving his cousin from his exile. Especially if he alone has kept faith with him, and knows Bisclavret owes him for that loyalty.

'I would know his capabilities,' you say, half an answer and far from a promise. 'Is there much hunting, on his estate?'

'Not of boar. Largely hares, foxes. We haven't the land for deer.'

We. Interesting. 'Then this will be a test of his mettle, too, I suppose. Will you be riding with us?' Properly, he should ride with his own lord, but you're sure the man can spare him, if it will put Bisclavret at ease to have a familiar face beside him.

'If my lord can spare me a horse,' says the cousin. 'My own will not be fit for hunting for some time yet.'

'Oh, have no fear about that. I will ensure you a mount.' Your father loved his horses, possibly more than he loved his son; his stables are the finest in the land. 'I'm going to the stables now, to arrange one for Bisclavret. I will have them saddle one for you, too.'

'Sire, you are too kind,' begins the knight.

You flash him an unkingly smile. 'I am a man alone in his own home. What have I to lose by cultivating friends? Fear not, I'll speak to your lord and ease the sting of his loss; I'm sure he'll not begrudge me the use of you. Be at the assembly when the huntsmen return, and I'll find you there.'

He doesn't blush as easily as his cousin, but his embarrassment and pleasure is plain nonetheless in the pink tips of his ears and the stammering way he thanks you for your attention. A novelty, still, to have men grateful for these scraps of friendship, when for so long you have been too unimportant and unwanted to be worth befriending by any but the other outcasts and exiles scrabbling for a place in a court they don't belong to.

But that is melancholy speaking, and ill becomes a king.

You make your way out of the keep and into the courtyard, still sheltered by the castle walls but with a sharp bite to the air nonetheless. It's past Michaelmas, and winter is rushing in – too fast for one newly crowned, who has had no time to ready his kingdom for the cold months. At least this wave-tossed peninsula of yours has gentler claws than the inland courts you've known these past years; here there will be less snow to besiege you in your castles, a lighter frost. But storms will harry the coast and keep the fishermen from their work, and an ill-prepared kingdom is a kingdom that starves.

Your own death of cold would be carelessness, but the loss of your people would be cruelty. If they do not live to see Candlemas, it will be your sin to answer for.

The stables have changed little in your time away. You even think you recognise a few of the grooms as they hasten around you, making preparations for the hunt. You enquire after Bisclavret's horse, and they gesture towards a stall at the end of the row, and you squash your inane anticipation as you walk towards it.

You see his horse first: a reliable-looking dun courser with sorrowful eyes. One of her forelegs is swollen, though the grooms have taken care of her with their poultices and bandaging. She snuffles despondently at your empty palm and consents to your touch, but your hand stills when you catch sight of Bisclavret.

He's still asleep, curled up in the straw like a servant boy. He's twig-thin and birch-pale, wearing only his undertunic and that with the sleeves loose. His chausses are torn, the left almost ripped from his leg entirely; his bare feet are obscenely white against the muddied floor. His hands and face are filthy, his hair tangled, a scratch across his cheek.

'Bisclavret,' you say, coming a little further into the stall. 'Bisclavret?'

He was taken ill, his cousin told you, but you cannot see how wine-sickness would have left him in this state. He is so still that for a moment you fear he is dead.

'Bisclavret,' you say again, more loudly, and this time he stirs. You see the moment he becomes aware of your presence: the crease of concern in his forehead, the tightening of his muscles as the discomfort of the cold air registers to his underdressed body. He looks down at his feet first, then at you, and you see his mouth curl into an oath or some utterance of despair as he realises the aspect he's presenting. 'Be easy. I won't judge you. Are you well?'

What a foolish question, when he is clearly not. But he pauses a moment and then nods. 'Yes, I'm well,' he says. 'I was …

taken badly, last night. I am not used to the wine. I will be fit to hunt, if still you want me there.' His words are unsteady, dealt out one by one like coins or blows. 'I'm sorry, sire, that you saw me like this.'

'Rare would be the man who has never been found dishevelled after a feast,' you say, and press him no further about his disarray. 'Come. I will arrange for a bath, and clothes, while we wait for the huntsmen to return. By the time we break our fast, you will have entirely forgotten your wine-sickness.'

He is taller than you, and broader-shouldered; nothing of yours will fit him. But the servants will be able to source something – hunting clothes of your father's, maybe, stripped of ornament and destined to be remade into something new.

'I thank you, but ...' he begins, and then abandons whatever argument had leapt to his tongue, perhaps remembering that you promised him clothes even before finding him like this.

'Then it will be done. Come. Your cousin will ride with us. He tells me boar hunts are rare on your estate.'

Bisclavret pushes himself to his feet, wincing. 'This is true,' he acknowledges. 'Though I am aware of the principles. I hope I will not disappoint you.'

And you will endeavour not to disappoint the court, and the shade of your father. 'It will be a fierce chase. And boar can be dangerous, even to a hale man. I could call a physician to examine you, if you have any doubt about your fitness to hunt.'

'No,' he says quickly, and then recalls his manners. 'Thank you. I am uninjured.'

But he stumbles, and when you extend your hand to steady him, his grip betrays both his strength and his need. His feet are bruised and bloody, belying his claims to health. 'Are you quite sure?' you ask him. 'It would be no trouble.'

'I am well,' he insists.

If he is determined not to see a physician, you won't force him. But you look doubtfully at his bare feet, and observe, 'You have lost your boots.'

'... Yes,' he admits, reluctantly, as if for a moment he intended to claim otherwise.

'I will find you another pair. Can you walk as far as the keep or will I ask the servants to bring water for a bath here?'

'Don't put them to that effort,' he says. 'I will manage.'

It is your right to put them to that effort. You are their king. But you don't feel inclined to remind him of that, when he has finally forgotten to call you *sire* or to look at you as though it causes him pain to regard the gold of your crown.

You take him to the kitchen, on the basis that the ever-burning cook fires make it the warmest place within the castle walls and he has not stopped shivering since he woke. They're startled to see you darkening their door, but usher Bisclavret inside with promises that he will be bathed. From there, it's easy enough to ask a servant to seek out clothes sturdy enough for hunting and fine enough not to shame the man.

With those orders dispatched, there is nothing left to be done but to return to the stables and select a mount to be saddled for Bisclavret, and a second for his cousin – the steadiest hunters your father ever had trained. The horses remember you, at least, and as they press their soft noses against your neck and breathe warm breath in your face, you feel a little more like you have come home, and not exchanged one exile for another.

But still the court is changed, made new – and Bisclavret is a part of that strangeness, his presence altering everything around. Perhaps this is a natural curiosity about an untested man who might be a knight, but it feels stronger than that. Fascination has ensnared you, novelty only part of the tangle of desire. His reticence, his blush, his almost-refusal, as though he owes no oaths … He is something new, this fellow exile, and you have only scratched the surface of understanding him.

You would know him for who he is, if he will allow you to see.

The hunt will test him. The hunt will test you both.

5

Him

Pathetic. He couldn't manage a single night at court without the wolf ripping itself out of his skin. He'll be lucky if he wasn't seen; he's still not sure how he stumbled back into the stables, wretched and hardly human, to sleep off the exhaustion and the pain of the change. And to be found there by the king—

Bisclavret doesn't know whether to treasure the memory of the king's hand in his, supporting him as he stumbled, or whether to bury it beneath the humiliation of having revealed himself as one so base and bestial as to be unable to sleep a night in the hall without fleeing for the stables like some over-whelmed peasant. What manner of man would behave in such a way? Not one a king would be inclined to raise to knighthood and his inheritance, that's for sure, and who could blame him, when it is so abundantly apparent that Bisclavret is unfit for it?

He's lucky the king didn't insist on calling the physicians, who would bleed him until he fainted, if they didn't summon a churchman to chase the demons from inside his head. If there were a cure, he'd have found it years ago. He purged himself often enough when he was younger, seeking out herbs deadly to wolves in the hope of killing it. Forgetting – not caring – that some of them are deadly to men, too.

At least it was never his mother who found him in these

moments of despair. It was his cousin, once, when he was fourteen and wretched and wishing for nothing so much as an end to it. His cousin who nursed him back to health. He has yet to repay that debt, and the greater one incurred by his cousin's faithfulness in keeping his secret; maybe that's why he's still here, allowing the castle servants to wash him and dress him in somebody else's clothes. He cannot reward his cousin's faith while he has nothing, but once he has secured his inheritance, all will be different.

If the king sees fit to restore it to him, after what he has seen.

It will sting, Bisclavret thinks, to return to his exile now that he knows what he is missing. Now that he has tasted his father's life. The feast – yes, it was overwhelming, all the noise and people and colours and smells. Maybe there was something of the wolf in him even then, and that's why he couldn't bear the cacophony of scents, and why the colours were too bright and every instinct screamed for him to *run*. His body ached as though the warmth of the fires caused his joints to swell and push against themselves, and he should have known then that it was coming, but he was distracted. Caught out by the soft gold of the king's hair, his kind smile, the exhausted shadows beneath his eyes.

But it was also so full of *joy*. The food, the fire, the fantasy of belonging. Sitting at the king's side while he enquired, quite sincerely, about lands and names and wants.

Are you here to beg me?

He's here to take whatever he can get, whether it's another minute or a lifetime of pretending he's human.

It's odd to be dressed by another, but the clothes the servants have brought him make it necessary, with side laces in places he can't quite reach and sleeves that need to be sewn tight to his arms. Quite the fine man he'll look, when they're finished;

he tries not to think how troublesome these fastenings will be should the wolf return again, though he hopes last night's disaster has earned him a few days of humanity.

He runs his hands over the soft wool, wondering at the feel of the cloth under his fingertips. It is always his hands he misses most, when the wolf comes. They look so fragile, now that he is himself: fingers so easily broken, nails so easily chipped. The tendons standing out below the skin may as well be ribbons, fit for nothing but adorning the braids of a woman's hair.

A woman. The thought snags a memory. There was a woman, wasn't there, at the feast last night, on the dais with the king? He saw her watching them. Wondering, perhaps, why the king was speaking with a man so poorly dressed, a man who hasn't even sworn the fealty he owes. She can't be the king's sister – it's well known that he's an only child, for his mother died when he was still a babe, and the old king never took another woman to wife. Heartbreak or disinterest, the rumours can't agree. Some other lady of the household, then, but who?

The servant finishes arranging Bisclavret's mantle – that, at least, is his, one small fragment of familiarity amidst the muddied and clouded selfhood bestowed by the borrowed clothes. Impulsively, Bisclavret asks, 'The woman. At the feast. Who is she?'

The servant looks startled by the question, but doesn't need to ask which woman he means. 'The king's ward, my lord,' he says. 'Daughter to his father's favoured knight, may God rest both their souls.'

Ward. Well, that explains her presence in the castle. No doubt she's under his protection until she marries. 'Does she hunt? Will she ride out with us today?'

'On a boar hunt?' says the servant, incredulous. 'No, my lord. But she has a taste for falconry.'

Of course. No lady would join a boar hunt; he had briefly forgotten the danger the day offers, the rarer thrill of a riskier chase. It is a shame, though, that there will be no opportunity to pursue her better acquaintance, for in the glimpse he caught of her at the feast, she had the same quick smile as the king, a certain laughter in her eyes. He would have liked to know her better.

Never mind that. 'I have been promised weapons. Where will I find them?'

The servant gives him directions, and Bisclavret leaves the warmth of the kitchen and embarks on his search. He is gratified to be met with no questioning when he arrives, so the king must have sent word: they readily equip him with a crossed spear and a long dagger. His own sword, in the stables with his saddlebags, is ill-suited to hunting.

From there, there's no further reason to delay returning to the stables, to collect the fine bay courser the king has had saddled for him. She's finer than his own horse, though it feels disloyal to think so, but she's steady, too: he knows it at once from the way she ducks her head to his touch and stands perfectly still, awaiting a rider. He is at no risk of this mount startling on the chase.

It stings, a little, that he will prove himself in borrowed clothes, with borrowed weapons, on a borrowed horse – the king's fancy, unequal to those who bring their own hounds to the hunt. But at least his equipment will not put him to shame.

The assembly is embarking on breakfast when he arrives, the king deep in conversation with the returned huntsmen about their findings. He glances up, catches sight of Bisclavret, and raises a hand in both greeting and summons.

Hesitantly, Bisclavret gives the horse's reins into the care of a groom and weaves his way through the crowd to the king.

'Good morning, sire,' he offers, as though their earlier meeting did not occur.

The king eyes his new clothes. 'A marked improvement, I would say, wouldn't you?' he comments, with a twist of a smile to ease the sting of insult towards Bisclavret's older clothes. 'I'd allow that you would keep them, but alas, they are not mine to dispose of. Still, we'll have better made up for you in no time.'

He speaks as though he intends for Bisclavret to remain at court. As though it would be no remarkable thing for the king to give new clothes to this countrified noble with only a handful of acres to his name. *Yes*, whispers his heart, triumphant: *yes, let me stay*. But Reason, ever cautious, reminds his heart of the unwelcome truth: *it's impossible*.

'You are most generous, sire,' he says at last, as neutrally as he can. The king himself looks well this morning, though he has traded the silk and embroidery of his coronation gown for plainer wool. The warm coppery orange of his tunic over his red chausses speaks of autumn leaves and the warmth of hearth-fires, fitting colours for an October chase; the white fur trim of his mantle will keep out the chill.

'Sire,' begins one of the huntsmen, and the king recalls himself.

'Ah, yes,' he says, but before he gives them his full attention, he adds, 'They've found us a fine boar, Bisclavret, quite ready for the hunting. You should eat; you'll need your strength for the day ahead. Look, here's your cousin.'

And sure enough, his cousin is moving through the crowd of men and dogs towards them. He's set aside his mail and livery for hunting clothes, and carries his own spear.

'Now,' the king is saying to the huntsman, 'you say he was moving west, but—'

'I looked for you last night,' says Bisclavret's cousin in a low voice, drawing him away from the king. 'After the feast. I had

35

found you a place to sleep, but you were nowhere to be seen. Bisclavret, did ... was it ...'

'Nobody saw me,' says Bisclavret, which is as much an answer as *Yes, it was the wolf*. 'I was careful.'

His cousin chews his lip. 'Are you well enough for this hunt? I know the wolf can leave you weak.'

It can – it does – but today the bitter ache of his ill-fitting skin is muted beneath the thrill and excitement of the chase ahead. Whatever else Bisclavret is, he is a hunter, in a wolf's skin or a man's. He has never had the chance to test himself against a boar before, but he welcomes the opportunity. One last chance, he thinks, to taste the life of a knight, before he returns to his own lands and his own life.

'I am well,' he assures his cousin, and pretends to believe himself, but underneath his borrowed clothes he feels again his ever-shifting bones and knows there is only so far he can push himself before disaster.

'If you need to leave ...'

'I am well,' he insists, a little more firmly, though he knows his cousin is merely concerned for his comfort. He is the only one who has ever understood the pain of the change, the only one who has ever been more concerned for Bisclavret than for the sheep the wolf kills or the paths it treads in the woods.

His cousin nods, acquiescing with grace. 'Then today is your chance to prove yourself the equal of your father.'

The *equal*. A joke. His father was a knight, well-trained and experienced; Bisclavret can claim only adolescent sparring with his cousin for his sword-work, though many long and lonely hours he spent swinging around a blunted weapon until it felt like an extension of himself. His father would have thought nothing of hunting a boar – he would know the technique of it in his bones and in his blood, not merely in his head, the product of hearsay, the way Bisclavret does. Just as he would have known his own father as a man and not a story, a body and not merely a name. Though perhaps it's for the best that his father never knew his wolf-sick son.

'Aye,' he says at last, dragging himself from his reflections. 'And when I have his land and his title, I will be safe.' Safe and secluded and rich enough to pay compensation for the animals he takes when the wolf is hungry. Safe, and nowhere near the court, or the king.

Bisclavret glances again at the golden-haired man who invited him here. He has put aside his heavy crown, exchanging it for a slim circlet. There is an earnest animation in his face as he discusses routes and habits with the huntsmen; he gestures emphatically, his hands darting like swallows.

One hunt, Bisclavret promises himself. Then he will swear his oaths, as master of whatever land is his, and that will be the end of it. He will not let the court seduce him; he will not let his dreams become too glorious.

Let me stay, howls his heart, but there is no place for desire amidst this careful balancing act of wolf and man. Better to have the loneliness of exile in his own body than the glory of the court without his proper shape.

Better to be no knight at all than to bring the wolf into the king's halls.

6

You

✦ ✳ ✦

The hunt is continuity: youth, exile, kingship, all of them joined by this bright thread of the horse beneath you and the call of the horns and the fierce joy of the hounds as they run, chasing down the boar as it crashes through the undergrowth. Your swirling thoughts settle, the winds that stirred them dropping to stillness, all your fears of inadequacy slipping away. You're awake to every detail around you: each shaking leaf, each shrilling bird, everything a fearful mind tunes out.

Even the knowledge that it's a test can't erase the thrill of it. So you are being watched, measured, judged by your father's standards and the standards of his men – what of it? They will not find you wanting. Not here in the woods, which are not so different, after all, from the woods of your exile.

The company, though, is better.

Bisclavret is here. You catch sight of him, now and again, out of the corner of your eye, and your heart lifts in triumph. *He's here.* He rides well, even on an unfamiliar horse, and when you dare turn your head to look at him, you see a vicious smile lifting the corners of his mouth, a new light in his eyes.

alive alive alive alive alive

The woods shake under the thunder of hooves, the beaters driving the boar ever forward, the well-trained hounds never forgetting their quarry no matter how many smaller beasts cross their path. The huntsmen were right: the boar is a strong one. He keeps his speed, though his low, heavy body has to fight through the undergrowth that the hounds leap over. He knows these woods, in the way that you intruders do not. Perhaps he thinks there's safety somewhere for him, if he can only run for long enough.

But even the strongest beast tires eventually. The dogs have caught up with him; he turns to face them, tusks at the ready, sword-sharp. There's a risk he'll gore them, if he's not gored first, and you pull back your horse and reach for your spear, but the animal is already moving again, path erratic, and you can't judge the angle. If you miss, and anger the boar—

He charges forward, snarling. Behind you, somebody mutters an oath, and you hear them turn their horse's head away, preparing to flee. You cannot think of doing so yourself. You're frozen in the face of violence and danger, unable to remember how to loosen your hand around the spear you're gripping so tightly you feel it might splinter into pieces at any moment. He is heading straight for you, for your horse, and you cannot move, the delight of the chase dissipating in an instant. This is not like the deer-hunts of your youth, nor yet the pursuits of your exile, where few eyes marked your progress and even fewer passed judgment on you. The crown is yours – the laws are yours – the kingdom is yours – but this, this test will affirm you as king in the eyes of all your barons or it will mark you as a weakling and a failure, unguided by God's hand, and the echo of your father's disappointment resounds in your ears like the hunting horns.

A thin film of cold sweat coats your skin beneath your clothes. You try, again, to raise the spear to strike, and your panic-locked fingers fumble, such that you're lucky not to drop it. What an ignoble way to die, before your reign has even truly begun, and how feeble the human will is, to hesitate now when you have never before hesitated to hunt. Some king you will make, flinching from the blow, without even a knight or favourite beside you to strike true in your place.

The boar is getting closer. It is too large, too fierce – the huntsmen shouldn't have chosen this target. But of course they wanted to test you against an enemy anyone with a shred of sense would fear. Wanted to know if exile had hardened you, but now, in this moment, all you see is death advancing towards you, and violence turned upon you, and your heart is as soft and weak as it ever was. You are afraid. You are afraid to die. You take a breath to better speak your prayers, and—

A spear flies from somewhere to your left and strikes the boar unerringly, burying itself deep, all the way to the guard.

He roars, furious, injured, as the hounds dive towards him. One falls back, stomach torn by a tusk; another takes its place, the smell of blood hot in the air. Only a brave man would dare get close enough to finish the job, and risk being gored himself. The kind of man who could make a throw like that, and hit a boar in motion from horseback, perhaps.

You keep your horse very still and turn your head, knowing already who you'll see at your side.

Bisclavret.

The boar holds his complete attention, as though the rest of the world has ceased to exist. You know how he feels – your own gaze drawn to him, the rest of the court fading in your awareness. He is already slipping down from his horse with the long dagger in his hand, seemingly unconcerned by the bellowing beast that longs to savage him. The dogs are blood-drunk and hunt-sharpened, and another man might have balked at getting among them, wary of their teeth or hesitant to cause them harm.

But Bisclavret moves among them fearlessly, part of the pack, a hunter among hunters. He gets behind the creature – good, he knows that much at least, you should have checked – and the unsheathed dagger is a fierce one, a sharp one, one of your father's finest, but it looks very small in his hand, shorter than the tusks of the animal, and he has never hunted a boar before, he may not know to keep clear, he may not—

You want to look away. You can't bear to see the moment blood blooms across those borrowed clothes of his and his blush fades to deathly pallor. But you're transfixed by him, by the strands of hair that fall in his face – still he wears his head uncovered, his hair long – and by the unyielding strength of his intent.

Somewhere behind you: '*Pater noster, qui es in caelis, sanctificetur nomen tuum. Adveniat regnum tuum—*'

His cousin. Afraid for him. You are afraid too; you feel that fear all the way through your thighs as they keep the destrier beneath you from shying away from the slavering boar. Even the best-trained warhorse still fears death. And this animal – enormous! Twice the size a boar should be, at this time of year, you're sure of it – has the air of death about it, teeth bared.

The dagger falls.

The boar, silenced, collapses in gore.

Blood fringes Bisclavret's sleeves. He remains there a moment, still, as though waiting to be certain, but you know the boar is dead. A fine, clean blow like that will have pierced straight through to its heart, heedless of the creature's armoured back. Even a seasoned hunter would be proud of it.

Finally, Bisclavret looks up. Something in his expression is vicious and bright. Another man might have apologised for robbing his king of the kill at the first boar hunt of the season, the first hunt of his reign, the day after his coronation – and you would have respected him less for it. But Bisclavret only with-draws the dagger and steps back to let the huntsmen unmake the fallen beast and give the hounds their reward. He crosses to you, and offers you the dagger, hilt-first.

'Sire,' he says, 'my blade and my fealty are yours.'

Oh, he's a clever man, a cunning man. Framing his request like that. No begging and no bragging: no *give me my lands* and no *look at what I can do*. But it's there, anyway, unspoken. Look at what he can do! Unscratched, unharmed, untouched but for the blood on his sleeve, and a boar dead at his feet after a throw you wouldn't have been able to make yourself. If the art of the chase is the art of war in miniature, then he is a warrior his enemies should fear.

And this, too, is clever: to give himself to you, to make his victory yours, no shame and no condescension. A true king has men like this to fight for him.

'You have a deft hand with a spear,' you say carefully, taking the bloodied knife from him, 'and a precise one with a dagger.'

He inclines his head. 'Thank you, sire.'

'I would be curious to know how you fare with another weapon. A sword, perhaps.'

He glances at his cousin as though seeking reassurance, and then back at you. For a moment, you fear he'll say his exile offered him no opportunity to learn, for that will make it more difficult to convince your men to welcome him among them, if they must first serve as tutors.

But he says, 'I am a fair enough fighter, though perhaps I lack the polish of the court.'

A diplomatic answer. Acknowledging his failings and leaving the next steps in your hands.

'Polish can be acquired,' you say, 'if the metal is good. You will have to show me.'

He has a hunter's smile, fierce as the boar he killed. 'Are you challenging me to combat, sire?' he says, with a hint of humour.

You cannot hide your own smile, joyous and broad.

'Bisclavret,' you say, revelling in his name, 'I am planning to make you a knight.'

* ✳ *

Exile brought you few friends of the sort your father might have hoped you would make – warlike princes with armies ready to ride to your defence in case of invasion, measured kings who might keep your borders from ever being harried in the first place. It brought you, instead, quieter and stranger men: clerics and abbots and scholars. And, most of all, a travelling scribe, lately a novice of the Cistercian order, seeking a place for himself at a court that would welcome his foreigner's hand and irreverent smile.

He'd made a poor monk, he told you, but he still lived by the rhythms of it, the prayers shaping his days. He's lived the life of a scholar too, and of a merchant and a warrior and a dozen other things besides, though he doesn't look old enough to trail so many stories, perhaps eight and twenty. You stopped asking him about his past after the first weeks of your acquaintance, for you suspect he spins his yarns from figments and dreams. Maybe if they were all stirred together in a melting pot until the embellishments boiled away, you'd be left with a glimmer of truth, but it was always his mysteries that drew you to him. That, and the fact that he, too, was alone and foreign and an outsider, though he had better the knack of making himself liked and certainly of making himself useful.

When you returned, you brought him with you.

Now he is your scribe, your record-keeper, and he has set to work repairing the damage wrought by your father's neglect of his books and charters. You have found him a drier chamber, away from the dank, damp corner where your father left his documents to the ravages of mould, and whenever you call by, he has found some new story worth copying in a crumbling codex, or a land charter that needs honouring. Your seneschal would prefer you leave such work to the chaplain and his clerks, rather than entrust it to a stranger, but the chaplain has little time for ancient stories, and in any case, your scribe is one of the only men in this castle who is not a stranger to you.

If anyone can discover the fate of Bisclavret's father's lands, a quarter-century after they slipped from memory, it will be him. And if the lands are gone, bestowed upon somebody from whom you cannot take them back, then he will know, too, what other inheritance you might give a knight.

He is hard at work when you arrive, scoring new parchment with lines for writing. He doesn't glance up, but his mouth curls into an insouciant smile as though he knows you by your walk.

'I did not know your father,' he says, 'but by the state of these books I suspect it would be reasonable to assume you have visited them more in the past month than he did in twenty years. The question that remains is whether you are here to see them, or to see me.'

'Both, on this occasion,' you admit.

'I'm honoured. Are you here to tell me you intend to commission a beautiful illuminated gospel-book? That you have convinced your seneschal to be less grudging with his purse-strings when I beg for parchment that isn't coarse and full of so many holes you'd think the poor sheep met its death in a thorn bush? That I am to have better ink, so that I might not spend my days rescuing each page from its spots and spattering?'

'Not today,' you say, regretfully, though you really must

speak to your seneschal about the matter. 'I have a question of inheritance that needs answering.'

He puts down his stylus and rule. 'Do I sense a story? A fair unknown come questing in search of his father's place and a sword of his own?'

You narrow your eyes. He has a faint look of dishevelment, as always, his modest sleeves pushed back to save them from the ink that stains his fingers, and his dark hair loose and tangled around his face. 'Who told you?'

'You mean there *is* a fair unknown?' he says, a gleam of interest in his eye. 'How exciting. I had rather thought they were the stuff of stories, but if stories are living at your court, well, then, you will be a fine king.'

He is likely the only person who believes as much. 'Neither unknown nor fair,' you admit, 'but yes, a young man seeking his father's inheritance. Bisclavret. A posthumous birth. His father died in service of mine some twenty-five years gone.'

'*Bisclavret*,' echoes the scribe, considering the name, and gives you a smile. 'And he has impressed you, has he, this stranger of yours?'

Your cheeks grow hot. 'He excelled himself in the hunt.'

'Ah,' he says, a little too knowingly. 'Well, then, I shall endeavour to determine what was done with his lands, and will report to you when I find it, if the worms haven't eaten the charter in question. Was there anything else you needed, my lord?'

There is a gentle mockery in his deference, a mischievous edge to his smile. You did not only bring him here because you had need of a court scribe. You brought him because you were lonely, and he was there; because he is a storyteller, and you felt your own threads unravelling; because when the nights of your exile were coldest and hardest, he was the one who warmed them.

It would be wise to forget this.

You have not yet succeeded.

'Only this, for now,' you tell him. 'If his lands cannot be returned, find some other estate of equal value. Bring word to me when you have succeeded, or have me fetched.'

He inclines his head in acknowledgement. 'As you command,' he says, drily, and takes up his work again.

7

Him

$\ast \; \divideontimes \; \ast$

He wants this. He fears this. He asked for this. He is unworthy of this.

He is still wolf-sharp from the hunt, but his skin is his own, such that he almost feels it safe to sleep in the hall near the fires and not pass another cold night in the stables. Almost, but not quite; Bisclavret has not lived this long by being incautious. At least his injured horse provides him with an excuse, though few would expect a man to tend the beast himself when there are grooms equipped to do so.

He sleeps hard and dreamless, which comes as a surprise, for he cannot stop thinking of the hunt: the king ahead of him on his destrier, so steady and assured until the final moment. Was that fear? He didn't think it wise to wait long enough for the court to be sure either way, and the boar would have savaged him, given the chance. Any man would have taken action to prevent it. *Should* have taken action. And yet only Bisclavret moved.

Do the others not love their king, or were they, too, afraid? Perhaps they should train some courage into themselves, the way they do with the hounds, since they don't have the wolf's savagery in their hearts to carry them through the battle.

The morning dawns cold, his breath misting the air. He takes a quiet moment with his horse – she is healing, slowly; she will carry him home when all this is done – and then he brushes straw from his hair and emerges into the stables proper, where a servant informs him that he is wanted out in the courtyard, where the knights train.

The king wants to test him. Bisclavret is unsure whether he will pass. His adolescent sparring with his cousin cannot compare to the training of a knight, and his own practice – alone, wielding a stick or a broom handle or whatever blunted sword substitute he could find – will not have made up the difference. He has done his best: every fighter who has passed his mother's estate in recent years has been watched and interrogated and begged for guidance. As time went on, he began to test himself against them, and he has won more of those bouts than he has lost, but that ... that means nothing. Surely here, at the court, any who see him fight will immediately know the failings of his education.

And the king will send him home, back to his mother's lands, no more a knight than when he started.

Perhaps that would be for the best, speaks Reason, but he has lived his life within the bounds of such limits and restrictions, and they have so far failed to keep him safe. No matter how careful he is, he isn't permitted to keep his body. He can avoid the world and keep himself hidden and do everything a wolf-sick man could reasonably be expected to do, but it will make no lick of difference to what he is. The wolf comes whether he is careful or not.

He is *tired* of listening to Reason.

It's in this stubborn mood that he emerges into the courtyard, where he is hailed by a man – a knight, he assumes, for he's wearing mail under his green surcoat, and a fine sword at his waist. A younger man than many of the old king's retainers

Bisclavret saw at the feast, not quite a decade older than himself or the king, and one with a friendlier smile than the others.

'Quite the feat yesterday,' he says cheerfully. 'A bold man to claim a kill like that without even swearing his fealty first, but the king seems to have taken a liking to your daring, and few could fault the sureness of your hand. Any would think you were an expert boar hunter, and yet I hear it's an uncommon pastime for you. Such quick aptitude puts us all to shame.'

Bisclavret's stomach twists at the thought of these knights judging his skills and his choices, and the resentment that he might spark in them with a misstep. His mother did not teach him this, the proper way to behave among his peers. 'Thank you,' he says unevenly, because he needs to say something.

It appears to be enough. 'I've been told to equip you,' says the knight, eyeing him, 'but I note you've already got a sword. May I see it?'

Bisclavret draws it from its scabbard and passes it to him, oddly nervous for the judgment. It was, he believes, his father's sword, but that's only guesswork based on its place in his mother's coffer, for she kept it hidden from him and it was only after her death that he took it up. He has had it repaired and sharpened, the wrap on the handle replaced, so that it no longer looks as though it has lain unused for two decades, and it's a good fit in his hand, but that doesn't mean it will meet the standards of one of the new king's knights.

The knight in green considers it carefully and with a murmur of appreciation. 'A fine blade,' he pronounces eventually, and hands it back, 'but you'll need something blunted for a bout like this, and it would be a shame to dull these edges. You didn't bring another with you, I'm assuming?'

'I did not anticipate the need for a second sword,' says

Bisclavret, simply and honestly, and the knight laughs and claps him on the shoulder.

'And why would you! Come. I will see you properly outfitted.'

To be outfitted means, apparently, passing through a hall crowded with other knights, all of whom eye him with interest; Bisclavret feels hot, and avoids their gaze. It's foolish, really, to be so shy in crowds, but his mother's estate is not so large that gatherings like this are commonplace, and he has spent little time among large groups. He half-expects the knight in green to notice and tease him about it, but if the man marks it at all, his only response is to quicken his pace and lead Bisclavret all the more rapidly through to their armoury.

'You won't need mail,' says the man confidently, testing the weight of one sword and then a second. 'That undertunic will do – are the sleeves well for you? You'll likely want a cap, though, unless you wish your hair in your face at every moment.'

He's never liked head coverings, though he wears them when he must. Perhaps that's the wolf in him, desperate for the breeze in his hair. 'What does the king expect of me?' he asks. 'I know little in the way of proper drills, though I have those of my own creation. I fear he'll see me as terribly rustic.'

'Oh, it's entirely up to you how you warm up,' says the knight, and hands him one of the swords. 'How's this? No – too light for you. I knew the other was a better fit. Here.' He swaps it for the other sword, and he's right; this does feel a better match. Only then does the man glance up and see the confusion on Bisclavret's face. 'He intends to see you spar, of course. He didn't say as much?'

Bisclavret swallows. It may be that he can show his skills best when sparring – it is familiar, after all – but unless it is his cousin they ask him to fight, he doubts he'll be a match for these men of the castle. No doubt they have their own techniques, refined and polished, and he will falter in the face of them ...

'Who ...' he begins, and has to wet his lips and try again. 'Who does he wish me to fight?'

'He hasn't specified.' The knight in green seems pleased about this, rather than concerned. 'I was hoping it would be me, if I'm honest, after seeing you yesterday, but he may have a different mind.'

There are worse fates, probably, than to lose to this man, with his easy welcome and ready smiles. No doubt the king trusts him, or he wouldn't have sent him to prepare Bisclavret for this test. But he'd hoped ...

Well. He doesn't know what he'd hoped. He never truly believed he would find himself in this position, no matter his cousin's encouragement or the stories he told himself.

'And if I acquit myself well enough,' he says, 'I suppose everybody will be eager to welcome me as his newest knight?'

The knight in green hesitates long enough for Bisclavret to guess the answer. It's as he expected. Most of these men will have been in the old king's service since adolescence at the latest, gradually distinguishing themselves until they might be dubbed knights. Bisclavret is a stranger, with no history of service – as yet, he has not even sworn himself to the king. Of course they would resent him.

'One might wonder,' he says, sparing the man the effort of explaining this politely, 'whether he were deliberately trying to aggravate you all.'

At that, the knight laughs. 'No, certainly not that, whatever grudge any might hold against him. He's young, and new to ruling, and he has been gone too long to count any of us among his confidants – natural enough that he should find another man with no fixed loyalties and seek to know him. He can't know if any among us hold him in the same esteem we held his father. We spent our youth together; we were friends, once, and he trusted my judgment, once, but whether that trust remains … it's hard to say. But I would not hold it against him that he feels adrift, or assume he acts out of ill-will towards any of us.'

There's a fondness in his voice, and a certain sadness, too, though perhaps his grin is intended to hide it. This is a man who knows the king, in a way that Bisclavret does not. 'His father sent him away,' says Bisclavret. 'Kept him from knowing his own courtiers and knights in the moment of his crowning. Why?'

'Oh, there was no intention of *that*,' says the knight in green. 'I daresay the old king thought he'd rule another score of years, and give his son plenty of time to form his friendships here. No, it was only the usual. A father concerned that his heir didn't have the mettle to follow in his footsteps. Thought he was a little too soft, inclined towards stories more than swords, and didn't feel the weight of his duty. That he was tumbling one of the grooms likely didn't help, though God knows there's enough of that around and still the kingdom has children to spare, so his father must have known he'd grow out of it.'

This is a startling speech from a knight about his king, even a king newly-crowned whom he knew primarily as a youth. 'Is that true?'

'The groom? I wouldn't say such a thing if it weren't.' He doesn't seem particularly concerned by this, but Bisclavret can't shake the feeling that he ought to be, that there is something strange and wrong about a king's son offering himself to a servant, when there is such a gulf between their positions.

In any case, he hadn't been asking about that. 'That he's more for stories than for swords.'

'No,' says the knight in green immediately. 'He's the best

fighter among us. Always has been. If he likes stories too it's because he's human, and don't we all? It'll be interesting to see what his time away has made of him, though.'

Bisclavret would like to know that too. To know the measure of the man to whom he owes his fealty.

'Come,' says the knight after a pause. 'He will be here soon, and your muscles will serve you better if they are warm.'

There's wisdom in this, but that makes it no easier to follow the man out into the courtyard again, where they are acquiring an audience – other knights and grooms and hangers-on, despite the early hour, eager for the entertainment to come. Bisclavret does his best to ignore them, stripping off his overtunic and testing the sword in his grip. It doesn't feel as natural as his own, but it's close enough; a few experimental drills, and he thinks he has the measure of it.

And it is ... welcome. Calming, almost, to have this weapon in his hand, as though he is once again a gangly youth playing at knighthood with his cousin, no weight to the dreams. It banishes the wolf, who knows no weapons but his own teeth and claws, and grants him a firm humanity with each precise stroke through the air, the sword's blunted edge cutting away his misgivings.

He's so lost in the drills that he hardly notices the general babble of the crowd falling silent, the air suddenly prickling with tension.

Belatedly, he lowers the sword, and turns.

The king is there. Resplendent in colour and furs, his hair as golden as his crown, he regards Bisclavret with an eager interest.

Bisclavret bows his head. 'How would you have me, my lord?' he asks. 'Is there a particular knight against whom you'd have me test my skills?' He tries not to glance across at the knight in green, halfway familiar and therefore halfway to an ally.

The king does look at him, however, and at the others gathered, and then back at Bisclavret, gaze steady. Then he raises his hands to the fastenings of his cloak and begins to undo them. 'I think I would have you try yourself against me, if you would.'

Bisclavret takes a step back. 'Against you?' he says.

'I can see already that you're skilled enough. And I am ... dusty and unpractised, and desire to brush away the cobwebs with a moment's novelty.'

Is that all he is, a novelty? Bisclavret raises his eyebrow and smiles. 'If you wish, sire,' he says. 'I'll endeavour not to hurt you.' He feels a faint glimmer of satisfaction when this prompts murmurs of outrage from the spectators, and a huff of laughter from the knight in green. He will never fit in this court if it has no space for humour, no tolerance for defiance. Better to know that now, before they think to let him through the door.

The king's mouth curls into an answering smile. 'Perhaps I would welcome a challenge,' he says, and raises his hand to call for his sword. 'I am *most* interested to see what you can do, Bisclavret.'

8

You

＊ ✸ ＊

You'd planned to leave the fighting to one of your knights, but the sight of him dismantles your intentions.

He seems uncertain of his own skills, but there's care in his movements as he runs through his drills, each angle studied and practised until it flows unthinkingly. Few men of your acquaintance have mastered such precision of technique, and even fewer have disarmed you with nothing but a smile and a handful of words.

When did you last have a fair fight? You can't remember. You've rarely had the opportunity to spar against an equal these last few years – if you can be called Bisclavret's equal. He has the body of a man who hasn't rested a day in his life; despite his slender frame, he has broad, strong shoulders, and you see the muscles shift beneath his undertunic as he moves.

You avoid his gaze as you warm up, relearning the feel of the sword in your hand, but when, by accident, you catch his eye, you are all the more grateful for the blunted edges. His attention is totally, unwaveringly, on you, and for a moment you have a sense of how it feels to be a hapless deer in the forest, in the breath before an arrow is loosed.

Your knight in green – a man you knew well once, in your youth, and still trust implicitly – has appointed himself the bout's herald and judge. He clears the spectators to the edges of the courtyard, giving you space, and then he steps back, calling for the fight to begin.

You regard Bisclavret. He regards you. For a moment neither of you moves.

And then—

He's fast. Faster than you expected, almost too fast to block, but you meet his sword and twist away. There's a thrill to being unarmoured and vulnerable to bruising, though the blunted swords would cause no real wound. You gather your strength and your speed and go on the offensive, forcing Bisclavret to match you blow for blow. His footwork's a little clumsy; you exploit it, slipping inside his guard, but only once, and then he realises what you've done and corrects himself, learning as he goes.

The crowd fades away. Their jeers and heckles, their shouts of encouragement, may as well be the whistling of wind through the trees. You forget where you are, forget the duties of kingship that wait for you, seeing only the swords in your hands and Bisclavret's face as he calculates his next attack. There is fierce joy in his dawning smile. It begins as surprise, the first time you parry one of his feints and nearly twist his sword from his hand; it transforms into delight when he manages the same, moments later, and you stumble to avoid being disarmed.

He feints, twists, catches you in the ribs with the flat of his blade. It will bruise. You stagger under the impact, the pain resounding through your torso and startling a gasp from between your lips. It's a pure kind of pain, a clarity-bringing pain, and though the crowd sucks in a breath and Bisclavret hesitates, unsure whether he's allowed to strike you like this, your grin only widens and your efforts redouble.

Before long you're both panting, dripping in sweat.

Bisclavret's hair falls over his eyes, overlong, and as he brushes it aside, you take advantage of his distraction to strike his wrist, hard enough that he almost drops his sword. With a sharpened blade, he could have lost the hand; as it is, he hisses in surprise and pain, before swapping his sword to his left hand. And that's a trick you didn't anticipate. He's slower and clumsier on this side, but stronger than you'd be, trying to do the same – it's never occurred to you to fight with your left, and it throws you off-guard, unable to properly counter his moves.

An oversight, surely. A kingdom should not be so easily brought down by a sinister opponent. You'll have to make that good, when next you have the chance to seek out a sword master for your own education.

The fight continues, but it's awkward now, slow, and neither of you has the skill to drag it out. Finally, you stab your sword down into the ground and hold up your hands. 'I yield, Bisclavret.'

He lowers his own sword hesitantly, as though anticipating a trick, but you don't move. You're not sure that you can, leaden with exhaustion. The rest of the world begins to intrude on your reverie, the colours of your knights' clothes bright and demanding attention at the edges of your vision. Bisclavret's undershirt is soaked and clinging with sweat, and you know your own must look much the same, but you cannot keep the grin from your face.

'You must tell me who trained you,' you say, earnestly. 'I haven't had a fight like that since—' Then you break off, unable to recall a bout that left you so exhilarated.

Bisclavret is flushed red with exertion, so it's hard to tell if he blushes now, but certainly there's something bashful in his expression as he says, 'I am largely self-taught, sire.'

It makes sense, of course; he's rustic, countrified, his father dead. And yet at the same time it doesn't, because he's so *good*, so quick to learn, enough to put any warrior to shame. 'You expect me to believe you've not sparred before?'

'Of course not,' he says, and inclines his head towards his cousin, among the crowd of spectators. 'We played at knighthood often enough in our youth. Still, I had little formal training.'

'But—' You shake your head a few times, stunned. Beaten in a fight by a man with no formal training – you should be furious. Instead you're delighted, and more than a little in trigued. What, you wonder, would he be capable of, if given the chance? 'Most impressive.'

Servants approach with cloths to wipe your faces. You'll need to bathe, next, and have a physician examine your bruises, though you think there's little real harm done. You'll need to rest, too, after all that.

'You are too kind, sire,' says Bisclavret, rubbing his sore wrist. 'It was an honour to spar with you.'

'Well, it won't be the last time. Come. You will need a bath, and there are arrangements to be made, if you are to be a knight.'

'Sire—' He pauses, glances away. 'On that matter, I would speak with you. Alone, if such a thing is possible.'

You're puzzled by his serious expression, but a consultation with your knight in green secures you the armoury and a few moments without interruptions – save for Bisclavret's cousin, who accompanies you. You're about to send the man away, but Bisclavret says, 'No, let him stay. He knows well enough what I plan to say, I'd imagine.'

'That your health is too delicate for knighthood?' says his cousin, baldly. 'That you should be allowed to retreat back to your mother's estate and pretend that this never happened? That you intend to spend the next twenty-five years hiding, as you have done until now? Yes, I rather fear I do.'

60

Bisclavret winces. 'You know that I ... that I am ... unfit for this, that however much I want it, I cannot take it.'

'I know that as a youth you dreamed of knighthood and as a man you fight better than anyone,' retorts his cousin. 'This is your inheritance. I will not stand idly by while you forsake it because your courage has failed you. I beg your pardon, my lord,' he says suddenly, as though remembering himself. 'I should not have spoken so in front of you. It is ... it is an old argument.'

'So I see,' you say, eyeing the pair of them. You had suspected already that it was the cousin's doing that brought Bisclavret to court, but you'd thought, briefly, that their aims were aligned. And nothing you have seen of Bisclavret so far suggests he lacks for courage. 'What is it you would say to me, Bisclavret?'

He chews on his lip for a moment. 'Sire,' he says at last, 'I came here seeking my father's place and my father's lands, I will not deny that. I did not expect your favour and I did not expect your attention, but I thought – hoped – that you would grant me the small boon of my inheritance. And then, I thought, I would retreat there, to my own lands. I ...' His gaze darts to you as though he anticipates an interruption, but you say nothing. 'I will serve you, sire, in whatever capacity you ask of me; I will fight when I am needed, and train men to do likewise, but I cannot ... I cannot stay here at the court, so far from my own home.'

His belief in his unsuitability, whatever underlies it, appears unshakeable – but you cannot understand the difficulty. 'Is it your lands you fear for? A good steward may take care of them for the best part of the year. Of course, you'd need to travel to see them on occasion, but—'

'It's not that. My cousin is not wrong, when he attributes my loss of courage to my health. It isn't as strong as it could be; it's one of the reasons my mother never brought me to court before.'

You'd wondered; he might have come alone, if she wasn't well enough to travel. 'What manner of weakness ails you? My physicians …'

'They cannot help me,' he says, with a glance at his cousin. 'I have been bled and purged and bathed and it has not helped. I have … I am … Sire, it is not madness of the true sort that troubles me, but madness it might become, amidst the noise and the crowds.'

Madness. You eye Bisclavret again, carefully, as though you might see a sign of it in him. You have no great love of noise and crowds yourself, most of the time, but you would not make a claim like this to escape them. 'Your father was a baron,' you point out. 'I know not yet the full extent of his lands, but they will be far more substantial than your mother's dower, and so will your duties, and the men you owe to me.' You have no desire for war, but still the kingdom must be ready for it, should such a day arrive. 'It will be no quiet retreat. I fear granting your inheritance would be more a burden than a gift, if you are so unsure of your own capabilities.'

You do not intend to keep from him his birthright, but he must see, surely, that this ends either with a return to his exile or rising to his father's place, and the latter will be a new life, one he has not known. And you … you mislike the idea of losing him to exile again. Of losing the chance to see what he might become, to tease out the hints of the stubborn, irreverent man you glimpse hiding beneath his shyness. To hone the edge of his rough-hewn beauty and make it something you can bear to look at, without feeling that the air has been stolen from your lungs.

There's a heavy silence, and then his cousin speaks: 'Let me help him.'

You both look at him in surprise; you recover first. 'What manner of help were you thinking?'

'I will serve as steward on his father's estate. Help to train his men, help keep the readiness for war, so that he carries not the burden alone. You would ... you would need to release me from my service to my lord, sire, that I might do this without shame or reprisals, but I would do it willingly.'

'I would not take your knighthood from you,' protests Bisclavret. 'We were to be knights together. To have you serve me as steward, it's—'

'A waste?' interrupts his cousin, with a self-mocking smile. 'I am a knight in service, Bisclavret, landless with little hope of inheritance. I am better spent helping you, at least until you learn the way of it, and have men you trust to serve you in place of me. It was to aid you that I was sent to you in our youth, after all.'

You consider this. It is no trouble to you if the cousin truly wants this, and it would aid Bisclavret. But it does not solve the issue at hand. 'And with your estate cared for, will it be able to spare you to the court? Or do you maintain that you could not live here?'

Bisclavret looks tormented. 'Sire, I ... I will do as you command me, and I cannot claim I do not want this. But I know myself. I know what I can withstand. This is beyond me.'

You think of that first night, of Bisclavret absent from the hall; the way you found him, in the morning, looking as though he had fought his own nightmares to return to you. Was that a reflection of this infirmity, or wine-sickness of the usual kind?

You think of the challenge in his voice when he offered you his oath. You well believe that he wants this – so whatever it is that keeps him from accepting it, it must be something grave, such that he cannot even speak the truth of it to you.

There is a knock, and then your knight in green looks into the room. 'I'm sorry to intrude, my lord, but your … scribe is here to see you.' His hesitation means little, you're sure. He's not the sort to judge you; if anybody is being judged here, it is the scribe, for being a stranger, and unacquainted with your knights.

'Show him in,' you say. It has been only hours since you instructed him to look for Bisclavret's father's lands, and you didn't expect news so soon.

Your scribe is looking almost respectable now, halfway to a cleric in his dark, sober clothes, his tangled hair hidden by a cap. Only the ink on his fingers gives him away – that, and the sly curve of his smile. He holds a roll of vellum, which he hands to you. 'The charter you were seeking, my lord,' he says, and glances at Bisclavret with barely concealed curiosity.

'My scribe and custodian of books,' you tell Bisclavret, by way of introduction. 'I set him to the task of identifying the location and fate of your father's lands.'

'A welcome distraction from the state of the records,' says the scribe, kissing Bisclavret in greeting and then, by way of afterthought, his cousin. 'You must be the fair unknown about whom I've heard so little.'

'I …' Bisclavret colours, laughs a little. 'You make a story of me, master scribe.'

'Ah, as is ever my task,' he responds. 'I see you've been fighting. I am sorry to have missed it; I'm sure it was a sight worth seeing.'

The blush deepens. 'I am sure your work was grateful for your attention.'

'Oh, I'm sure it was,' says the scribe, and his smile widens. 'At present I'm at work at the copying of a collection of lais and romances, if the parchment with its holes doesn't defeat me first, and if I'm not sent in search of too many more half-forgotten charters.' He nods to the roll in your hands. 'Aren't you going to look at it, my lord?'

You unroll it, skimming the painfully complex hand of some long-forgotten scribe with a wince. Your scribe may be foreign enough to give the seneschal a headache with his abbreviations, but he has a fair hand, monastery-trained, and the scripts of the present age are a little easier on your eyes than those of a century or two ago. 'This records only the granting of the land to Bisclavret's father's line,' you say. 'It is ...' You hesitate, reading the description again. 'Why, it's scarcely an hour's ride from here. Perhaps less, to the most easterly border, which is ...'

'Firmly bisecting part of your finest hunting forest, yes,' says the scribe, with some apparent amusement. 'It seems the woodland was once cultivated, but your father conveniently forgot this, when it offered his deer more space to roam.'

You read the charter again. 'But you've found no record of it being granted after his death?'

'It was given to nobody. Whether this was carelessness on your father's part or avarice, I can't be sure, but those lands remain in the hands of the crown. You could restore them today, if you chose to.'

An hour's ride from here. Land on the very edge of the forest. Perfectly suited to a fine hunter, perfectly within your capacity to grant, and none could see it as undue favour, for they were his father's lands. It is the most elegant solution to the situation that any could have offered you.

You look up at Bisclavret, who is staring at the parchment in your hands as though it is a saint's relic, miraculous and holy. 'What say you, Bisclavret? No need to remain at court, with a home so close. You may keep your father's lands and join us for feasts and tournaments. And you would have hunting rights.'

He wants it. You can see well that he wants it. 'Those were truly my father's lands?' he says. 'He lived so close to the court? No wonder my mother—' But his voice cracks, and he breaks off before finishing that sentence. You wonder what would have completed it: *No wonder my mother wanted them back. No wonder our exile wore so heavily on her.*

'They were your father's, and they will be yours,' you say. 'And you will be a knight, without the madness.' This with a light tone. – you do not truly believe him mad, though it's quite the figment to concoct, in place of whatever his true infirmity might be.

'A knight,' he whispers, wonderingly. 'I will … I am to be a knight.'

His voice breaks on the word, breath stolen by joy and wonder. You exchange a glance with your scribe; he has a pleased smile, to have enabled such delight, though elsewise his expression is as sharp and curious as ever.

Bisclavret's cousin, less wonder-struck, says, 'Sire, he will need time to return to his mother's lands and make arrangements with his steward. We will leave tomorrow, if it please you. I anticipate that we will be returned within a fortnight. Will that be enough time, do you think, for clothing and weapons to be made or fetched for him, and the ceremonies to be arranged?'

He will make a fine steward, brusque and efficient like that, but you feel a pang of dismay at the thought of losing Bisclavret so soon. You had … well, you had scarce thought about the practicalities, beyond a vague idea that he would be dubbed and raised to brotherhood within a day or so. Of course it can't be so; the castle chaplain would have your head and months of penance for demanding such a thing without the proper preparations, and your scribe will need time to set the record to rights.

'A fine plan,' you agree, reluctantly, 'and I will speak to your lord and have you released from his service.' Then you look back at Bisclavret. 'And you will swear to me as knight and baron, and nothing less. Perhaps it is for this that the weather waylaid you on your first journey to the court. One might almost see the hand of the Almighty in it.'

He swallows hard. 'One might indeed,' he says.

And, like that, he is yours.

9

Him

✦ ✹ ✦

The day has an unreal air to it. Bisclavret allows the servants to chivvy him away to another bath, and dresses once again in his own clothes, shabby as they are; with a journey ahead, there is no need for anything better. He makes arrangements to travel, trying not to think too hard about where he is going and why for fear that, when looked in the eyes, these impossibilities will splinter and disappear.

But that his cousin witnessed it, he would think the conversation with the king had been a dream.

The impossibilities: that the king should want him for a knight at all; that his father's lands should be intact and waiting for him; that they are so close to the court as to allow him both freedom and concealment; that his cousin will give up a small piece of his own dreams to help him; that when he hesitated to accept what he was offered for fear of the wolf inside his skin, the king worked to persuade him otherwise.

The king *wants* him. Will bend rules to make space for him. It is like breathing fresh air after two and a half decades of drowning.

He'd thought if he gained anything from this, it would be the king's pity, inheritance restored because it was his right and nothing more – perhaps some small portion of land that represented only the least lucrative corner of his father's estate, a softer and easier exile but an exile nonetheless. It was all he dared hope for. He certainly did not imagine this.

You will swear to me as knight and baron.

Can he? Does he dare? The wolf is at bay for now, but he can still feel it, haunting his bones. The hunt made it restless, the unfamiliarity of the court made it worse, and the fight with the king ignited every trace of savagery within him and stirred it into motion. What if it returns just as he is raised to knighthood? Better not to rise at all. He knew that almost before he'd lowered his sword to accept the king's surrender, and he'd tried—

He did not expect, somehow, for his cousin to intervene. He is more used to his kin trying to limit him and to hide him. His mother would have kept him shackled to the loom like a girl, if she'd had her way of it; she would not have armed him with anything larger than a needle, and he would have lived a quiet life, a safe life, until the wolf tore him from it.

But his cousin and the king, they demand more of him. His cousin he understands – the man will benefit as much as he, though life as a steward will offer less glory for a young man than a knight's life, and one day perhaps he'll want to return to the latter. The king, he understands less. Oh, he noticed the man's lingering gaze, his interest; he can't imagine what it is about him that draws the king's eye, but drawn it is.

Unbidden, the words of the knight in green come back to him: *he was tumbling one of the grooms.* Is that what the king seeks? Is all of this a seduction, from a man with the power to command him with a word? The idea settles oddly in his stomach. He is not used to being desired, and he can't give the king what he wants. Not with the wolf lurking inside his skin.

'Bisclavret,' says his cousin sharply, and he has the sense that this is not the first time his name has been called.

He pulls himself with difficulty out of his thoughts. 'Yes, cousin?'

'So you *can* hear me. I thought perhaps you'd left your wits in that stable you slept in.' Beneath the sharp words, there is relief: he is not entirely joking. He's ever feared the wolf will take Bisclavret's mind along with his form. 'Are you well for the journey? Tell me now if you are not, that I might make arrangements.'

Arrangements. By which he means an alteration of their route to pass by some woods somewhere that he might let the wolf off the leash like an over-spirited hound in need of exercise. Bisclavret appreciates the consideration, but feels nevertheless the humiliation of need.

'I am well,' he says, which feels truthful, this time. How he will feel when he bids farewell to the estate that has been his gaol, however, he cannot say. Perhaps that will be what shakes him loose from his humanity.

His cousin makes a noncommittal noise and continues saddling the borrowed horses. Their own will remain here, so as to allow speed without injuring the beasts further.

'Is there something on your mind?' Bisclavret asks him, after watching for a moment or two. 'If you have something to say ...'

'I will have several days to say it, while we travel,' says his cousin. 'And a lower chance of being overheard.'

That bodes ill for the kind of conversation it might be. 'Before you say anything, then, let me remind you that you pushed for this. If you have any regrets or concerns, recall that I was on the verge of accepting exile as my lot and knighthood as nothing more than a childhood game.'

'Yes, thank you,' says his cousin. 'I am well aware of that.'

He will say nothing more on the subject until they are on the road – just the two of them, without company, for the sake of speed and cost. It may be the last time Bisclavret travels like this, for there will be expectations of a baron to travel with servants. The prospect of a life of company brings both joy and dread: that he will not be alone, as he has so often been alone, is everything he has wished for, and yet it brings with it the impossibility of secrets. How will he conceal the wolf from them? Will he be known, exposed, shown to the world? He could not bear that.

Some miles from the castle, his cousin says, 'Tell me truthfully. How much of your fear is habit?'

'I beg your pardon?'

'Your mother carved shame deep into you. I am aware of that. To my eye, you manage the wolf well enough; I have never known you hurt anyone or anything larger than a sheep. I see no danger in this new life – less, perhaps, than staying on your mother's estate, which is too small for you, and drives you to hunt too far afield. Your father's lands will grant you hunting rights, and are far larger, with some good acreage left without the interruption of tenants, such that you may remain concealed.'

It is delivered in a crisp manner, as though he has been evaluating this question all night. 'But ...' prompts Bisclavret, for he knows there is more than this.

'But you are afraid. You know the wolf better than me, of course; you know your needs. Are you afraid because you have grown used to being so, or because there is some real danger I have not considered?'

It is a mercy to be asked in this way, unflinching and honest. If only Bisclavret had an answer. 'I have been afraid all my life,' he says. 'I have not known how to protect those around me except by withdrawing. This change threatens to unbalance me, and what effect that will have on the wolf, I cannot know. Perhaps it is perfectly safe. Perhaps the king invites disaster, and does so unknowing, and I would not put that on him. That he offered me this at all ...' He shakes his head. 'Still I cannot fathom it.'

'They are your father's lands,' says his cousin. 'Had he waited a few more weeks to die, you would have had them all along.'

'You know it's more than that.' Would he have been a knight, if that had happened? Would he have ridden beside the king, hunted with him, sat beside him at a feast?

'I know that you have the king's favour,' says his cousin, and though his tone is even, there's something in it that catches Bisclavret's attention.

'What does that mean?' he asks.

'That he looks at you like a starving man looks at a feast. That is a dangerous position to be in, Bisclavret.'

'I have no intention of—'

'What do your intentions matter? This is a king we're talking about. A new king, his friendships at court not yet solidified. The man is alone – any fool can see he's desperate for friends, to win the love of his father's retainers, to know which of his knights are loyal beyond their oaths and which are looking ever for fairer weather. He is a crowned exile, and his attention is on you because you, too, are an exile and an unknown and have no prior loyalties with which he must compete. You were never sworn to his father. You underestimate how much that means to a man still finding his footing in a kingdom that no longer knows him.'

Bisclavret is stunned into silence. After several wordless moments, he manages, 'Why give up your place as a knight to be a steward to me? You could advise kings. You have a canny eye for politics.'

His cousin laughs, some of the tension broken. 'I am the youngest son of six brothers,' he says. 'My life has been an exercise in observing needs and alliances, and positioning myself to best catch the favourable winds. I know how to watch a man for his intentions, and I am telling you that the king is adrift. A baron who could situate himself as a reliable support at a time like this would profit well from it, but if the king proves rash, profligate, quick to make enemies, then that will be a difficult bond from which to extract oneself with honour. And he is young, untested. It is hard to know what manner of king he will be.'

One unlike his father, Bisclavret suspects, though having never met the old king, this is a supposition based on hearsay. The king does not seem rash, but that he is so intent on knighting a man he hardly knows – and surely no man of his father's type would have brought a scribe as friend and ally upon returning from exile.

'And yet you manoeuvred me such that I must accept the honour he has done me,' he points out.

His cousin shrugs. 'It is your inheritance. If this life truly suits you so ill, you will return to your mother's lands and plead infirmity, and the king will remember that we warned him of your fragile health and accept this excuse.'

He has a quick and calculating mind, planning steps ahead. He has taken Bisclavret's secret into his care as his own and learned to hide it with clever words and keen observations. It is a valuable talent, and a still more valuable friendship. 'I will still owe him men and service. If there is a war ...'

'Then let us hope there will be no war.' His cousin raises an eyebrow. 'I did not forsake knighthood only to calculate your rents, Bisclavret. I meant it when I promised to help train your men, though I'm not the fighter you are, and I will be your

74

sworn man. If such a time comes that you find another steward, perhaps I will be your knight, and wear your livery.'

It is a kindness, and a practical one. But it sits uneasily with Bisclavret. 'As children we played at knighthood together. As equals. Not one in service to the other.'

'We were children,' says his cousin. 'There was never a world in which that was true. I have ever been the sixth of six and my father poorer in rank than yours. Service or the Church was always my fate and,' he adds, with a wry smile, 'I am not suited to holy orders.'

He's right, of course, but for so long exile seemed the only fate Bisclavret might hope for, and that made a strange parity between them.

'I will be glad of your service,' he says at last, 'and of your friendship, and whatever guidance you might offer me. But when my father's lands are steadied, when we have unravelled the neglect and made them once again an estate worthy of a baron, and when you have trained another steward to see the currents of power that you see, then, cousin, you will be a knight again.'

His cousin smiles. 'And I will be glad of it. But there will be plenty of work to do first.' They ride a little further in silence, and then he says, 'Will it be difficult, do you think, to say good-bye to your mother's lands?'

Impossible, and also a relief. 'They have been all I have ever known,' says Bisclavret. 'I will be leaving behind a life. But ...' This journey is wringing more truths from him than Confession. 'But I am also leaving behind a great loneliness, and that is a blessing. And I will have the lands safeguarded, and should I ever have a daughter, they will be hers, and if I ever wish to return, they will be there. It is no true parting.'

None of this will cut the bonds that have tied him to this

life of secrecy and distance; it will only loosen them, slackening the ropes to give the illusion of freedom. He would do well to remember that. It will make it easier to bear, when the wolf robs him of it all again.

As it must. As he has always known it will.

You will be a knight, said the king. It was a promise more than an order, and still it sank into his bones like a command. The king desires it, and it will be so.

But even a king cannot command a wolf.

10

You

*

Sparring set aflame what was smouldering before; absence fans the fire. Part of you is sure that if you could only act – if you could take Bisclavret by the hand and lead him aside and forget your place and his – it would fade into nothingness, a simple infatuation, and you would be free of it. But left alone, the wanting grows and consumes, until you fear it will burn its way out of your flesh and leave a brand for all to see.

He is gone, in any case. A fortnight without him; a fortnight to have the arrangements made. A fortnight for the bruises he left on you to fade, and your raging blood to still to coolness.

You had no choice but to surrender the fight and give him the victory: he would always have won, and to prolong it would have shamed you. Your body aches still with the memory of blows, and when you undress to bathe the next day, your hip is purpled with bruising and your skin burns for his touch. In the polished bronze mirror, you see the mess he has made of your ribs and arms.

You would have let him do worse, but for your men watching.

The bath eases the aching and tames a little of the heat inside you, but it does not soothe your hunger or make rational your mind. Your disordered thoughts spiral into chaos, interrupted by the memory of him – of his smile, of his sword-work, of the body beneath his clothes, of the way it felt to be the sole object of his attention. It's for the best that he's gone; you can imagine the trouble you might have made for yourself, otherwise, trying to keep a fair distance.

When you are dressed, you proceed to the chapel to make arrangements. The chaplain there is almost as newly raised to his post as you are: he's a young man, younger than the dour bishop who taught you your letters and Latin as a youth, and far milder in temper.

He is not surprised to hear of Bisclavret's knighting, which means word has already spread through the castle. 'A man cannot be knighted until his soul has been made ready for it,' he informs you. 'When he returns, I will need to take his Confession. He will profess his faith and keep his vigil.'

'You think his soul unready?' you say, with a glimmer of mischief, squashing your disappointment that the ceremony must be delayed another day beyond Bisclavret's return. 'Why, he is a good Christian man.'

He could be none of those things and you wouldn't care. You suspect the chaplain knows this, though he has been your confessor only since your return from exile, and spared the bulk of your sins and indiscretions.

'It is as much a part of the ceremony as the oath,' he says. 'You know this, my lord. You kept your own vigil.'

You did. It was a lonely night spent making yourself right with God and your own heart before taking up the sword. You wonder, still, whether God really minds. If He notices at all. In your father's day, there were no such vigils; were his knights less holy for it? None of them rode out to answer the call of popes and kings; they had enough to worry about at home without concerning themselves with holy war. But the spectre of it fell heavily over your childhood nonetheless.

'Very well,' you say, at last, though you wonder how Bisclavret will cope with a night under the chaplain's watchful gaze, if he cannot even bring himself to sleep in the hall. 'Though the man is practically a hermit. He must have done many years' vigil under the stars before now, and made enough peace within himself for a lifetime. Certainly enough for a knighthood.'

The chaplain's eyes narrow. 'Anyone would think you were treating this lightly, sire.'

He has you there. 'I wouldn't dream of it.'

'Mockery is unbecoming of a king.' Is that *disapproval* from this mild-mannered chaplain of yours? That's new. You have never crossed him before, happy to let him minister as he sees fit. 'Even the purest heart must be made ready for service, and I know nothing of this man. When he returns, send him to me, and I will prepare him.'

'So be it,' you say, and cross yourself in half-sincere deference. The chaplain raises an eyebrow at that, but he lets you leave without imposing penance for your impertinence. That is a relief: you have much else to organise, and no wish to aggravate him.

You have other duties, too, a fact your seneschal is keen to draw to your attention. The role of a new king, it seems, is to give gold and clasp hands; to receive fealty and hear petitions; to visit those tenants who might benefit from alms after summer storms left their farms battered and fatigued. You must be seen, so that all might learn to love you. They don't know you, but nor did they know your father as anything more than a distant figurehead, so that matters little. They would kiss the palm of any man in a crown who paused long enough to hear their troubles.

You meet a newborn child. They say they'll name him after you, but you tell them to give him a brighter name, a younger one – one with less to weigh it down. Their uncertain smiles suggest they can't tell if you're joking, and you wish you knew, too, how much of that was jest. But you hope nonetheless that they don't name the child for you. All you did was touch his brow and laugh when he clasped tiny hands around your finger; there must be fathers, uncles, grandfathers whose names are a better fit.

You meet older children, too. A small boy tells you he wants to be a knight, and you encourage him with tales of great deeds and chivalry. A girl tells you the same, and when you glance over at her mother you see the woman's concern, though you can't be sure if she's afraid you'll punish the girl for her dreams or merely trample them. You do neither, and tell her the story of a damsel rescuing a captured knight to repay him for his favour, because it is the best story you can offer her.

Two brothers, at odds with each other, bring a petition to you concerning their inheritance. Two sisters, penniless, beg a dowry from the castle's coffers, for they'll make no marriage without one. A poacher hunting in your father's forests – your forests – is brought before you in chains, to be made an example of, and you regard him for a long moment.

'Were you hungry,' you ask him, 'or merely sporting?'

'My lord,' begins your seneschal, but you hold up a hand to silence him.

'I would have his answer.' You turn back to the man. 'You did not hunt a doe or hart. You trapped hares. That to me speaks more of hunger than of greed, but I would know your defence.'

The man is trembling, but he manages to meet your eyes. 'I had three sons and lost two to the sea, sire,' he says, 'initially as fishermen until they were drowned last winter. Now my third son and I try to keep body and soul together on land scarce large enough to keep goats and the last of those fell sick with a fever. We've no coin to buy more and no crop large enough to live on.'

Perhaps it is a lie. A figment, a story, designed to evoke pity. Your father would have thought so. He'd have fined the man if he were in a good mood and had his hand in a foul one, if he let him free at all, though all outcomes would have required him to concern himself with matters of justice and not merely the pursuit of his pleasure. No doubt your seneschal expects a firm hand and a similar violence from you, to prove to your people that you are no soft-hearted boy to be trifled with.

But a king can do worse than to be known for his kindness. 'Give this man a goat,' you tell your steward. 'No – two goats. And coin enough to feed them for the winter.'

'Sire,' the seneschal protests, with real dismay in his voice. 'If you allow poachers to evade punishment, you—'

'Will gain a reputation for mercy? What a tragedy. Perhaps if I ensure my subjects do not starve, there will be no call for poaching. Who's next?'

More of the same, it seems: more tests of what flavour of justice you might mete out, more signs that your father's interest in his land and people had waned before his death. It was not the weeks of waiting for your return and coronation that left lands mismanaged and tenants starving, but the years that went before them. You will have your hands full for some time restoring your kingdom to prosperity, and that's assuming no greater trouble – no raiders from the sea, no invasion from the east.

When the day is over and you are finally freed from duty and the weight of your crown, you find that there is somebody else who wants your attention: your ward, sitting beside you as you eat.

It is strange to think of her as such, when she is almost your own age and no niece or daughter. Perhaps a sister, in another life, if your father had not sent you away and you had had the chance to know her better. Perhaps a wife, if you did not know already that you will marry for political ends if you must marry at all.

Still, she is under your protection, and you have been neglecting her these last days, your mind full of other things.

'I hear you are winning the hearts of poachers and petty thieves,' she says, with a touch of laughter in her voice. She is dressed almost as finely as you, in her silk bliaut with its embroidered hem and full, draping sleeves, her hair in long braids wrapped with ribbon. A narrow circlet keeps her silk veil over her hair.

'Better to win the hearts of thieves than the hearts of nobody,' you answer her, affecting the same lightness of tone. 'Am I inciting such rumour already, or do you take a particular interest in petitioners?'

'A little of both,' she says. 'One never knows whether the next man to stand before you in the hall will be there to ask for my hand.'

You glance sharply at her. You have not spoken of her marriage, and while you are half-aware that such petitions and proposals are inevitable – a man would be a fool not to know that marrying a king's ward might better his standing, to say nothing of her beauty and charm – you had not particularly thought of them as imminent. This was, you realise, an oversight of ignorance.

'Did my father ...' you begin, and trail off, unsure what you are asking her. It is close to half a year since her father died, and she has been reliant on the crown's charity since then. 'Did my father involve you in such things, at all?'

She tilts her head noncommittally – not quite a nod, not quite a denial. 'He assured me that I would have some choice in the matter,' she says, 'but choice means little when you know nothing of the hearts of the men who desire you, only their name and lineage.'

You consider this for a moment. It is likely you will know no more than the name and lineage of whatever woman you one day marry, but those who enjoy not the privileges of kingship should carry not its burdens. 'And is it marriage you seek?' you ask her. 'If a cloistered life would suit you better ...'

A laugh, slightly nervous. 'No, sire, marriage is more to my liking than that. I had some years in the cloister as a girl and while I'm grateful for my learning, it is not the path for me.'

No doubt she is more learned then than you, and has a fairer hand. 'Then marriage it shall be,' you tell her, 'but when any man comes seeking your hand from me, I will ensure that you may talk with him, and hawk with him, and share whatever other diversions might suit you, before I ask you for your answer. If that suits you.'

A shy smile. 'That settles greatly my worries, my lord. Thank you.' But there is something else she would ask of you, you think, watching her pick at her food and open her mouth, once or twice, as though trying to shape a question and struggling to find the words.

'Speak,' you encourage her. 'There is nobody here to listen. What is on your mind?'

This is not entirely true – there are servants, of course, waiting to refill your cup or bring you another dish of food, and others seated elsewhere in the hall. But here on this dais, it is only the two of you.

'Your new knight is on my mind,' she says at last. 'The one who was here, at the feast ... *Bisclavret.*' She says his name almost the way you do – wondering, luxuriating, tasting each syllable. 'He will swear his oaths soon, will he not?'

'Yes,' you answer cautiously. 'When he returns from putting his mother's lands to rights.'

She makes a thoughtful noise. 'What manner of man is he?'

'A brave one in the hunt and a shy one at a feast,' you answer; it is as much as you know of him. 'An exile, new to courtly life and easily overwhelmed by it.'

There is a moment's pause while she ponders this, and you eat a few more mouthfuls. At last, she says, 'Is he courteous? Kind? What aid does he offer to those in need? Is he easily tempted? How would he treat a maiden, if she came to him alone?'

You are ashamed not to have thought to learn these things about him. You might guess at courtesy, read respect into his shyness and expect aid from a man who saved you from the boar, but there has been no opportunity to test his other qualities.

'He strikes me as a good man,' you say weakly.

A nod of acknowledgment – disappointed, you think, in your lack of answers – and then she says, 'Send me to him.'

'I'm sorry?'

'When he returns. The priest will hear his Confession and test his faith and creed, yes? Let me do likewise. I will see if he has the qualities of a true knight.'

You cannot, in that moment, explain the feeling such an idea arouses in you. Yes – a test of his loyalty and his courtesy is well for an untried knight, and a stronger temptation than your own ward with her fair hair and smiling eyes couldn't be found for all the wealth in the world. But if he were to fail . . .

You would not expose your ward to that humiliation, and you would not weather well the disappointment of finding Bisclavret so weak. And – and you do not like to think of him touching her that way.

For her sake, of course, that she might keep her good name until her marriage, and nothing more.

'You would do this?' you ask her. 'And if he proves himself uncouth—'

'I do not think he will,' she says. 'I watched him at the feast. I think he is a fine man. But better for you and I both to be sure.'

True. 'Then,' you say, a little reluctantly, 'when he returns, you will go to him, and tell me afterwards how he behaves towards you.'

Her smile widens. 'Yes, my lord,' she says.

After that, your impatience for his return only seems to grow, but the days pass without sight or word of him. You attend to whatever business your seneschal directs you to, and when the day's work is done, then come the minstrels and storytellers and musicians all – more of them every day, it seems, for word that you're more inclined to patronage than your father must be spreading. They bring new lais and romances and have an eager audience among the knights and ladies, though many of their tales are already familiar to you from your exile. There, every feast brought some performance, poets and jugglers alike competing for attention and bread, and you miss it, a little, here in this small kingdom of yours with its quiet, dark castle. Your father had little time for letters, beyond the necessary, and gave scant gold for music, such that the best of your kingdom's harpers have long since left to seek their fortunes elsewhere and the best of your storytellers with them. Perhaps you can tempt them back, now that you are king. Perhaps you can make of this hall a place of joy again.

It should be enough to fill your days: the work and the sport, the contemplation and the dreaming. But your thoughts grow scattered, and when the last night of a fortnight has passed and there is still no word of Bisclavret, you give up on keeping your frustration buried, and go in search of the only man who will not judge you for it.

Your scribe is working when you let yourself into his chamber, half hidden among his book-hoard with its sturdy codices and neatly piled scrolls. They look better cared for than ever they did in your youth, and if he keeps at this rate of scribing, there will be plenty more of them soon, for he has a voracious appetite for stories and appears single-mindedly determined to rival the book production of any monastery, one man that he is.

'If it's another charter you're seeking,' he says, continuing to write, 'you'll be pleased to know that I've imposed some order on them, that they might be easier to find.'

'Not that, today,' you say. 'It's you I came to see.'

He puts down his pen. 'Ah. A distraction.'

'Something like that.'

His smile is back, but different now. 'Will you tell me what you seek distraction from, or am I to guess? I hear your seneschal's been plying you with criminals for judgment, but that seems not to be something you'd seek me out about. There's little else in the winds of rumour, unless it's that your Bisclavret ought to have returned by now, and hasn't.' He eyes you, and laughs when your expression gives you away. 'I thought as much.'

He misses little, even in this dusty corner, half-buried in vellum, and even when few in the castle know and trust him enough for conversation. 'Perhaps we might spare the speaking,' you tell him.

His expression turns wicked. 'I see. It's that manner of distraction you need. But you're so beautifully dressed for court, my lord.' He gestures to your fine clothes. 'Really, I'd not want to treat your servants' handiwork lightly.'

His teasing is the only thing that hasn't changed since you first met him. If ever he treats you with deference, you will leave, and never ask him for this again. 'I'm sure you know the trick of the fastenings.'

He raises an eyebrow. 'Me? Oh, but we had no silks and fine things in the monastery, and I am only a humble scribe ...' His fingers have already found the laces that hold your mantle closed, and are untying them with ease, letting the heavy furs fall to the floor. 'I wouldn't know where to begin.'

You take his hand and guide it to your belt. 'Begin here,' you say, and he unclasps it and draws it away, gathering it around your sheathed sword and placing both carefully on the desk.

'And now?' he says, and you show him – *and now? and now?* – until he's taken from you all the armour of kingship and all that's left is your undertunic, thin as clouds, pushed up around your waist, and nothing is real but his fingers on your skin and yours tangled in his hair and the scrape of unyielding stone against your back.

It's not enough. But he is warm, and real, and *there*, his lips hot as brands against your skin, and you can almost lose yourself long enough to forget why you were trying in the first place.

II

Him

❋

Bisclavret has not been alone with a priest since his mother died.

Now, fatigued from another journey delayed by rain and poor roads, is not the time he would have chosen to change that. They gave him a chance to bathe and eat, but sleep, it seems, must wait until this is done, for he had no rest at all before they bundled him into the chapel for this testing of his faithfulness.

There was no time even to greet the king; he hasn't seen him since before he left for his journey. Though perhaps that's for the best. The way the king looks at him – it flays him, lays him bare. He feels known, in a way he's not sure he's comfortable being known. There is something unsafe about those looks. He doesn't believe for a minute that the king would act in any way that might harm him, but the power of that knowing threatens to violate his sense of self, of boundaries, of what will bring him peace and what will unmake him.

Every time he meets the king's gaze, he's half certain the other man can see the wolf there, lurking behind his eyes. One day, the king will know him for what he is, and the threat of it is terrifying – and exhilarating. He can do nothing but hide from it.

In that respect, being confiscated by the castle chaplain is a welcome reprieve from a reunion he wasn't ready for. In other respects, it is ... harder.

The chaplain asks, 'Do you speak your prayers, son?' and for the span of a heartbeat, Bisclavret almost tells the truth: *yes, every time my body warps in on itself I beg to be allowed to die.* Instead, he hesitates, and the chaplain's brow creases into a frown. 'I am not expecting you to keep the hours, but this should not be a difficult question to answer.'

'I pray,' Bisclavret interrupts. He doubts the chaplain will send word to his mother's estate to confirm his attendance at Mass, but in any case he has missed few services, though often his mind wanders and his prayers echo more the desperate pleas of his heart than the words of the priest: *Lord, I will endure this if you give me the good days, the human days, the memory of having hands.* The wolf has kept him from the church on occasion, he cannot deny that, but if the Almighty forgives a shepherd who shuns the Eucharist to mind his flock then perhaps He might extend the same grace to a broken man tending the animal that lives in his skin.

'You will keep your vigil, nonetheless,' says the chaplain, 'whether or not the king thinks it necessary.'

This has the air of an old disagreement, and one to which he was not privy. 'I have no objections to that,' he says, which is not entirely true, for he can feel the wolf ache in his bones even now, and a night alone in the chapel carries little appeal. He hopes only that it remains an ache and nothing more until all of this is over, but it would be a lie to say he has not imagined them dressing him in armour only for the wolf to burst out of it, splintering the mail into tiny useless fragments. It seems strange, after all, that he might be allowed another skin when he already has two of his own. 'It will not be the first night I have spent alone with God.'

The chaplain gives him a small smile. 'Then this will be no hardship. I will hear your Confession first, and we will take the Eucharist together.'

Confession. It will not bring him peace nor cleanse him of his demons, and in recent years he has all but abandoned the practice, letting months elapse without absolution. How, after all, can he name his sins, the acts he commits when not in his own skin? Is it even truly a sin for an animal to give in to rage and hunger? He doesn't see the birds and beasts trooping to the confessional.

But he cannot make excuses now, so Bisclavret bows his head obediently and speaks the familiar words, faltering only when he comes to articulating his transgressions.

'I have told lies, Father,' he says finally. 'Not because I wanted to, but because I believed it was safest that way. That the truth would hurt others, as well as myself.'

The chaplain eyes him keenly. 'Have you lied to the king?' he asks.

Bisclavret would not think it a confessor's place to ask such questions, but he supposes it is a little different, when you are confessor to a king and your penitent is about to be knighted. He has to stop and consider the question for a moment: *has* he lied to the king? Not in as many words. The king has not said to him, *Come, Bisclavret, tell me, are you wolf-sick?* And he has offered no false explanations for his nature. If he has told a lie, it has only been a lie of omission.

'No,' he says at last, content that this is an honest enough answer. 'I have never lied to the king.'

The chaplain nods. 'Have you anything else to confess?'

There are few enough opportunities for sin, living alone in exile. There are few neighbours whose possessions he might covet, few married women with whom he might wish to commit adultery. He knows that in his wolf's shape he has taken animals from fields in the dead of night, but he has tried where he can to compensate those losses, if they are not his own beasts that he takes.

He says, 'Sometimes I am guilty of the sin of despair.'

The chaplain looks at him. 'Tell me what is in your heart, my son.'

My son. The word carries no weight, spoken by a priest who is father to all, but it brings a lump to his throat regardless. Has anyone ever addressed him that way? His mother would call him by name, when she acknowledged him at all; his father never had the chance to call him anything – *and the better for him that way,* his mother used to say, *that he never had the shame of seeing you.*

He swallows. 'Sometimes I think it would be better if I were not alive.' He sees the look on the chaplain's face and adds, 'I have not … I would not attempt self-murder. I know well enough the teachings on the matter and I've no interest in damnation, and besides which, I maintain a stubborn hope that better days may yet come.' He has been human for days now. Weeks, in fact; the wolf may have tinged the edges of his long journey home, but he has not slipped from his skin since that first night at the castle. Maybe he is recovering from this bout of weekly transformations, and will know peace for a few months. 'But still it is hard to avoid the darkness when it creeps in, and it brings with it doubt.'

'You struggle with faith,' says the chaplain, not exactly a question.

'I struggle to see the Lord at work when everywhere I turn I see the shadow of the Adversary.' He doesn't *think* this is heresy, but he avoids meeting the chaplain's eyes anyway, in case he has never known what it is to wrestle with God. 'I have a condition, Father. It is … it is akin to madness, though it seldom lasts more than a single night when it comes. I am like a sleepwalker, wandering the woods, lost to myself. It frightens me to realise how little control I have over my own body and mind, and sometimes I lack hope that I will ever recover that power. At other times I'm not sure I have ever had it at all.'

'And that brings you to doubt the Lord's goodness?'

'It brings me to despair.' Bisclavret looks down at his hands. 'It feels like I will live my life always as though sleepwalking, never one thing nor another – not sane nor a lunatic, not a child nor a man, never fully grasping anything. I have remained in exile because it is easier there to be unmade and not have it witnessed.'

He is confessing everything and nothing at the same time. He waits for the chaplain to give him that sharp-eyed look and ask if there is more to his condition than he is saying.

He does not. He says, 'It is difficult, when our health is not our own, to hold fast to trust in the Lord.' There is new sympathy in his expression. 'I have struggled myself with pain, of a kind which neither physicians nor prayer can fully banish. We are told that the Almighty has plans for us, to prosper us and not to harm us, but it is hard to fathom how any plan can involve such suffering. I have felt this same despair, this loss of self that comes from the absence of control.'

Bisclavret did not expect such understanding from a man of the cloth who carries his self-assurance like prayer beads, familiar and comforting. He swallows hard and asks, 'How do you defeat it?'

The chaplain does not look at him as he says, 'I have tried to see myself as Job, my faith tested by misfortune. Then, at least, there would be some purpose in it, and if I am true to my God, it will come to an end, and I will have my reward.'

93

This is a bitter disappointment. He finds no solace in the idea of suffering for some holy game or unseen test, played out by forces beyond his ken. 'Does that help, Father?'

'Not in the least,' he says, looking back at Bisclavret, and his kind smile carves deep lines around his eyes. 'We are supposed to be saved through Christ, with such evils defeated. It gave me strength, perhaps, in my youth, but it has long ceased to be a comfort. I tell you this only so that you know I have wrestled with these angels too.'

'What now, then?'

'Now, I take each day as it comes. I accept that I will never have control, and allow my pain to be only part of me, not my entire being. I hold to the knowledge that there is a greater plan, though little I can see of it. I count my blessings, and let the pain pass over me.'

He speaks the words as though they're easy, but his expression, his lined face – lined in a way a young man's face should not be – says otherwise. This is, perhaps, a question he still grapples with.

Bisclavret says, 'What else is my being, but this?'

'A knight,' says the chaplain, and blesses him. 'For your sins as you have confessed them to me, and for those you have not, seek both penance and peace in the praying of the psalms. I will be back shortly to administer the Eucharist.' He holds out his psalter, and Bisclavret takes it. 'Bisclavret, for what it is worth ... the king sees great potential in you. Perhaps your fortunes are turning.'

He musters a smile. 'Perhaps.'

When the chaplain has gone, he opens the psalter with trembling hands, but for all that the book boasts clear script and fine illumination, it remains impenetrable to Bisclavret. He has yet to confess his illiteracy, another symptom of his inadequacy for knighthood; the chaplain must assume either that he can read or that he has the psalms by heart, and he cannot claim such piety as that. But he dredges some few words from his memory: *Miserere mei, Domine, quoniam infirmus sum; sana me, Domine, quoniam conturbata sunt ossa mea. Have mercy on me, O Lord, for I am weak: heal me, O Lord, for my bones are troubled.* Troubled, yes, that's one word for it, but what mercy may the wolf claim?

This is a mistake. An abomination. He should have confessed and had it over with, allowed the chaplain to take the lead. Perhaps they would have had him killed, perhaps merely sent back to his exile; even that would have been better than the endless torment of waiting to be discovered.

But he wants this. He wants knighthood. He wants the oath, the service, the brotherhood; he has always wanted it, since before he understood the twists and turns of his life's path.

And if God did not want this for him, would He have formed in him this desire and allowed this opportunity? If this is not his path, why is it so difficult to turn from it? For once in his life, he is being led somewhere that he wants to go, and he is not minded to argue with that.

Still he chokes a little on the Eucharist, and tastes his blasphemy on his lips as he swallows. Still he feels the impostor as they take the candles away, one by one, leaving him alone in the dark chapel. Still the doubts threaten to crack his resolve, interrupt his prayer, rob him of his dreams.

But the cold stone beneath his knees grounds him, and a shaft of moonlight slices the altar with its insubstantial blade, and Bisclavret keeps his vigil.

✳

The woman is golden-haired like the king. Dressed in silks and furs like the king, too, fit for a princess. Bisclavret remembers her from the feast, but he did not expect to see her here, in this chamber adjoining the hall where he has been brought to be clothed for the ceremony. She slips in, speaks quietly to the servants, and to his surprise and dismay, they nod and disappear, leaving him alone with her.

'My lady,' says Bisclavret, flustered, and not solely because he is dressed only in his undertunic, barefoot and bareheaded. 'I was not ... should you be here, unchaperoned?'

'Do you pose a threat to my virtue, Sir Knight?' she asks, with a smile.

He wouldn't dream of touching her, even if she weren't under the king's protection, but he hasn't the words to say as much without casting some slight on her beauty and her charms, nor still to make it convincing. 'I am ... I am not a knight yet,' he stammers instead.

'And yet you trail stories in the way of the finest,' she says, and steps closer to him. 'I hear you defeated the king in single combat.'

'Combat it was not,' he says, a little desperately. 'Friendly sparring, that was all, and he yielded, when well we might have continued for some time. My lady, I am certain this is not allowed.'

She makes a reassuring hushing noise, as though to a child. 'The king knows I am here,' she says, and if that is true then it eases slightly the sense of danger, but only increases his certainty that this is a test. Bisclavret wishes he knew better how to pass it. 'Tell me about your home. Your mother's lands, those you have but lately left.'

He has only until the next sounding of the church bells to dress, and no notion of how much longer that might be, but if the king has sent her then he must indulge her curiosity. 'They were small. Wooded on one side, the hills on another. Largely heath more than farmland, though there was a little of that. We were too far from the sea to count fishermen among our tenants, so winters could be hungry.'

Is this what she wanted to know? Her expression doesn't change. She looks at him with appraisal, her clear eyes evaluating every inch of his body. Her gaze does not penetrate his human skin the way the king's seems to. She sees a man. Only a man. But what does that mean in this moment, when she has sent the servants away, and ensured they are alone together?

'Were you loved, there?' she asks. 'Did you have a pretty maiden of your own? Perhaps several?'

Does she ask for the sake of narrative or for the sake of law; is she concerned that someone might lay claim to inheritance from him, or that he might be distracted from his duty and torn in his loyalties? In either case, the answer is the same. 'No. I was quite alone.'

A peculiar smile on her face. 'Then you are untested,' she says, and steps even closer, close enough to lay her hand on his chest, to feel his rapidly beating heart through the thin linen of his undertunic. 'We might change that.'

'No.' Too fast, too brusque, but he's already pulled back from her. A night at vigil in the chapel has left Bisclavret fortified against temptation. 'You are ... very beautiful, my lady, but I will not touch you. You are the king's ward, and I am unworthy, and I will not violate my oaths before I have even taken them.'

Her smile, to his surprise, widens. 'Good,' she says. 'Then I will help you dress for those oaths.'

Stupefied, he cannot immediately process this change of direction. 'I beg your pardon?'

'It would be a poor knight to swear into the king's service who did not act courteously towards a lady. Your hesitation does you credit and your polite tongue more. Now allow me to help ready you, for the servants will not be back for some time, and the ceremony awaits you.'

Bisclavret is momentarily weak with relief that he seems to have passed this trial. 'I can manage perfectly well by myself,' he says, although he is not at all certain that is true.

She clucks her tongue disapprovingly. 'It is no shame to be dressed, and I am as capable as any squire or page.'

It isn't that he is ashamed. But there's a shocking intimacy to it, to her hands on his legs as she helps fasten his hose, new and bright with royal dye. No more for him the simple colours of undyed wool and linen, or the cheap blue of woad. The armour is less familiar, and the sensation of permitting her help ever more alien: she eases the padded gambeson over his head and then the mail hauberk; laces the mail chausses around his calves; reaches around his body to fasten his belt over the fine bright surcoat in the king's colours. Her movements are quick and efficient; perhaps she once helped her father with his armour, that she knows so well the fastenings and the best way to arrange his tunic into comfortable pleats beneath the layers.

Her touch is feather-light and safe as a hearth, and the weight of the armour is grounding. Each piece is like a bandage, another skin, a shell encasing him and binding him together, all of his selves locked up tight. He thought perhaps it would feel like losing something. Instead it feels as though something is coming together.

She takes a step back and regards him, appraising her handiwork. 'There,' she says. 'You are almost ready to be dubbed, Sir Knight.'

'Almost?' he echoes.

She reaches out and touches a strand of his hair hanging loose about his face. 'Let me braid your hair for you,' she says.

'That will keep it from shadowing those eyes of yours.'

His head will be bare for the ceremony, no coif of mail or helmet to hide his expressions from the king and all who have come to watch. He might well wish for the slender defences of his loose hair to conceal his thoughts. But he is aware that the length of his hair is unfashionable, an echo of decades past; the men here at court wear theirs cropped far shorter, and their beards likewise neat. On that front, at least, he fits in; he keeps himself clean-shaven, a small act of reclaiming skin from the wolf and anything that might remind him of it.

'Very well,' he says at last, and sits. She is as efficient with the comb as with the rest of his armour, braiding his hair and twisting it away from his face.

When she's done, she drops a kiss to his forehead. 'For luck,' she says, with another smile. 'I must to the king and my place there. You know your part?'

If ever he knew his part he has lost the knowing of it; he feels as though he's waking from a dream, only half-remembering who or where he is. How unafraid she was. Touching him as though he were any man, any knight, no care for the lurking wolf. How unfamiliar the press of her lips to his forehead, a blessing his mother ceased to offer him some years before she died. He'd forgotten the unique benediction of a woman's care.

She sees his stupefaction in his face and laughs. 'The servants will fetch you, and bring you to the hall,' she says. 'All will be well, and you will be a knight.'

Yes. A knight. Dressed in the armour in which she dressed him, made by her hands. He opens his mouth to thank her, but she is already gone, and he is alone again.

He stays there, unsteady, unravelling, until the promised servant comes to tell him that it's time, and then he finds his feet again and goes forward to meet his future.

12

You

His hair has been tied back from his face in intricate braids, the curls and tangles oiled away. His skin is clean, pink-cheeked in the cool air of the throne room. They've made for him a surcoat of green and burnt gold, and mail so polished that it shines like moonlight. Your ward returned some moments ago with a smile and a nod that only you would understand, and you know then that he did not touch her, but her touch is everywhere on him, lingering like perfume: in his hair, teasing out the tangles; drawing tight the fastenings of his clothes; resting on his skin.

You permitted it. You wish, absurdly, that you had not.

He wears no cloak, no helmet, no armour around his head and neck. His throat is pale and exposed, and you see him swallow as he approaches.

The words of the oath are as familiar as a prayer. It has been much less than a month since you received it from the rest of your nobles, a seemingly endless stream of fealty, a flood of kisses pressed against your hands and mouth. But for a moment you cannot recall them. All you see are his clear eyes, looking up at you. The contrast between his dark hair and his pale skin. The harsh, straight lines of his eyebrows. You look at him and feel as if you are drowning in wanting for something you cannot have.

The chaplain prompts you and you stumble through the

questioning, the words of the promises he must make. His responses are softly spoken, as much breath as speech, and you strain towards him to hear the quiet words. His Latin is rough; it lacks a churchman's polish, but he knows the shape of it, and the formal patterns of the oaths expected from him. He swears to serve: with taxes in peace, with his body and with men in war. To answer your call and to stand at your side. It is a friendship any king is owed and it is too much to ask. You want it desperately.

When the words are spoken, he kneels before you, waiting for the bestowal of his title, and all you can see is the graceful curve of his neck as he submits.

You knight him with shaking hands, and he kisses your feet, your hands, your lips, as is proper, each fleeting touch an impossible tenderness.

Sir Bisclavret.

He wears a small, secret smile, one he keeps biting back as though afraid to show his joy. But what you feel is wonder: wonder that he is here, that you have his oath, that you will not lose him again to exile.

You fasten the sword-belt around his waist, and then you take his hand and turn him to face the gathered crowd – your knights in their brightest livery, the ladies in their finest gowns, all the castle servants dressed for feasting. They cheer, the musicians striking up a tune, and it is time for ritual to give way to celebration: oaths to wine, prayers to song. You have hardly let go of Bisclavret's hand before he is swept away by his cousin to take his place among the knights.

As you stare after him, momentarily bereft, you can still feel his lips against your skin, the trail of his fingertips along your hands where he took your help to stand.

Somebody touches your arm, startling you from your

yearning. You turn to see the chaplain, whose joy, it seems, is tempered by concern. 'Be careful of him, sire,' he says.

You frown. 'What do you mean? You think he intends harm to me?'

'Not at all. I bid you take care not for your sake, but for his.' The chaplain looks across at Bisclavret, being slapped on the back, kissed, embraced by all the other knights. 'I do not think life has been easy for that young man.'

You follow his gaze. It stings a little to see the easy brotherhood of the knights, which once you hoped might be yours. Now their friendship comes ever with the added weight of favour, of service: it is wholehearted and impossible to return. They would see no insult in sleeping on the floor at the foot of your bed, that they might claim such intimacies with their king, and whatever you may offer them in return is nothing compared to the whole of their life and body and honour, as they have given it to you.

Bisclavret will not even sleep in your hall. And yet he offers himself nonetheless into your service.

'He seems hale enough to me,' you say at last, remembering that the chaplain awaits a response.

'Not all bodies that appear whole are as strong as they look. He is ...' A polite hesitation, pausing before disclosing secrets given in confidence. 'He has a more delicate nature than perhaps you are used to, in a knight.'

You nod. He said as much himself. 'He has, perhaps, a wilder soul than most, unsuited to a cage,' you say, as though you believe it's as simple as that. 'But his father's lands – his lands – are close enough that he may keep his own seclusion and sleep under his own roof, should he need sanctuary away from the court. He seemed to think that would help.' You would give him that distance willingly, if it will keep him here by day.

'Sire,' begins the chaplain, but whatever reprove he's about to utter, he thinks better of it, and simply says, 'I will keep the both of you in my prayers.'

You suspect, coming from a priest, that that is a barbed statement. But you thank him and move away to join the feast, and you do not have to pretend merriment when Bisclavret is there, when Bisclavret is a knight, when he catches your eye and smiles, just once, without hesitation.

The musicians begin a jauntier tune, and there is a cheer as those assembled gather themselves for dancing. Your knights have brought their wives and sisters to this feast, and the colour and laughter of the women illuminates the hall. Pairs and circles form organically, lines interweaving; the knights join the dance as merrily as the rest, heedless of the weight of their mail.

Bisclavret is dancing with your ward.

She stands out, even amidst all the finery of the court on a feast-night. Her long braids of fair hair have been neatly woven with silk ribbon, and her bliaut is resplendent with gold, all buttercups and sunlight. The embroidery around the cuffs of her sleeves is so fine it must have taken a dozen women to complete, and all of that pales beside the joy of her laughter as she spins, hands clasped in Bisclavret's.

A moment later, a second laugh joins the consort, a sweet-voiced lyre to her bright flute. Bisclavret.

He is no skilled dancer, clumsily fumbling the steps as though it is the first time he has ever danced them. And well it might be: you assume his mother hosted few dances, and he would have had no call to study this footwork with the solitary diligence he dedicated to the sword. But he is gaining confidence as she leads him, as the circle joins, as the people swap partners and come together and break apart again.

His laughter warms you. The sight of him happy, when he has

worn a crease between his brows like a jewel since the moment
you met him, is balm upon a sore you had hardly noticed. But
something cracks, too, at the sight of that happiness being
found in the crowd while you wait alone by the side of the hall,
afraid to join lest your crown ruin the fraternity of the dancers.

You would have him happy. But for a moment you wish that
happiness were to be found with you, and not in the arms of a
woman, however bright her sunshine smile.

You find yourself with a cup of wine in hand, and don't remember calling for it. It's welcome now that it's here. You take
a sip and retreat to stand against the wall, out of the way of
the dancers, so that you can better watch their revelry. There's
pleasure to be had in watching the patterns they weave, spotting
the unexpected pairings among the dancers – some reluctant,
fleeing each other as soon as a tune ends, and others coming
together for dance after dance as though they can't bear to let
go of each other's hands.

'That's quite the storm-shadow on your brow,' says a voice
beside you.

You glance up from your wine. 'Have your books spared you
for the evening, then?' you say. 'How sporting of them, to release you for a feast.'

'I came to give your seneschal the charter that will restore to
Bisclavret his land,' replies your scribe, with a wry smile. 'But
I would not have missed a knighting, in any case.' It is odd to
see him here, when never at that court of exile did a scribe have
a place at a feast. 'All the kingdom has turned out to see the
man who has won his spurs from you. And there are rumours
aplenty about him.'

You scowl. 'There's no call for them.'

'No call for rumour about a man who came from nowhere
to slay a boar and save your life, only to then defeat you in

combat? You underestimate the human appetite for stories.'

'That is a story grown in the telling,' you protest. 'The boar was a long way from goring me, and friendly sparring is hardly combat.'

'I'm only telling you that which the people are whispering to each other. A king should know the mood of his subjects.'

You narrow your eyes at him. 'You're mocking me.'

'I wouldn't dare.'

'Then speak plainly, or go back to mouldering with your books.'

He pretends affront, but his smile is back before you've had time to miss it. 'He's a beautiful man, my lord. Wasted in exile. How lucky for the both of you that he has been restored to his proper place.'

And that's a sly remark and no mistake, but it's not as though he's wrong. There's something striking about the way the torchlight catches Bisclavret's profile as he whirls his lady around in a wild circle, laughing all the while. You didn't know he had it in him to be so carefree.

'And he's found somebody he favours, I see,' he continues. 'The rumours hadn't picked up on that yet.'

You think of telling him that you sent her to Bisclavret, to test his courtesy, but he would only pity you for it. So you say, 'If I wanted your commentary, I would ask for it.'

'And if you wanted a distraction,' he says, voice low, 'you would ask for that too, I suppose.'

From another man you would think that was a threat, a reminder that he knows too much about you and holds too much power because of that knowing. But he is still a stranger here, and whatever his knack for accruing secrets, he is not the sort to spread them, or to break confidences better kept vouchsafed.

'I am distracted enough,' you say. Confess.

He smiles. 'This isn't distraction,' he comments. 'This is you tormenting yourself. Watch him all evening – it'll change nothing. He's happy. You have made him a knight, you have given him a gift, and even your ward is charmed enough by him to braid his hair and dance with him and will no doubt continue to do so for as long as he will let her. We know how this story ends.'

'How do you know?' you ask before you can stop yourself.

'It's predictable,' he answers, and swallows a little more wine.

'Not the story. The hair. How do you know she braided his hair?'

He gives you a pitying look. 'Was it another of her ladies that you sent to him, then? Or did she ask you if it might be her, to know best whether he was courteous? Permission to flirt and tease and try to draw from him bad behaviour that was not there to be drawn?'

You reel, momentarily stunned. 'Predictable,' you echo numbly. A stranger here and still he sees the mechanisms by which the court ever turns, its seasons and its tides.

'It's how these things go.' He drains his cup. 'Will you dance, my lord, or does that crown on your head come attached to a rod all the way down your spine?'

There is no good answer to that. You cannot dance with a scribe, especially a foreign one, brought home from a kingdom neither of you belonged to. No matter how little you care about inciting rumour, there are some hierarchies that cannot be violated.

'I would rather not,' you say, which is a lie and he knows it. He doesn't challenge you, however, but wanders away, and for a moment you think he means to abandon you, until he returns with a jug of wine pilfered from a servant and uses it to fill your cup again.

'Tell me about your Sir Bisclavret,' he says. 'I know the tale of his father's lands, but not how you came to learn of it.'

You should have seen the interrogation coming. 'Poor weather,' you say. 'He should have sworn his oaths with the rest, but he and his cousin were delayed.' You gesture vaguely in the approximate direction of his kinsman, now dressed in fine court clothing as befits a baron's steward. 'His cousin begged forgiveness, and I had the story from Bisclavret then. For a man seeking advancement, he was curiously hesitant to ask for it, and when it was offered – well, you saw him, he practically had to be talked into it.'

'Hmm.' Your book-wrangler regards them both, knight and steward, with a sly gleam in his eye. 'If there's a story there I could learn it, if you wished me to.'

You shake your head. 'Bisclavret has offered as much truth as he is willing to offer at this time. I would earn his trust and his friendship honestly, and with it the rest of his story.' In the meantime he is happy, and you are left watching him dance.

You sigh. It's a deep sigh, and a melancholy one, and your companion looks sideways at you.

'If this feast is such a trial to you, I'm sure nobody would object were you to slip away.'

'They'll notice,' you say.

'Noticing isn't minding. Concoct some excuse about a pain in your head and they'll not bother you for the rest of the evening.'

'And then what? Spend the night in my chamber, alone and resentful? A poor occupation for a king.'

'Nobody said you had to be alone.' Another man might have said that with a leer. But although there's an edge of mischief in his smile, his expression is simply kind. He has always been kind, even when you were a prince of nothing, seated by the door at every feast and sleeping far from the hearth at night, heir to too small a kingdom to be worth cultivating as a friend. If he hadn't been, you would not have brought him home with you.

Still, you should be more careful. Yesterday's encounter was reckless, exposed, and while a king may do as he likes and have few chastise him for it except perhaps his confessor, there are too many watching to see how you handle these first months of your kingship, and you would rather not start your reign with a reputation for hedonistic carelessness.

You watch for a moment longer, but the joy has faded. 'Some air,' you say at last. 'I won't leave entirely. But I'll take a turn or two around the courtyard, and be back before I'm missed.'

'Do you want company?'

He asks it so simply and frankly, like you're any man. 'Yes,' you admit. 'I would welcome it.'

And you work your way through the crowd to the door, stepping out into the cool night air and leaving Bisclavret behind with your knights and your ward, your family his and your home surrendered to him.

13

Other

＊ ✳ ＊

barely past the walls it all collapses:
humanity. reason. the boundaries that keep chaos
from the door and the wolf from the world.
these fine clothes are a better prison and a worse defence
than anything they might build, knots and laces
snagging and snarling at skin like traps in the forest,
impossible to untie with fingers becoming claws
and hands – *don't take my hands don't take my hands* –
lost and sharpened and made new.

ever the change comes like prophecy, unwelcome,
abrupt – *I thought I would have longer* – truer
than truth and more hated for it – *this is what I get
for believing I could be a knight.*

stripped back and twisted open, the lies
are a poor armour, unable to guard against the bite
of the self. some hungers are never satisfied.
some emptiness is never filled –
I thought this had stopped –
and lies are wood-bitter, poison-sharp, nothing

compared to a hunt and hunger.
a few weeks of humanity and wholeness
is that so much to ask for?
hope's a lie too, a pretty one, if knives
can be pretty. but in the end a wolf is hungry
and hunger must be fed.

soft thoughts, safe hearth, yearning for a voice
like sunlight and hands like dancers
but that's a trust built on lies and means as much
as a dream – *she saw the truth she saw me*
only me only the man – in the end the wolf
is as true as the man – *this is not who I am.*

but what self is there in the trees and the taste
of the wind, what being in the night howls its name?
I refuse to be defined by my dismantling
by these moments of unmaking I refuse—
we are all made of our collapse.

I am more than this I deserve

more

than

this

the wolf is hungry like the man is hungry,
a desperate emptiness, starving for freedom
and this small moment of a future.
but all we are given is this: always again this,
always again this – *I thought it had stopped* –
and hope's pretty blade is a cousin to despair,
impossible to outrun and swift as pity.

it drowns you in your own reflection, creeps in
with the blackness at the centre of your eye.

I deserve more than this

may as well run just for the thrill of it
just to taste blood just to feel like you're moving
like you've ever had any power at all

14

Him

He spasms back into his own skin sometime after dawn.

The air is fresh, thin mist dissipating in the pale sunshine. The trees are stark outlines against the foggy white of early morning, and the ground is thick with dead leaves, autumn on the verge of surrendering to winter.

He's naked, and without clothes the change looms again, ready to drag him under. If he can't dress himself and convince his body it's meant to be human, he'll slip again into the wolf and this time, he fears, he won't come back.

He always fears that. That one day he won't come back. But the fear is strongest in these moments when his body has forgotten its proper shape and he has no way of reminding it. He doesn't even know where he is, though it has the look of the royal forest, so perhaps he didn't stray too far. He was at the castle, yesterday. Did he make it into the trees before he changed? He can't remember. He doesn't know. There were so many people; God, what if he didn't get away in time?

But he'd remember. He would have stopped himself before he hurt them. He has to reassure himself of that, when the memories are fuzzy and disjointed because the geography of a wolf is painted in scents and shapes that mean little to a human.

He is not wholly lost, even in the depths of his wolf-sickness. Only changed.

Bisclavret runs his fingers over his face, as he always does when he returns. He's not sure what he's checking for. Perhaps it's the sheer relief of feeling eyebrows, eyes, nose, mouth, the tug of his fingertips against his own lips reminding him that he has a mouth and that he has hands.

He has hands.

He begins to stumble towards the outwood – perhaps there he'll have a hope of orienting himself and finding some way back to his abandoned clothing. The roots of gnarled oaks snag his feet, threatening to trip him; he's helpless as prey compared to the wolf's loping grace. Does he miss it? He's not sure. There's always a period, when he first comes back, when his mind isn't certain what skin it wants to be in, only that whichever he's currently in isn't it.

It'll pass when he finds his clothes. He hopes. It usually does.

It's cold, out here in the forest. When the winter comes properly, it'll bring new dangers: he'll need to ensure he doesn't freeze to death while he's a new-skinned cub stumbling pelt-less among the trees. He survived last winter only through careful planning, never straying far from home, but this year already feels different. New lands, a new home, paths he hasn't yet learned, and a new resistance to the careful limits he's built up over the years. The castle and the king and the lady – they've tangled the carefully separated threads that form his life, made a mess of it.

He's almost to the edge of the trees when he hears footfalls.

No. No, they can't find him here, not like this. Naked and wandering the king's forest like a witless poacher. He tries to remember whether he hunted last night, and whether he'll have killed any of the king's own deer. He hopes not. He may be a knight now, with his father's hunting rights to some of these woods, but it will still cause trouble.

A knight. What a joke. He's a naked, terrified man with a wolf beneath his skin that threatens to steal him away. He can feel the shift coming, the aching as his joints prepare to twist inside out, and all he can think is, *not again.*

The footsteps come closer, swishing through the fallen leaves. They're making no effort to conceal their approach – most likely, they have no idea that he's here. He needs to concoct a story before they stumble into his path, but his mind is still half-wolf and ice-cold, and excuses fail him. There is no reason he can give for being naked on somebody else's land that will make it any better.

The footsteps halt. He stays perfectly still, half-concealed between the trees, and hopes they leave before the wolf comes back, but they don't move.

After several agonising moments, they break the silence. 'I brought your clothes.' His cousin. He sounds wary, and distinctly unimpressed, but not hostile. 'I thought you might not find them. They were … scattered.'

There's a rustling, as though he's placed the bundle on the ground. Bisclavret coughs and it's half a growl, but he manages to say, 'Thank you.'

'I'll wait for you outside the wood.'

His cousin retreats. When he's sure he's alone, Bisclavret darts forward to pick up his clothes: his own linen undertunic, only lightly torn, and the fine gambeson his cousin had made for him for the ceremony; simple everyday braies and chausses; his boots, brushed free of mud. His mail and surcoat must be elsewhere. He doesn't know how he got out of them.

When he's presentable and the sting of shame has receded a little, he follows the sunlight to the edge of the trees. His cousin is leaning against a drystone wall, arms crossed. He looks relieved to see Bisclavret.

'I wasn't sure you'd come back,' he says, 'without your clothes.'

'I came back,' says Bisclavret. 'But I might not have stayed.' He thumbs the fabric awkwardly, feeling it brush against his skin, willing his body to understand that *this is you this is who you are you are human.* 'Thank you.'

'Here.' His cousin pushes himself forward, and takes charge of the laces Bisclavret couldn't manage, just out of reach of his fumbling wolf-scratched fingers. Every fastening he tightens seems to bring his skin a little closer to his bones. 'You gave me a fright.'

'Did I ...' Bisclavret's mouth is dry. 'Was I seen? I don't remember leaving.'

The other man has changed out of his feast clothes, but he doesn't look like he's slept much. 'You made it to the forest, just. I gathered your clothes before the king or his knights stumbled upon them and started asking questions. I didn't see you change; you were already amidst the trees by then. By the grace of God, nobody else did either.'

His tone demands reassurance, or at least excuses, but Bisclavret has few to offer. He tries anyway: 'It was overdue. You know we were lucky, on our journey, that the wolf let me be. After everything, I might have expected it sooner.'

'Everything?' his cousin echoes.

'The hunt, single combat, our journey, Confession, a vigil, the ceremony ...' And the lady. And the sights and the colours and the fact that the change was already there, waiting, because he'd been too many days without it. He was deluding himself to think he would be allowed peace for long.

There's a pause, and then his cousin says, 'I must say, when I urged you from your exile, I thought you had more control over it than this.'

'I know you did,' says Bisclavret tiredly. 'I tried to tell you otherwise.'

'Perhaps I was wrong to push you.'

'Perhaps you were.' It's too late now. He's sworn his oaths, accepted a blade from the king's own hand. 'Perhaps this is inviting disaster. Perhaps it is unsafe. But then, you said to stay in my exile was unsafe, lest the wolf be tempted to roam too far. The truth is that I have never been safe, and I will never be safe, for I can neither escape the wolf nor hope to control it. The best I can do is try to live despite it – which I thought was the philosophy you were encouraging me to adopt. You cannot now drive me back into fearful timidity because the limitations of that idea have made themselves known.'

'I have no intention of doing so,' says his cousin, with more patience than his bitter tone warrants. 'If I wanted to hurt you, I would not have ridden half the length of the forest looking for you so that I might bring you your clothes.'

Only now does Bisclavret notice the horse, tied to a branch a little way off, blithely cropping the muddy turf and ignoring them both. 'Where are we?' he asks. 'How far did I come?'

'All the way into your own lands,' says his cousin, and his expression softens into half a smile. 'Perhaps the wolf in you has some sense after all.'

His own lands. Bisclavret looks around him in new wonder: the woods, their glorious autumn colours already fading to the muddy grey of winter; the heath before him; what looks like farmland beyond that. There will be the manor, too, the house he should have grown up in, but has never seen.

'The wolf has as much sense as I do at any other time,' says Bisclavret, distractedly – *his own lands!* – and his cousin says,

'Yes, well, no wonder he would put you in such danger, then,' with enough humour in his voice to ease the sting of insult.

The relief of being in safe territory gives way once more to fear. 'Do you tell me true, that I was not seen? Why does the king think I left so suddenly?'

'He had already excused himself. I told his seneschal you were wine-sick, and that I would see you safely home.' He adds, with faint amusement, 'He advises that you must learn to hold your drink, lest you find yourself cheated at dice by the knights.'

Bisclavret forces a smile. 'If that is all I have to fear, then I would be a luckier man than I deserve.'

'We both would be.' His cousin takes a breath. 'Bisclavret, as your steward I am sworn to be honest with you, and as your kinsman I would not choose to lie. I am afraid.'

His cousin has had various reactions to Bisclavret's condition during their lives. Disbelief. Confusion. Doubt. Disgust. Hope, far more tenacious than Bisclavret's own. But if he has ever before been afraid, he has not admitted to it.

'Afraid of what?' Bisclavret asks, waiting for him to say: *you*.

'That somebody will be hurt by this. That you will be hurt by this, or that you will hurt another, and be in turn tormented by the knowledge and the guilt of it. I saw you, last night, with the king's ward. The way she looked at you, and you at her ...' There is a new uncertainty in his voice. 'Do you intend to court her, Bisclavret?'

'I had not thought so far ahead.' He can't court her. What kind of marriage could a wolf-sick man offer the king's own ward? 'What concern is it of yours?'

'Every concern,' retorts his cousin. 'The same way that your land is my concern, that your health is my concern. For the same reason that I came out here looking for you this morning.

But also for her own sake, that she should not be injured by this.'

'I will not hurt her,' says Bisclavret. 'And you have no reason to fear me.'

'Bisclavret,' says his cousin gently, 'I am afraid *for* you.' He reaches out and plucks a leaf from Bisclavret's tangled hair, letting it fall to the ground with the rest. 'I wish you all the joys of knighthood, and I will be at your side to guide your lands to their flourishing. I know you do not lack caution, but ...' He takes a breath. 'This hope is new for you, as though the sight of the lady has changed something, and I am afraid of what it will do to you if your hopes prove unfounded.'

He knows, then, the shattering of Bisclavret's heart every time the wolf comes back after a long absence. He knows how dangerous that fall from grace can be.

'Cousin, I must be allowed to hope,' says Bisclavret softly. 'I cannot live my life never looking ahead to better days nor celebrating them when they come for fear that Fortune's wheel will once more plunge me into sorrow.'

'The fall is greater from a height.'

'So is the view.'

His cousin's smile is sad, and Bisclavret feels close to weeping. 'I'm trying to protect you,' he says, 'the way I always have. You know that, don't you?'

Of course he knows that. His cousin is the only kinsman who keeps faith with him: keeps his secrets, made those thankless journeys to his home in exile, brought him food and news and cheer. It is a debt he will never repay, for it has kept him alive.

But his cousin cannot protect him from the wolf, just as the king cannot command it.

'I am a knight,' he says. 'I can protect myself.'

15

You

Bisclavret is absent a good week after the knighting, and you try not to dwell on it. Of course he is absent. He has new lands to survey and attend to, a home to settle into – it may be a month or more before you see him again, and nobody would think him negligent in his duties to you. Still, you had thought he might call by the castle once or twice in that time, seeking advice or company.

By the eighth day, you've half convinced yourself you imagined the whole thing. The ceremony. Your newest knight. It's a distant, feverish dream, becoming less real the more you try to grasp it. You are better letting it fall into the shadows of memory.

Resolved to do so, you step out into the courtyard where your knights have met to spar and practise – and there he is.

He's sparring, hand-to-hand, stripped to his braies, with your sharp-tongued knight in green, equally unclothed. The two of them grapple, and it seems impossible that the slight Bisclavret might prevail against his more heavily-set opponent, but he's lithe and fast, slipping under the other man's arm and throwing his weight off-balance. Perched on the fence or leaning against the wall are other knights – some drinking, a few eating, all jeering and heckling the wrestlers from the comfort of warm clothes and a safe perch.

You've seen them like this before, testing each other's limits, but never with such delight. They're laughing as Bisclavret knocks the knight in green to the ground and punches the air in triumph, only for his fallen opponent to hook a leg behind his knees and bring him crashing to the mud. As he collapses in a heap, the knight bounds upright and lets loose a roar of victory – prematurely, it appears, for Bisclavret has already rolled onto his knees and is moving to topple him again.

'Interesting man, your Sir Bisclavret,' says a familiar voice.

You don't take your eyes off the fighters and their smiles. 'A funny turn the scrivener's trade has taken, that you now regard not books but a brawl.'

'Ah, not a brawl, surely. It's not as vicious as all that.' You look at him then; predictably, he's grinning. 'They've been at it all morning. I've yet to see one of them beat your Bisclavret. He fights like no knight I've ever met – there's such grace to it.'

Bisclavret moves with a fluidity that's hard to match, but that's not what has caught your attention – your gaze has snagged on the small scars that glimmer white against his sun-dappled skin. A dozen small wounds, by the looks of things, and some of them deep. They're marks you'd expect to see on a man who has been fighting all his life, not one only lately recalled from exile.

More pieces of him that you don't understand.

'They seem to be enjoying themselves,' you say, and resent the staid, disapproving tone that creeps into your voice against your will and gives you the air of a humourless cleric.

'They love him,' your companion informs you. 'The castle rings with praise of him. He vanished that first night – they say he was badly taken by the wine, and stumbled off to be sick. Since then I'd say a half-dozen of them have called on him in his home, and found a courteous welcome there, though it's taken until today to lure him back here. He may be rustic and unpolished, but he has the knack of making himself liked. Look,' he adds, gesturing to the fight, which Bisclavret has won. 'They're cheering him for beating one of their best fighters.'

They love him.

How easy it is for Bisclavret. How readily he has come into this world, into this life, and made a place for himself in it. But you, for all you grew up here and thought you called it home once, still feel the castle's welcome as conditional, and you wait always for the moment when it will be taken away again. When you will be sent away, again.

Your sharp-tongued knight has spotted you. Pulling his green tunic over his head, he hails you from across the courtyard, and immediately the others look up, calling out greetings, jumping to their feet in respect. Bisclavret is panting; he pushes his hair back from his eyes and grins at you, a feral grin, before he tames it into something more appropriate.

'Good morning, my lord,' says one of the knights. 'Have you come to wrestle with us?'

A burst of raucous laughter at that – though not, you think, in mockery of you, but of those who might try themselves against you. You feel a surge of warmth at the idea of trying yourself against Bisclavret, and squash it. 'I came to see what manner of trouble you were making for yourselves,' you say, and then add, in a lighter tone, 'and to escape the seneschal's lecture on the cost of candles. He claims we are being too profligate, so I thought I'd best ask you how well you fare at seeing in the dark.'

'I can read as well by moonlight as I can by day,' offers one knight, with a lopsided grin. 'Which is to say not at all.'

His fellows jeer, offering good-natured teasing; some were tonsured in their youth, and are as literate and Latinate as any cleric, and the large part of the rest will have their alphabet or more, but there's always one who takes to the sword more readily than to letters, and abandons his schooling at the first chance. 'Careful what you say, for we're watched by a man of words,' you tell them, and gesture for your scribe to join you. 'You've met few enough of these men before, have you not? Make better your acquaintances, for I would have you all as friends and brothers.'

There's a pause. Then your knight in green steps forward to embrace him. 'I hear you're late of a Cistercian monastery,' he says. 'What was it that lured you away?'

While they talk, you turn to Bisclavret, who is hastily emerging from the undertunic he has just pulled over his head. You try not to let your eyes linger on the way it clings to his sweat-soaked skin, too warm from fighting to shiver yet in the frigid air. 'I'm told you have been entertaining visitors,' you say, in such an even tone that you're proud of your own restraint. 'Is your father's manor to your liking?'

'Yes, sire,' he says, 'though a little worse for its abandonment, and we will be hard-pushed to patch every leak in the roof before the winter storms set in. But it is no discomfort I have not weathered before, and in a far finer setting. My cousin has found excellent servants, though I am still growing used to such a large household.'

Behind his words linger a dozen stories. 'I am glad. And I am glad, too, that your wine-sickness seems to have done no lasting damage.'

He flushes red. 'Forgive me. I had not intended to leave so early, and without bidding you goodnight. I am only lucky that my cousin took care of me.'

He would not have found you there to speak to, even if he had stayed, for you let melancholy drive you to bed unfashionably early. But shame keeps you from saying so. 'There isn't a man among these knights who hasn't found himself in the same position,' you assure him instead, clapping a hand to his shoulder. 'And the lady spoke most highly of you.'

His blush deepens, and he cannot meet your eyes. 'She ... she said that you gave permission. For her to help me before the ceremony.'

'I gave the permission I was asked to give,' you say. 'The interest in you, however, was all hers. I believe she enjoyed your company.'

For the most part it is possible to forget that he is an untried exile with little experience of the court. But to see him stammer over the question of a lady – then he seems more rustic than ever, and more charming. You note the way his blush spreads to the skin of his neck, the tips of his ears, and wonder how it would feel to press your lips against it. Whether you would be able to discern the heat of it.

One thing is clear: if you remain here much longer, your thoughts will run entirely wild. 'I am needed indoors today,' you say, with all the dignity you are still able to muster, 'but I have a mind to train tomorrow. Will you be here?'

He hesitates a moment, and then nods. 'Yes, my lord,' he says. 'I will be here.'

You would hear him say that over and over again, if you could find an excuse to ask it. But all you say in response is, 'Good.' You turn to the rest: 'Come, scrivener. I need your pen. You will have to save any further fraternising for another hour.'

'My pen and ink are at your service,' says your scribe lightly, and extricates himself from the crowd, falling into step beside you as you return to the castle and pass through the hall to your own chamber.

Inside, you sit down on the edge of your bed and wonder

what it is you might do with this futile, wordless desire that weighs down your heart and threatens to consume you.

You cannot give it to Bisclavret. Even if he wanted it, it strikes you that he would not allow himself to take it – and he does not want it. He is already half-smitten, his heart captured by your ward and her smile. An outcome easily foreseen, if you had thought to look for it, but you dared not, with this ever-growing need inside you. You have not felt a longing so powerful since the throbbing pangs of adolescence. Normally, desire is brief, fleeting, easily dissipated, but this – this threatens to choke and swallow you, the intensity of it, and you need ... you need a moment's rest from the sensation that something is expanding inside your ribcage and threatening to burst out, or you will not be able to bear it.

Your story-dealer, ink-spinner, scribe, and companion – he clears his throat and says, 'This business for which you need me ...'

An excuse, to escape the torment of Bisclavret's blushes. You pat the bed next to you. 'Will you sit here,' you say, 'and just ... hold me?'

Often you find some delight in letting him use you, but you have no taste for that today. You lean tentatively against him, and after a while he puts his arms around you. Very gradually, you shift into a horizontal position, tangled in each other's limbs, breath hot against necks. He says, in a voice so low it's hardly audible, 'Is it that bad, how your Bisclavret makes you feel?'

'I don't have words for it,' you confess, and curl tighter against him. 'Only this ... sense of *loss*, for something I never had.'

You expect him to offer solutions, or some wise or witty line of poetry from one of those old books of his. No doubt they have plenty to offer on the subject of love, and plenty more on the theme of desire. But he doesn't. He braids his fingers with yours, holding your hand tightly, and finally whispers, 'I'm sorry.'

He has nothing to be sorry for. You want to tell him that this is not his place, that you did not invite him here so that he could comfort you, that he has a part to play and this is not it.

But you cannot bring yourself to voice the words, so you pull him a little closer, and let yourself weep for the hollow ache inside you that you cannot understand or fill.

16

Him

✦ ✷ ✦

The lady again. She helps him with his armour, and the heavy mail turns to light in her hands, shimmering silver between clever fingers. The laces and fastenings of the rest are nothing to her. He should learn the trick of it himself, or else find an eager squire to help him, but he's loath to lose the simple intimacy of her hands as she binds him into the strange new skin he's been given.

She has bold, bright eyes, and she watches him intently. Sometimes he catches her staring, and she never flushes and looks away: she holds his gaze, stalwart and steady, waiting for him to react.

He doesn't know how to react. He doesn't know what it is that he wants from her.

He wants ... safety. He rides home each night and finds it in his barred door and the quiet peace of his father's manor, despite the ever-present sound of rain finding its way through the holes in the roof, the furniture lost to woodworm, the coldness of the bare walls with no hangings to keep out the chill. It helps to know that he has a place to retreat to, a way out when everything becomes overwhelming. But still it's lonely, to turn his back on the lights of the castle and make his daily pilgrimage to a place that has yet to start feeling like his own. Each morning when he rides out, he thinks to himself: *today I will stay*. Each night, he feels the wolf in his skin and leaves before it becomes more than a phantom. With enough time alone, enough quiet and stillness, he can persuade it back to sleep, but here amongst the noise and the lights it wakes up and demands attention.

His cousin waits for him most nights – always, ostensibly, with some question or decision to justify the waiting, but it's clear he is watching to be sure Bisclavret comes back. To be sure he comes back human.

And he does. Mostly. He's careful. He can do this, if he has his lonely nights away from everyone else, and never pushes the boundaries of his capabilities.

He feels as though he will spend his entire life being careful. He would like, for once, to be free.

And the woman – she's not freedom, as such. But he feels safe around her. Her touch is gentling; it doesn't wake the wolf. When he's with her, he feels as human as he ever does, and when she looks at him, it's clear that's all she sees. There's no sense of being stripped bare the way there is when the king's gaze rests on him a moment too long.

Maybe that's why he says, 'Perhaps this afternoon, we might visit the castle gardens together.'

Her smile is the sun breaking through thick clouds. 'I would welcome it,' she says. 'There are few flowers at this time of year, but there's beauty still, if you know where to look.'

He looks at her and wonders where else he could possibly turn his eye. 'Then you will have to show me.'

And she does. She is chaperoned, as ever, by her kinswoman – an aunt or suchlike, greying hair all but entirely hidden beneath her cap and veil, with a strict enough air, but she seems to approve of Bisclavret, for she always gives them enough distance to feel that they're alone. Bisclavret assumes, nonetheless, that his behaviour is being observed, and reported to the king, and tries not to examine too closely how he feels about the king watching him by proxy even in these moments of intimacy.

They walk together among the kitchen herbs that fill the air with their sweet scents, and he tells her about the rosemary that his mother grew from a cutting from the local monastery, which like enough still flourishes beside their home, if the servants have remembered to tend it. She tells him about her own mother, and the loom she inherited from her; about her weaving, and the colours that make her happiest. By the time they pass from the kitchen gardens to the orchard, her smile has grown into laughter like daylight, and his own smile creeps unaccustomed across his lips.

This late in the year, there are no apples left clinging to the branches, nor any other fruit that he might offer her, so in place of such sweetness, he finds himself telling her stories he has long kept close to his chest. About his father the knight, whose legacy loomed over the family long after he was gone, and in whose shadow he has always lived without knowing the man who cast it. About his mother and the strain that exile put on her – second only to the strain of being mother to a monster, which was what undid her, in the end, as it would anybody who looked into a cradle and felt only horror at what they saw there. He may as well have killed her himself.

Bisclavret refrains from mentioning that part, though something about the lady invites his confidences. Nevertheless, he thinks she understands the true nature of what he is telling her, the loneliness and the love and the resentment all, though her own stories sound different resonances.

By the time they hear the church bells ringing for Vespers, they are no longer strangers to each other. Bisclavret walks her to her chamber – up a small stair, at the other end of the hall from the king's own room – as though he is courting her, and perhaps he is. He knows not if this is friendship or something else, nor what she wants it to be, and he will not humiliate himself by asking.

'Wait here for a moment,' she tells him, and he does. She returns with a long, woven strip, such that she might have worn as a belt, made in all the colours she said brought her joy. Carefully, she wraps it around his own waist; it is just long enough, over his winter layers, to tie. 'There. Now you may wear my handiwork and my colours.'

He swallows the lump in his throat and takes her hand that he might kiss it. 'You do me too great an honour.'

'I have spied you at training,' she says, with a small smile, 'and more than that I have heard tell from the grooms and the servants how well it is that you acquit yourself. So it seems to me I best make known my favour now, before you have the whole kingdom in love with you.'

In love. The words hang half-spoken in the air between them, though she neither confirms them as her own feelings nor makes to deny them. Bisclavret looks at the gift she has given him – tablet woven, he thinks; his mother taught him, once, to occupy his idle hands, but he never had the knack of patterning like this – and his hopes and affections and fears flood through him all at once, tangled in each other, because *he can't do this*, but something about her makes him believe that he could. She sees only his humanity and, in her presence, so does he.

'I will wear it with pride,' he tells her.

And he does, over his armour and his surcoat in the king's colours. The first time he appears in this array to train as usual, the other knights bombard him with questions and the king wears a strange look, as though he is not sure whether or not he approves. And why should he? Bisclavret's lands are fine enough, but she is the king's own ward, and she will marry someone far greater than he, someone better educated and better attuned to the rhythms of courtly life.

He says as much, when the king remarks that he has seen her watching their training. Immediately he regrets it, in case it appears that he is declaring his intention to court her. But the king only says, 'I promised her that I would be guided by her desires, when it comes to her future. So far she has given none of her time to the men who come angling for her hand. She enjoys walking with you; she speaks of it gladly.'

It's as good as approval, and yet there is something cool in the king's tone. He will be guided by her desires, perhaps, but he would prefer them directed elsewhere – is that the truth of it?

Bisclavret tries to push the issue from his mind in favour of thinking about his sword-work, but his preoccupation must be showing, for after they're done sparring, the knight in the green surcoat announces that he's taking him into the village for a drink. He'll acknowledge no objections. 'You succumb too easily to wine-sickness,' he says, with a mischievous gleam in his eyes. 'I have appointed myself your tutor, the better to teach you to resist this enemy.'

The castle's ale-wife brews a fine ale, and jealously she guards the secret of her recipes, but she has fierce competition down in the village, and there's one woman in particular who is the true mistress of the art. Her husband's farm is popular with locals and travellers alike, who find there entertainment and a drink and a bed for the night: it's a welcoming rest-stop for those ragged travellers who dare not beg alms at the castle gate, or those with miles to go and no taste for the austere cells of the monastery to the north. It's also a popular gathering place for knights in search of cheer and sport, away from the eyes of their

lords, their king, and the castle chaplain – though it would be
rare to see them there at this time, scarcely past Sext with the
winter sun high in the sky.

Despite the hour, they receive a ready welcome, and there's
an easy humour in the way the knight in green speaks to the
mistress of the house. He knows her children by name, and
greets the littlest of them, peering out shyly from behind her
mother's skirts. Soon he has secured for them both good-sized
cups of ale, and bread, too, to strengthen them after sparring.
And, most importantly, a place that they may talk without an
audience – save the curious eyes of one child or another, lingering in the doorway to delay their chores.

It seems the knight does not plan to interrogate Bisclavret
about his intentions towards the king's ward, nor to admonish
him for his inattention during their training this morning. He
speaks instead of the other knights, determined to explain their
histories and rivalries, their loves and losses.

'You've already made a fair impression,' he says, eyes bright
with ale. 'There's no danger that they'll see you as an intruder
now – but still, it's never easy to be a newcomer, and most of us
have been brothers since we first came to court as children. It's
time you knew more of us than our sword-work.'

'I have tried,' begins Bisclavret uncertainly; there have been
so many new faces to keep track of, and so little opportunity
to talk. He has begun, gradually, to match heraldry to names
and names to lands, but every time he thinks he has a sense
of it, one man or another will have returned to his estate and
somebody else come to court, and he must start again.

'I'm not reprimanding you,' says the other knight. 'I mean to
help.' He begins with a knight with hair like fire and a tongue
sharp as a whip. 'He's famous for his pride, and well he might
be – he was near unbeatable in a fight before you came to court.

I think it's a challenge to him that a man with so little formal training can rival his skill. But you've entirely different styles, and if you praise his footwork, you'll win him over in no time. And if you see him with a dark-haired lady, that's his sister, for all they don't look alike. Compliment her, but not too effusively or he'll think you mean to woo her. It would not serve you well to have a reputation for treating women lightly – better to avoid any misunderstandings.'

Bisclavret nods, more grateful than he knows how to express. He has felt adrift, these first weeks, unsure of his standing or how to behave among the other men. The knights have their jokes and squabbles, but they also have courtly manners, and their true feelings can be hard to perceive. Even when he is certain that their welcome is genuine, he is lost for how to convey his gratitude without seeming to grovel for their favour.

By the time the knight has finished articulating the foibles and characteristics of his companions, Bisclavret's head is spinning, both from the ale he's drunk and the amount of information he's been given. Every knight, it seems, has victories to his name and stories spun about him; they have saved innocents from harm or defended another's honour or achieved some noble quest previously thought impossible.

He learns that the knight with the emblem of leaping fish on his shield holds lands contiguous with his own southern border; to his west, his neighbour carries the heraldry of a lion, 'though little he's been at court this winter, for his wife's heavy with child and deathly ill with it, and he mislikes to leave her.' He learns that most have known the king since he was a youth, and some shared his tutors in arms and learning, though few were as close to him as the knight in green. Before his exile, at least.

'He trusts me yet, I'd hazard,' says the knight thoughtfully, 'inasmuch as he trusts any, but he is still feeling his way. All the more important, then, that you know the currents of power for yourself, so that you are not swept away in his wake.'

All of it is useful knowledge to be given – and all of it seems to confirm Bisclavret's own inadequacy. 'I don't know why the king made me a knight,' he admits, the confession escaping against his better judgment. 'Most would have sent me away when I arrived at their coronation feast rain-soaked and hours late, not invited me on a hunt. And then to keep me around …'

'Really?' says the knight in green, giving him a sideways look. 'You've no idea?'

Bisclavret's heart sinks. So it's that obvious, then; he isn't imagining the way the king looks at him, the banked flame of desire that smoulders in his eyes. No wonder he speaks so coolly of his ward's care for Bisclavret. *He was tumbling one of the grooms.* What Bisclavret sees in the king's eyes feels more dangerous than a youthful fancy. It shears straight through him; the king's touch, he imagines, would unravel all remnants of his human skin and leave him wild and vicious.

He wouldn't dare reciprocate it. Doesn't dare examine his own feelings long enough to know if he would want to; better not to know, when he can't. Never mind the curious warmth that comes with knowing he's wanted – this would unmake them both, and cannot thus be countenanced, even in his own imaginings.

And yet – yet he is sworn to the king, sworn to his service, and if the man should *ask* …

It would be a bitter poison, to lose the king's friendship that way, but safety would demand the refusal. He couldn't explain, of course; knowledge of the wolf would only make things worse. But if it is desire that raised him to his place at court, that gave him back his inheritance, then he cannot expect to keep it once that fancy fades, or is smothered by rejection. And he cannot pretend he earned this fairly.

The knight must read his thoughts on his face, because the sly mischief fades from his expression. 'Bisclavret, you were dubbed in recognition of your skill and your lineage. Your lands are yours and nobody doubts your prowess with a blade.'

'There is more to a knight than the ability to swing a sword,' Bisclavret points out. 'Or to kill a boar. Or even, one might think, being born of a noble father. A knight is brave and noble and courageous. Knighthood is about honour, and courtesy, and ...' He trails off.

'On what grounds do you think you fail to meet those requirements?' asks the knight gently. 'Courtesy means not the manners of the court, though often we mistake the two. You have shown nothing but respect to your fellow knights; you've responded with grace to both victory and defeat. You have skill far beyond the most of us, but no arrogance to speak of, such that it shames those who have thought themselves superior. And if the hunt is any test of your bravery, then none can doubt it, for you slew that boar more fearlessly than any man ever went into battle.'

Bisclavret flushes. It is gratifying to hear his best traits articulated in this way, but it cannot smother his shame. 'And yet you imply still that the king dubbed me because of his own desire.'

'I spoke in jest, and shouldn't have,' says the knight. 'Yes, I have seen the way he looks at you. It is clear to me that he harbours some interest beyond the usual. But I have known the king since he was a child, and I not much more than one. I watched him play at knighthood while I dreamed of it myself, and as we grew older, I saw him go from a boy swinging a stick around to a clear-eyed and high-minded young man who handled a sword like the best of them. I would not presume that I always know his mind,' he adds, 'but I'd hazard I know him the best of any of his men, and so I can tell you that while I have often seen him momentarily captivated by a pretty face, I have never known him to act rashly because of it.'

A pretty face. Is that how the knight sees him? Is that how they all see him? 'And yet he sent his own ward to test me before my knighting.'

The knight shrugs, taking a long drink of his ale. Then he says, 'He would not have done that if he thought you would fail the test. And he would not allow a man even the possibility of kinship with his own household if he thought that man was unworthy of it.' He adds, a little sharply, 'Or is your opinion of the king's judgment so low that you think him easily swayed to unwise decisions?'

'No,' responds Bisclavret immediately, chastened by the accusation. 'Of course not.'

'Yet your opinion of yourself is so poor that you doubt any who disagree with it. As though we are foolish, and unable to see for ourselves what qualities a man might possess – as though we have not the knowledge and experience to see your value for ourselves.'

It's a gentle rebuke, but it feels like a blow with the flat of his sword. 'That isn't what I meant.'

'It's what you said, meant or not.' He leans forward, clasps Bisclavret's hand. 'You may not be able to see your own qualities, but please, spare us the discourtesy of assuming we are similarly afflicted. The king may be young and untested, but he is not a king to place his own desires above the common good. He sees what I do – that you have the makings of a knight, and are fair worthy of your inheritance. And,' he adds, 'that you have a face the poets would write ballads about.' This is said with a teasing smile.

Bisclavret feels heat rise in his face, but this time no shame or discomfort feeds his embarrassment. 'The poets,' he says wryly, 'clearly have nothing better to do.'

At that the knight cackles, and pushes Bisclavret's cup closer towards him. 'Such is the life of a poet,' he says. 'Now drink. If there's one way in which you fail to live up to the men, it's your capacity for drunkenness, and I've taken it on myself to change that. The next feast will see you carousing with the best of them. And when we're done here, I'm under orders from my wife to bring you home with me, that she might get a look at the man who has all the court talking. So best to down it, or we'll keep her waiting.'

Bisclavret drinks, and feels the sparks of belonging ignite inside him.

17

You

✦ ✳ ✦

Everywhere you look, Bisclavret is there.

If you thought his absence unbearable, then his presence is worse, for you can think of little else but him. When you spar with the knights, you are perpetually distracted by the way he fights, fluid and dangerous as a river after a storm. Your gaze snags on the coloured belt he wears, declaring his affections for all to see; catches on his smile when your ward comes to watch him fight. Perhaps you should feel kinship with her, a shared admiration; perhaps you should be glad of the excuse to bring Bisclavret ever closer into your household – but all you feel is a strange, cruel jealousy, one that ill becomes you.

Still, you have learned courtesy the way prey animals learn survival, and you like to think no hint of your lovesickness is apparent to those around you. But the mask comes closest to cracking – to shattering entirely – the day you go in search of your scribe with some fabricated request for a letter you wish him to compose, and find Bisclavret in his chambers.

You're about to turn on your heel and go, but your knight spots you, rising from his seat with an apology already springing to his lips. The movement draws the scrivener's attention, and he looks up.

'How can I help?' he asks immediately, as though you have no relationship beyond the needs of a king for a fair hand to copy his scrawled epistles.

'I—' You look from him to Bisclavret. You cannot imagine what business they might have together. 'It's unimportant. I'll come back later.'

'No, by all means,' says Bisclavret, already gathering himself to leave. 'I wouldn't wish my presence to delay you. I can go.'

'I'll return later,' you repeat, and make good your escape. In your chamber, the door firmly closed, you sink to the floor. It shouldn't feel so strange to see the two of them together: you introduced them, and you have made it clear you wish your knights to welcome the scribe as a part of your household. There is no reason Bisclavret should not avail himself of the man's services.

And yet.

As you half-expected, your custodian of books comes in search of you a little later, letting himself in to your chamber without hesitation. 'I should have warned you,' he says. 'He asked me to teach him to read.'

Whatever you were expecting, it wasn't that. 'He did?'

'His exile, it seems, afforded few opportunities for a formal education; his mother's teachings were more practical than literary, and he can scarcely read his own name, let alone write it. He sought me out with the vague idea that I might be a tactful tutor, unlikely to pass judgment on his failings.' He sits down next to you. 'Of course I agreed immediately. He'll be vulnerable if he's not literate, and his steward handling it all.'

It ought to have occurred to you that a man who had so rarely left his mother's estate might not be lettered, but the thought never crossed your mind. 'Of course you should teach him,' you say. 'I might have suggested it, had I known.'

Your scribe's mouth twists in a knowing smile. 'But I ought to have told you when it started. You were taken by surprise today. I'm sorry.'

He doesn't owe you apologies, and you are being absurd even to find this situation startling. Bisclavret has half the castle in his thrall, his grace on the field matched only by his kindness, and that's as it should be. But you underestimated the effect it would have on you.

The effect *he* would have on you.

'I hear you hired a new sword master,' says your keeper of books.

Your father trained his own knights; there has been no man hired for the role since the master who taught you to fight as a youth passed away. Until now, you'd thought you might continue in the same way, for you are well able to train your own men. But after seeing Bisclavret fight, you know you will never be enough to nurture that talent – and you have begun to wonder what the rest of your knights might be capable of if pushed to their limits.

'The seneschal assured me the funds would not have gone to parchment or ink whatever happened,' you say, with a brief smile. 'But yes.'

The scribe nods. You have the odd notion that he would like to try himself against the man, though it would be un-fitting of his position. Against Bisclavret too, no doubt. You have never seen him fight, but you know he's capable of it: you have seen the scars that mar his skin, the remnants of a dozen bloody battles. He's evasive whenever you ask about them, as he is about any aspect of his past, but there must be a story; however harsh the discipline of his monastery might have been, no monkish scourge or mortification left those marks. Perhaps once he wore both sword and cross, though you'd have thought him too young to have waged holy war.

For a few moments you sit in silence together. Finally, you say, 'Has he told you much about his upbringing?'

'Little enough. I do know his mother taught him to weave and to sew and manage the housekeeping; it seems they had very few servants. His new estate must be quite an adjustment, though I don't doubt his cousin is well able for managing it for him. He's Bisclavret's heir, you know,' he adds. 'He had me draw up a charter that would ensure it. The cousin's the sixth of six and has no inheritance coming to him from anywhere else, and Bisclavret's had no contact with the rest of the family since he was quite young, but I suppose he still fears they might lay claim to his estate should he die unexpectedly.'

'Has he told you why?' you ask, then add, more petulantly than you intended, 'He has not spoken to me of his family.'

Your scribe purses his lips and says, 'Have you asked him?'

Not in as many words. In truth, you've spent more time sparring than in conversation. But neither has the man volunteered information, or shown himself to be open to such a discussion. 'Do you think he would answer?' you say. 'After all, I must have asked you a dozen times for your story and I have yet to hear it.'

He gives you that half-smile he always does when you needle him about his past. 'You don't want my story, my lord, though you may think you do. You'd lose all respect for me.'

Which only feeds your curiosity, but you have learned that pursuing that line of questioning will get you nowhere. 'And does Bisclavret feel the same way, do you think?'

He considers this. 'I think if he wishes to speak of his family, he will. No, he hasn't told me what manner of feud or falling-out has caused this estrangement. I also haven't asked. I suspect he would prefer to construct for himself a new story, free of the shadow of his exiled youth – a story of a knight in the court of the king. You could give him that. You have *already* given him that.'

You want more. But you don't know how to ask for it.

'You should go,' you say finally. 'You must have work to be doing, and it will not please the seneschal to think you have my ear.'

He grimaces. 'One day, perhaps, the man could start trusting me,' he says, but he gets to his feet and makes for the door without complaint. Then he stops and says, 'I can't make this easier on you, nor can I tell you honestly whether it will pass as an infatuation does, or grow the way passions do when left untended. All I can tell you is not to torture yourself, lest your hair turn white before you know it.'

With that, and the return of his usual grin, he leaves you be.

Infatuation. Is that what it is? Probably. You're behaving like a youth ten years your junior, and you're at risk of embarrassing yourself. As the day wears on, you try to force yourself to sober pursuits, but the business of kingship is tedious when your heart is elsewhere, and you cannot keep your thoughts from intruding. No wonder your father was so often in an ill temper, cooped up all day listening to reports of lands you've never seen, or the twittering of advisers over rumours of a war that will likely never reach you, even if it does eventually erupt.

In the end, your restlessness becomes so powerful that you abandon all efforts to tame it, and decide to go for a ride before your prowling aggravates your servants entirely. You have the grooms saddle your father's most vicious-minded destrier: the warhorse is trained to courage but has never welcomed any touch but your father's, and the effort of imposing your will on the intractable creature will occupy your wits and keep you from slipping into further rumination.

You mean to go alone – or as alone as you are ever allowed to be, now, with guards following at a discreet distance – but you're not far past the main gate when you hear the clatter of hooves on the stony ground behind you, and you turn to see your knight in green. He's dressed for a ride, his hair streaming in the wind.

'If I'd wanted company, I would have asked for it,' you say, trying not to sound unwelcoming.

'I thought I'd spare the guards the effort of keeping up with you,' he replies, with an easy smile. 'Besides which, not wanting company is not the same as not needing it.'

You scowl and spur your horse forward without answering. He follows, holding his tongue, and soon you're past the village and out of earshot of anyone who might care to listen. As you anticipated, the destrier is stubborn and high-spirited, and the presence of another horse has him minded to show off; your hands and thoughts alike are consumed by the strain of keeping him to a steady canter.

Eventually you slow so that the both of you can catch your breath, and your knight does likewise. 'Would it help to talk?' he says.

'Of what?' you snap.

He shrugs. 'Of whatever it is that has you so nettled, my lord.'

There's a fond, faintly sarcastic note to the honorific – a reminder that while you may feel you returned from exile a different man to the one who left, you are still enough the same to be unable to hide your mood from a man who has known you since you were only a boy. He was never quite your peer, always a few years ahead, but you had a friendship, and you've done him a disservice not to acknowledge it more since your return. You glance sideways at him, trying to gauge the extent of his knowledge. There's nothing of the scribe's knowing humour in his expression, but it's clear he, too, has an inkling of your mind. He has known you too long to be easily fooled.

'Bisclavret,' you say finally, and the destrier shifts beneath you as though the sound of his name sets him as restless as it does you.

'Ah,' he responds, and waits for you to elaborate.

'He is … he is the sort of man any king would wish for a knight, and any man for a friend.'

He raises his eyebrow. 'That sounds like something to be glad about. What troubles you about plucking such an excellent knight from obscurity?'

You shrug and look away. 'Perhaps the very fact that I brought him out of his obscurity. Have I not thrown in the faces of all my knights their service and training?'

'Have no fear on that account,' he says immediately. 'The men love him; nobody resents his knighting. We are only saddened for his sake that it took so long, for he should have been dubbed ten years gone.'

You believe him – your knights have ever been better men than you, not prone to jealousy, and this man knows their hearts the way few others do, and would not tell you falsely.

'You don't think me a fool, then?' you ask, in a voice smaller than befits a king.

'For returning a man's inheritance and bringing him back to his proper position? I can't think what could be less foolish.'

Of course it was *proper*, it was *right*, it was the *way things should have been*, and yet none of that was on your mind when you took his oaths from him. 'I suppose, over time,' you begin vaguely, 'it will all be … easier.'

'No doubt,' he agrees. 'My wife is of the mind that all change is disruptive until it is old, even when it is for the better.'

And there has been such a lot of change, these past months, not least your presence here and this crown on your head. 'A wise woman,' you acknowledge.

'The wisest, save that she married me.' His smile is fond. 'You're not alone in being caught out by a beautiful man once in a while.'

So he knows, then. Well, of course he knows. You were youths together, fighting with sticks in the shadow of the forest, and you have never been skilled at hiding your feelings. 'I wager she benefitted more from the entanglement than I will,' you say, only a little wistfully.

He cocks his head. 'Perhaps,' he allows. 'But you've his fealty, and he his knighthood, and few things bind a man more tightly than those.' He clicks his tongue, nudging his horse into movement. 'Shall I race you, sire? To the river?'

You hesitate, but the destrier is itching to run and part of you feels the same way, battle-roused without a fight into which to channel your passion. 'Sword drills before Prime for the loser,' you suggest.

'Before Lauds, surely, my lord,' he counters, 'for it to be a fitting wager,' and before you have time to agree or object, he has spurred his mount into action, his laughter ringing in the air as you begin your pursuit.

18

Him

It's been three weeks now, perhaps longer. Three weeks in his own skin, and more still to be thankful for. He whispers his gratitude in the chapel as he kneels for Mass like a man with nothing on his mind but knighthood. His Confession is still only half a truth but it feels like more than that, and he can neither hide his joy from the chaplain nor explain it. With the scribe's help, he traces the words in the psalter and feels the echo of their rejoicing: *in pace in idipsum dormiam et requiescam, quoniam tu Domine singulariter in spe constituisti me. In peace in the selfsame I will sleep, and I will rest: for thou, O Lord, singularly hast settled me in hope.*

For the first time in his life he has friends, true friends: the knight in green and his wife who make him welcome in their home; the flame-haired knight and his sister; all the men who have welcomed him into their brotherhood. He has the scribe and his patience, and the chaplain and his intercession. Impossibly, wonderfully, he belongs.

And the wolf has not come for three weeks.

He almost wishes it would, just to free him from the anticipation of it: the longer the wait, the harder the fall will be. But he's being so careful, and it almost feels like having control over it.

And when she helps him with his armour, the lady says, 'There is something gentle in you, Bisclavret,' as though she can't see the wildness and ferocity waiting to tear him apart.

As she spreads salve on the bruises he earns by sparring, she says, 'You are a good man,' as though he is no more or less than that.

And one day, as they walk through the frost-glittering gardens together, their breath forming white clouds in front of their faces, she says, 'Your father's estate must be a lonely place, without family to fill it. Do you plan always to live there alone?'

He cannot make sense of this question, doesn't know what she's asking. 'My cousin is the only kinsman with whom I have any friendship,' he says. 'There are no others whom I might invite there, and I … well, I …'

She takes pity on him, linking their arms together as she says, 'I meant a wife, Bisclavret.'

Oh.

'I have never …' He trails off. 'The opportunity has never …'

She stops walking, bringing them both to a halt. 'The opportunity is here,' she says, bringing his gloved hand to her chest, over her heart. 'I would marry you, Bisclavret, if you would have me.'

Others might see impertinence in this declaration, but Bisclavret is overwhelmingly grateful to know her mind so plainly, when he would never have dared to guess.

'You would?' She is an orphaned daughter of a knight, but she is also the king's ward, beautiful and learned, and he is far from her best prospect. He has so little to offer her, and so much to hide.

'I would,' she says. 'I would be your wife, Bisclavret. There is no man in the court that I love so well as you, and I hate to see you lonely.'

He has long ceased to think of himself as lonely, but it's true he's losing his taste for solitude. Perhaps one companion, one more person in his home, would not greatly alter the peace of it. She brings with her such calm that he can't imagine her presence doing anything but keeping the wolf at bay.

And she is lonely too. She hasn't said as much, but he hears it in her stories, and knows the loss of her father left her as abandoned in the world as the loss of his mother left him. The king has been kind to her, and her life in the castle is a comfortable one, but it isn't hers – just borrowed rooms and borrowed riches, waiting for the day when she makes her own home.

What harm could it do for two abandoned souls to find comfort in each other? She feels like safety: in her presence he is human. And she is kind. He has had precious little kindness in his life.

He knows what his cousin would say. What the priest of his childhood would say, or his mother, or his own common sense. To bring her home as his wife would be to put her in danger. Beyond that, she'll want an explanation for the nights that he's away, and he has none to offer her, nothing to say that won't leave her feeling spurned and neglected. And if they were to have children, would they also bear his curse? To his knowledge, his father was unmarred by any such monstrosity, but he has been given no other explanation for his own nature that might assure him of the impossibility of passing it down to a babe.

Perhaps (he thinks, clutching at desperate hope) it is some unique weakness of his soul that renders it incapable of remaining in a human body; a child, its soul shaped afresh by God, would not share this failing. Perhaps he doesn't have a soul at all, he thinks suddenly, and that prompts questions he'd like to pose to a priest if only he could find the words to express them.

In their sermons and prayers they speak of man being made in God's image, but what does that mean when his own shape is so changeable? Is it his soul or his body that reflects the Almighty? For if it is his body, then either the Lord is more strange than has been preached to him, or he spends at least part of his time outside of the glories of creation, some uncreated thing.

And if it is his soul … well, he has enough of his mind in wolf-shape to suppose that he keeps his soul, too. He is a human in a wolf's body, driven by a wolf's hungers without being slave to its desires, and his shifting does not take everything from him.

'I am sworn to the king,' he says finally, 'and you are his ward. I would need to ask his blessing.'

Her expression has been nervous, earnest, but now it fractures into a small smile. 'And will you?'

'Yes,' he tells her. 'I will ask him.'

The king has good judgment. The king will know in his heart if this is wise, and if he agrees, then all will be well, and a marriage will be well, and their children will be well.

But in his heart of hearts, Bisclavret fears – wishes? – that the king will see this for the danger it must surely be, and refuse him.

* ✳ *

It proves more difficult than Bisclavret anticipated to find the right moment to speak with the king. He could seek an audience as petitioners do, or catch him after their sparring practice in the morning instead of staying to exchange the usual banter with the other knights, but neither feels like the right environment for this conversation. He practises the request alone at night, trying to find the words, and still it seems presumptuous to ask for this and expect it to be granted. Part of him almost believes she was testing him when she asked, and will retract her favour if he proves himself so easily led.

The words of the knight in green come back to him: *You may not be able to see your own qualities, but please, spare us the discourtesy of assuming we are similarly afflicted.* He must trust her to know her own mind and express it honestly.

Still, he's close to losing his courage when he stumbles upon the king in the armoury. It's a surprise to see him there, diligently repairing some small damage to his hauberk as though he doesn't have servants to cater to his every whim. He has the knack of it, twisting rings back into shape and scrubbing away the rust that's accumulated in the poor weather, and he doesn't look up as Bisclavret enters, only says, 'If you've a spare hand, would you pass me that cloth?'

Looking around, Bisclavret sees the cloth lying over a bench and hands it to him. It's only as the rag changes hands that the king looks up, and smiles to see him there.

Bisclavret gestures to the armour. 'Is it fitting for you to be doing that yourself, sire?'

The king snorts, and it's hard to imagine a less regal sound. 'I have hands, do I not? This crown on my head doesn't render me entirely helpless.'

'I'm sorry,' begins Bisclavret. 'I didn't mean to imply otherwise.'

'No, of course you didn't,' says the king. He has a wistful look. 'A season ago, I was an exile who could scarcely persuade a groom to feed my horse without an incentive, so little did they care for me or any power I might one day hold. Now I must evade my own seneschal to be permitted to do anything useful for myself.'

'That must be ... strange.'

'Strange is one word for it.' The king twists his expression into a smile and resumes his work. 'As it happens, I have a busy mind and idle hands, and this struck me as a useful occupation for them both. Was there something you needed in here? If I'm in your way—'

'I came to borrow a whetstone,' Bisclavret admits. 'I expected to find the place empty at this hour. But now that I have you here ...' He pauses. The words are harder to find than ever. 'There is a matter about which I have been meaning to speak with you.'

The king lowers his work to his lap and sits up a little straighter. Aside from their training sessions together, they've talked little these past weeks. Bisclavret has become just another thread in the tapestry of castle life, unremarkable in his presence – and it would be a lie to say it hasn't been a purposeful act, for the king's keen interest unsettles him as much as it thrills him, an intensity in it that he doesn't know how to match.

'Go ahead,' says the king.

Bisclavret pauses, whets his lips. How to phrase it? How to make the request seem reasonable, conventional, within the bounds of his oaths and plausible for a man like himself?

In the end he puts it simply: 'I seek your blessing to take your ward as my wife.'

The king looks at him for a long moment, as though he's speaking a foreign tongue. Meaning seems to reach him only slowly, until finally he says, 'Your wife? And ... and she has indicated her willingness, has she?'

'She has. It was her understanding that you would allow her to act according to her own desires in this matter. I know ... I know that perhaps, as she is a member of your household, you might have hoped for a more auspicious match, but I can promise that I, at least, have troubled to know her before think-ing of this, and would treat her courteously. My lord,' he adds hastily, trying to remember that he is a knight asking a boon of his king, not merely a cursed wolf-thing begging to be allowed some piece of normality in his life.

The king puts down his cloth and regards his empty hands for a moment. 'Well,' he says at last, 'I can think of no objection, if you are both happy with the match.'

Happy. Is he? Bisclavret is unsure whether he was shaped for happiness, or whether the best he can hope for is to be more content some days than others, but perhaps in the end that's as close as anyone comes. 'You truly have no objections, my lord?'

The king gives a strange, jerky nod. 'If I marry, it will be for the kingdom, not for myself. No reason that she should bear the same burden. I promised her a choice in this matter and I will keep my word. And,' he adds, with a smile that wavers and fades before it fully takes shape, 'I can think of no better man than you to ask for her hand.'

Bisclavret swallows the lump in his throat. 'Thank you, sire.'

'Speak to the seneschal about her dowry; he manages her inheritance. And you're best off discussing the practicalities with the chaplain directly. May I trust that you will give her the good news yourself?' In that moment, he reminds Bisclavret of his cousin: efficient, his mind turning at once to the practical details, carefully skirting the issue of his wolf-sickness, except that it is ignorance, not tact, which keeps the king from the subject.

'I will. Thank you.'

'Go, then,' says the king, 'with my blessing.' And then he picks up his cloth and resumes his polishing as though the matter is settled and there is nothing more to be said. No warnings or admonishments, no attempts to persuade him away from a course that will inevitably result in destruction. Surely a king, in his wisdom and good-judgment, should be able to see the danger lurking?

But whatever it is the king sees when he pierces Bisclavret's soul with his gaze, it isn't the wolf.

Bisclavret goes.

19

You

His wife.

You saw this coming, almost from the first time she spoke to you of him, but still it pierces you like an arrow, startling and painful. You agree before you can think of a reason to refuse – and what reason, truly, could you give that did not also do her a disservice? – and he bows his head and leaves, giving you no opportunity to reconsider. But it would have changed nothing if he'd waited a month for your answer. You wouldn't take from him his happiness. You've seen how the weight on his shoulders lifts when he's with her; she smooths away the creases in his brow, gives him the comfort you cannot, and no true friend would rob him of that.

And yet.

And yet you watch him leave with the sense of something ending. And yet you know that when he is married, he'll spend less time at court (it's inevitable; it is the way of things). He will not want for adventure; he will lose his taste for the hunt, unwilling to travel far from home and his lady. It will become harder and harder to drag him from his bed in the mornings to ride out with you and, eventually, you will lose him.

Not immediately. It's never immediate, and you have known Bisclavret long enough by now to know that he will not shirk his responsibilities or break his oaths. He will do his duty and more, and he has exemplars enough to follow – there are others among your knights who are married, and they do not let it keep them from court. But neither are they unchanged by it.

And if he is married, then he is lost to you.

He isn't yours. He was never yours. He was never *going* to be yours, but the secret hope was a small lie you could tell yourself without guilt. No more the innocent pleasure of wistful desire: such a thing will always be wreathed in shame for the selfishness and discourtesy of it, for you cannot think that way of a man who belongs to another.

Whatever his lady is able to offer him – her gentleness, her safety, her beauty, whatever it is that draws him – isn't something you can give. If it were, he would have asked for it, you would have offered it, it would already be satisfied by these oaths and bonds that tangle you in each other's lives. And if you cannot be what he wants, then you must put aside your jealousy and let him find it where he will. To *help* him find it where he will, with all of your power and all of your heart.

This, too, is love: a sacrifice made willingly, to ease his darkness and bring him forward into something lighter.

But perhaps even a heathen before a burning altar might, for a moment, regret the blood spilled there and wish once again for the return of the slain beast. Is it not human, to be grieved by this kind of loss, by the knowledge that your beloved loves another? It may be a poor friend who resents his friends' joys, even when they come at a cost to himself, but you have always suspected you're a poor friend.

You go, as you find yourself doing too often these days, to see the only man in the castle to whom you can speak freely. Your chaplain is wont merely to look sympathetic and prescribe prayers as though they are the remedy to cure all ills, and your seneschal has little time for feelings when there is always work to be done; neither will offer you any comfort today.

Your scribe is working intently, his pen in one hand and a knife in the other, carefully shaping trails of neat black letters. Propped in front of him are his wax tablets, filled with scrawled and abbreviated notes on whatever story he is now transcribing. He must have heard it from one of the storytellers, or else begged a glance at a book they carried.

He says, 'You know, many would frown on a king taking counsel from someone other than his noble vassals. From a peasant and a foreigner, no less.'

'Is that what you are?' you say, taking a seat on the bench across from him. 'Even with all your monastery-learning?'

'Perhaps in the eyes of God we are all peasants. Or all noble.' He darts a smile in your direction. '*Omnes enim vos unum estis in Christo Iesu.* Nevertheless, I am no baron, to advise your rule and your choices.'

You consider this. 'It is not advice I seek,' you say finally. 'Only sympathy.'

He doesn't put down his pen, but he pauses in his writing. 'That, perhaps, a common scribe might offer,' he says.

It makes it easier that he isn't looking at you: you don't have to hide your expression as you say, 'Bisclavret is to be married.'

His brow creases for a moment. He resumes writing in silence, and only when he has formed the final letter of the line does he pause, glance up, and say, 'Will that make him happy?'

Your voice is unsteady as you say, 'I hope so. I would like to think it will. He – he seems to think so.'

'But it will make you unhappy.' This isn't a question: he can read that much on your face.

'It has no right to,' you say. 'I should be happy for him. I *am* happy for him – and for her. I wanted for her a kind husband who will treat her well, and she cannot do better. I want him to have what he needs, and that is not me. I have no reason to feel this way. I cannot resent him seeking out his happiness, wherever he finds it.'

'*Should* is a dangerous word when it comes to feelings,' he says, laying down his pen. 'Should we be sad when an elderly relative, who has lived a long and full life, passes away in their sleep? Should we fear death at all, when we are promised such delights on the other side? Should *any* love or hate or jealousy or happiness or grief exist? Perhaps not. Perhaps they are never justified. But we feel what we feel, and our hearts are no great respecters of reason.'

'That isn't the point,' you protest.

'I think it is,' he responds. 'You are holding yourself to an impossible standard, my lord. By all means, recognise that your feelings should not be acted upon, but it is no sin to feel them.'

He should know, after his time in the monastery, though you have the thought that some would disagree with his theology, and still others with his politics. A king should not have desires of his own. A king's heart belongs to his people, to his land; his own hungers are immaterial, and his follies a burden his people must not be asked to bear.

Your scribe picks up his pen again, and you watch him write for a few moments. There are as many words in your head as there are on his page, but they resist your efforts to marshal them into sentences. Finally, you say, 'I fear being replaced.'

'That's because,' he says, without looking up, 'you believe you are replaceable.'

The words settle oddly in the air, ringing with a truth you cannot deny. You are their king: if you die, the kingdom will mourn for you, and without a named heir, they will be left adrift. The crown will be fought over, and amidst the chaos and struggles for power, lives will be lost and others altered. Nobody could argue that your death would pass unmarked.

But would they miss you?

Would your knights miss you – your knights whom you are only now beginning to know again, after so long away, unwanted even by your kin? Is there anything you can offer Bisclavret that he cannot find elsewhere? His lands should have been his in any case. If you were gone, and another king crowned, he would swear his fealty again and all would continue as before. Nobody would think your loss too great to bear, once the tumult had passed.

He finds companionship amongst the knights. Happiness with his lady. Pride and honour in his armour and the strength of his arm. He does not need you.

But you need him. It's absurd, the intensity with which you need him. Your morning training sessions together have aroused in you a passion for swordplay that you thought lost, your childhood delight in the blade long since worn away by the weighty demands of your father's expectations. He has blown away the cobwebs of familiarity and reminded you of all that is surprising and delightful about the physicality of knighthood.

And he has woken the rest of your court in the same way. Your knights are bright-eyed. They fight harder, dare more, live more boldly because he is among them.

It is no wonder his lady loves him.

'I am replaceable,' you say. It is a relief to admit it, like giving your fear a name has tamed it. 'There is nothing about me that another could not imitate. I have nothing to offer him, or anyone else.'

Your scribe puts down his quill and penknife and comes over to you. He takes your hands in his; you hadn't realised they were shaking until he holds them still. 'One day you will learn that that isn't true,' he says. 'One day you will see yourself as the man I know, the one I chose to follow here, when I might have gone to any court in Christendom or crossed the seas in search of a more distant exile. In the meantime, you will watch your knight marry your ward, because you want him to be happy. And it will hurt, but you will bear that pain with courage, because you are a good man. I respect that. Anybody would, if they knew.'

You don't deserve his respect. You don't deserve the gentleness in his voice, the warmth of his hands holding yours, the care with which he assures you of your worth. Your father was right to send you away – he must have seen in you this unmanly envy, this bitterness unbecoming of a king. A better man would not feel this way. Bisclavret was never *yours*, you have lost nothing, you have no reason to feel bereft.

He wasn't yours, he wasn't yours, he wasn't yours.

'I wish I had forbidden it,' you say. 'I wish I had – I wish I had longer. I wish I could let go of these desires, because they are doing me no good, and I wish he was mine so that I didn't have to.'

'I know,' he says.

'I wish she didn't make him happy.'

'I know.'

'I wish I could be what he needs.'

He kisses your fingertips gently, less like an oath, more like a lover. 'I know,' he says again, and you believe him.

20

Him

✦ ✳ ✦

They're married three weeks later.

It feels impossibly fast, but they have the king's assent and no other kin to trouble them, and as such they find themselves in front of the priest before Bisclavret has a moment to catch his breath. His lady is resplendent in silk and gold outshone by her smile, and he wants this, he wants her, and he'll swear as much in front of witnesses and the king – but still a part of him wanted longer to reflect on it before this moment of union, with the prayers and blessings echoing in his ears and her hands clasped in his.

If she notices then that he is shaking, she doesn't comment on it. She is laughter and smiles as they feast, and he is a pale moon reflecting the sun's light. He toasts her. Toasts the knights. Toasts the king. Accepts their congratulations and well-wishes and finally bids them all a cheerful farewell as they return to his home.

And to his bed.

If asked an hour ago, he would not have said he was nervous, but now his hands tremble so much that he cannot manage even the fastenings of his mantle, the brooch impossible and the laces unyielding beneath unsteady fingers.

She helps him, quiet and competent as always, and he stammers excuses: 'I'm cold,' he says, 'just cold, it's only cold.'

And it's true there's a chill in the room, though the holes in the roof are patched now, and there's a strong fire in the hearth to take the bite from the air that caresses their naked skin. But he knows that's not the only reason he's shaking. He's terrified. He feels foolish and clumsy and incompetent in the face of her soft worldliness, and it's mortifying, anyway, all of this. His bare skin seems horrifying, even without the knowledge of what lurks beneath it.

What if the wolf comes, here, before he has a chance to get away? Will he forget himself, lose his form, warp and twist and destroy her? His skin is not enough. It has never been enough. It took many painful years for him to realise that clothes make the difference between shifts where he comes back and shifts where he almost doesn't; now to be naked feels like being flayed and helpless, at the mercy of the wolf.

She runs her fingertips over his bare chest and he shudders. She has seen him stripped before, has tended his injuries, but that was not the same as this. Not the same as being unravelled by her hands.

'Are you afraid?' she asks him, her voice full of concern. He knows that if he says yes, she'll stop touching him, and fetch their clothes, and they will sleep as chaste as churchmen. And he doesn't want that. He doesn't think he wants that.

'I want this,' he assures her, tracing her collarbones with the pads of his fingers, and then her shoulders, her arms, the impossible, perfect shape of her. His hands are still trembling, but they both ignore it: she is warm, and he will not let uncertainty make a coward of him. Bisclavret sinks back onto the bed and she follows, curling herself against him, legs twined with his. He leans his forehead against hers and feels her breath against his lips, feels the way the air mingles and their breathing steadies to match each other's rhythm.

He can't stop touching her. Now that he's started, her skin compels him. He draws spirals with his fingertips, tracing every inch of her arms, resting on her collarbones and throat. She's touching him, too: her fingers burn as they trail across his back, light as feathers. They're so close, her leg pressed between his thighs, her arms around him, his reverent touch on her cheekbones and drifting across to her ears, the pale vulnerable skin of her neck, the sharp jut of her shoulder blades. So close, and yet some final distance remains between them, a barrier uncrossed.

He should kiss her.

They're barely breaths apart. It would be so easy – hardly even a movement until his lips would be on hers, the natural expression of all the fealty and service he owes her. He has kissed her a dozen times before and thought nothing of it, just as he has kissed his cousin, the other knights, the king—

Unwanted, unbidden, comes the memory of the king taking his hand and raising him to his feet as a knight.

She could kiss him, if she wanted to. She could take the lead, instead of hovering there with her breaths matching his own. He wishes she would: he will happily follow where she leads, give her what she wants, if only he knew what it was.

What do you *want, Bisclavret?*

He doesn't know. He's wanted this, something like this, for what feels like a long time. Weeks. Months. Since the first time she dressed him in his armour. Since she gave him her colours to wear. Since he first saw her smile. He must have daydreamed about it a dozen times, imagined the feel of that mouth on his, and yet now that the moment's here, he's frozen like a deer trapped by hunters. His breath catches, ragged, and he knows she'll notice, because she's too close to him not to.

'You're shaking,' she whispers. He feels the words, breathes them in, tastes them more than he hears them. 'Are you sure you're—'

'I want this,' he tells her again. 'I'm … I'm nervous. But that doesn't mean I don't want it.'

She smiles, small and gentle and understanding, and he should kiss her now, but he can't. Why can't he? Why does he feel torn by his oaths, by everything he has sworn? He is hers, as surely as he is the king's, the entirety of his being in their hands, and he does not resent that debt nor hope to free himself. But the declaring of it – it's the declaration that's beyond him. It's easier to touch her than to kiss her. Easier to be touched by her than to be kissed.

He shifts slightly and the movement pulls her closer to him. For a moment she tenses, holding herself apart, and then she leans into the contact. Her skin against his is a shock of sensation he wasn't prepared for. She's impossibly warm, her breaths ragged and her heartbeat fast; he has the sense that she's exerting a great deal of self-control to allow him to dictate the terms of this moment.

He's grateful, and still it seems an unnameable cruelty, to leave this decision in his hands. He wants her to take the responsibility away from him. He has spent his life hiding from his own instincts and repressing the desires that would turn him inside out, until the very thought of acting on them wraps his heart in fear that stings like nettles. How is he to know now what it is that he wants, after a lifetime denying he wants anything at all? What if giving in is a surrender of another kind, one that robs him of his skin?

Besides which, he has never done this before, he does not know where to begin.

She ducks her head and presses a kiss to his neck. And then

another, a little lower. Soft, careful kisses at first, but she grazes his skin with her teeth and he shifts involuntarily in a way that makes her laugh, low and playful, mouth still against his skin. After that she's a little less careful, and he feels her fingernails against his back – not hard, but there, the small threat of an edge.

Her mouth is pressed against his collarbone. She lifts it, looks up at him. In her eyes is a question; on her mouth the faintest hint of a smile.

He kisses her. At first it's chaste, the kind of intimacy a man might give his lord. Then she sighs into his mouth and presses herself closer, deepening the kiss, and it becomes something else entirely – something new, strange, something that demands he follow her lead.

He allows his hands to drift lower, pulling her against him, and hers are there, too, matching him, suddenly urgent. She may have a confidence he lacks, but her movements are filled with fumbling curiosity, no more practised than his own. It makes it easier, to know that they are learning this together, though well she knows herself, enough to guide him inside her. He thought they were close before – now they are indivisible, entangled, one body blurring into the next. It steals his breath, and hers too, to judge by her gasp, but her expression is pleased, not pained, as he begins to move, and she pulls him closer and closer and closer and—

Afterwards, as they lie there, limbs trembling from exertion, he understands what it means to know somebody carnally. Why they call it *knowledge*. He feels terrifyingly known, as though he has given her some understanding of him that nobody else has – allowed her to perceive him in a way that should be private. She has seen, heard, felt his utter vulnerability, had him under her power, and he's exposed by it. It's a gift he gave her willingly, and still it frightens him, as though he's been stripped of some armour that was keeping the world at bay.

For a moment he feels skinless, half-shifted, naked in the forest. He's struck by sudden terror, haunted by phantom claws tearing through his fingertips, and he jolts away from her so abruptly that he's out of the bed and on his feet before she's opened her mouth to ask him what's wrong.

'Where are you going?' she asks, as he pulls on his tunic, his braies, anything to remind his body what shape it should be in.

'Nowhere,' he says. 'Everywhere. Away. I don't know.'

'Bisclavret …'

He cannot stay. If the wolf comes, he can't promise he'll have the strength to stop it from hurting her. If not with his teeth then with the knowledge of him, because she can't know, she can't see this, not when she still looks at him and sees a man. God, she has seen more of him as a human than anyone ever has, understands better the shape of his humanity, so why should he take that from her? Why should that be taken from him? If he had a choice he would always be a man, always be here, always lie in her arms with her fingers on his skin, reminding him that he's human.

But he isn't. And he doesn't have a choice. He stumbles from the room, ignoring her calling after him, and pushes his way out of the house and into the night with ragged breaths tearing at his chest. They might be sobs. They might be howls. He doesn't want to change. He never wants to, but he wants it even less now, when he still has the memory of her softness and her kisses marking his skin like tiny brands.

The cold air pulls at his skin, trying to rip it off him. He staggers towards the forest and has hardly reached the outwood when he falls, knees hitting dirt, hands scrabbling at tangled roots. He can feel his back arching until it threatens to break, the change baring its teeth before it bites.

Not like this.

It is always like this.

Bisclavret gasps, and sobs, and the wolf rips the humanity out of him, and as the colours of the forest shift and alter and the smells and tastes of the air burst across his senses, he feels the echo of her fingertips on the skin he no longer wears, and then he loses even the remnants.

21

Other

✦ ✸ ✦

the air is wintergrief and rust-sharp.
it tastes of fear – *am I far enough away?* –
and fear smells like guilt and guilt like blood.
she has married a monster, shackled herself
to a wreck to be ruined on the rocks
of her affection – *did I get far enough away?*
did she see me-not-me become this?
this is a ruin that smoulders like a torch
held to thatch. its smoke, bitter as a warning,
sings of a grief too close to be escaped.

I cannot go home not while she is there
I will not bring the wolf there
I will not frighten her with this – and home
like hope is fragile, contingent on human hands.

I should never have bound her to me
to the wolf to this ugliest of truths

the wolf-skinned are better served by forests,
exiled to a bed of leaves or snow –
some place here will be safe

I can curl up there and sleep away the hours
and hope to wake in my own skin –
sleep is a way of waiting for an ending,
hunting a way of hastening it, and what
is a small death to a wolf's hunger?

I am not the wolf
I am caught by it
ensnared by it
tangled in its fur
but I am not it I am human

and humans hunt too and this,
this chase, *par force de loup*, no huntsmen needed,
is better and faster and bloodier
than any with horns and hounds.
and a wolf alone shares trophies with no one
and a kill alone is witnessed only by the moon
and the blood alone drips like regret to the dark earth
and is lost among the mud.

it's said (by men) that wolves have no names:
that names devour the silent cooperation of the pack,
the comfort-cruelty-community of a group –
I have a name –
but if a name dies when a whole becomes a fragment
then perhaps that's a greater grief than abandonment.
perhaps belonging is its own loss.

I have never belonged I have always had a name
even the beast in me knows I am something other than this

22

You

'Wolves, sire. We only tracked one, but where there's one there's a pack, so the rest will be close by. And there were three deer half-eaten in the royal forest.'

The huntsman is grim-faced, freshly returned from the forest. His tidings feel ill-fated. Your father was merciless in his hunting of wolves when you were a boy, and you who loved your hounds always thought it a shame when they dragged in the carcasses and hung their pelts on the walls. But you know better now, and fear the violence of the outcast hunters. They must be creeping back across the rivers and the mountains, slipping into the kingdom from the east like the invaders they are.

In your years of exile, you heard stories, plenty of them, of men who lose their skin and reason and go out wolfing in the night. The garwolf, they would call such a man locally. Humans transformed into mindless, violent animals, such that they might eat their own kin and enjoy the feast. The first time you heard the story, you dismissed it as a folktale; the second, as an embellishment. By the third you had begun to wonder what it was that haunted their woods, to give birth to such tales, for there must well have been something, and that something bloody-minded and sharp-toothed.

But these stories do not belong here. If such wolf-men ever

175

roamed your kingdom, they're long gone, hunted down with the rest, and these tales are unfit for Christian men.

When your knights hear the wolves are back, they'll want to mount a hunt. No time to waste: wolves left loose in the forest will become a problem. It's an ill season for riding out, though, the ground soft with winter mud, and the hounds sluggish with cold. All the more reason to address the threat before it grows.

You're interested to see how Bisclavret acquits himself in a hunt against wolves, and whether his fierce courage will serve him as well against them as against the boar. But you've not seen him since the wedding, now three nights ago. A messenger sent to his wife brought back the message that he has been taken ill, and that his cousin is caring for him. If you could, you would visit to see how he fares, but he has not been ill so long as to warrant such attention from his king, so you must content yourself with waiting.

'Very well,' you tell the huntsman, and turn to your seneschal. 'Have them make arrangements, and send word to those within a day's ride.'

He gives you a look that suggests he's noticed the lack of enthusiasm in your voice. Perhaps he wonders when hunting stopped being enough to give you pleasure, and you might wonder the same thing, except that you have known this ebb and flow of happiness all your life. It comes, and it goes; sunlight one day, shadows the next. You are deeply shadowed, now, wandering the ramparts late at night as though searching for something, with no real idea what you're looking for. Bisclavret's arrival brought a momentary colour to your life, but now that radiance is fading, and even he cannot stop the colour seeping away again, grey disinterest descending like rain.

The physicians call it melancholy, an excess of black bile, another excuse for purgatives and blood-letting; the priests are inclined to call it sin, or weakness at the very least, and recommend prayer and penance. You have tried both cures, in years past, and found little relief in either. Each time the fog descends you fear that this time it will never lift, and each time it does, and all is restored; this is the hope you must cling to, when the shadows are darkest.

Through this cloud of apathy you make your absent way to the stables, and there he is: Bisclavret, looking pale and drawn and very much as though he has been ill, a half-healed cut on one hand. His hair hangs loose around his face and he has a nervous, darting gaze, unwilling to meet your eye even as you ask earnestly after his health. It's not the behaviour of a man recently married who has been enjoying the delights of the marriage bed. It is the behaviour of a man who is afraid.

'Bisclavret,' you say finally, losing patience with his evasive answers. 'Something is wrong. Tell me what it is.'

He cannot disobey a direct order. Even so, he considers it. Tries hard. Eventually manages to say, 'I'm sorry, sire, but it's not something I can explain to you. It's …' He trails off. 'A matter of personal importance, not for the ears of others.'

'I did not judge you harshly when you spoke to me of madness,' you remind him. 'What else can there be that you cannot explain?'

'Too much, I fear, sire. I'm sorry.' He brushes his hair out of his eyes with a hasty, thin hand. The bones in his wrists are more prominent than they were four days ago, and you worry for him. How ill has he been?

'At least assure me that your wife is taking care of you,' you say finally, expecting that, at least, to be a request he could grant. But Bisclavret avoids your gaze, and it strikes you then that his dishevelled appearance means he came here without his wife's knowledge. 'In the Lord's name, you'll kill yourself if you don't rest. You shouldn't have come to court.'

'Maybe not,' he says. 'But now that I'm here, I hear rumour of a hunt?'

'Yes, they've spotted wolves in the forest, but—' You break off. The colour has drained from Bisclavret's face so fast you fear he'll faint from the rush of blood away from his head. He staggers and leans against the stable wall for support, coughing to cover the movement 'Are you well?'

'Wolves?' he repeats faintly. 'But there aren't – there can't be ...'

'You have a fear of them?' You're surprised by that. You didn't think he was a coward, to be brought to near-swooning by the mere mention of wolves. A hunter of his prowess is more than capable of protecting himself. 'I know they have been nearly gone from these woods for some years now, but my huntsman assures me we're plagued with them once more. Three deer have been found dead so far.'

Bisclavret looks ever more alarmed. 'Three?' he says. You wonder if his illness has damaged his hearing, or addled his brains in some way. 'No, that can't be, there can't be, there are no wolves in the—' He glances up at you. 'Where were they found?'

'In the royal forest,' you say, 'a little west of here, and— Oh.' You've begun to grasp the nature of his fear, for that forest adjoins his own land and any wolf might well slip from one to the other, poaching Bisclavret's animals and threatening his tenants and his household. 'I did not hear that they were as far west as your border, but well you might think to fence in your animals.'

'Yes,' he says faintly. 'Yes, that I might.'

'Are you sure you're quite well? What is it that worries you about these wolves?'

'Nothing,' he says hastily. Too hastily. 'That is, nothing that wouldn't strike fear in the heart of any man. I did not think there were wolves in your forest, and as for my own lands, I've walked them enough times now and never seen hide nor hair of them. It alarms me to think they could have returned without my knowledge, for I felt I was a better steward to the woods than to have allowed something like that to pass me by.'

Perhaps that's all it is. But there's more fear in his expression than you'd expect from a man of his boldness and courage.

'Will you join us on the hunt?' you ask. 'You might rouse your men to ride with us, since it concerns your land.' You think you would feel safer with Bisclavret at your side.

He shakes his head. 'I cannot. I'll send men, if you desire it, but I'm too weak myself to be hunting wolves at present, and you cannot wait until I'm recovered if you're to catch the culprits before they poach more from you.'

Of course he's in no fit state to ride out – he should be in bed. Had you been thinking straight, you'd have forbidden him even to contemplate hunting until he has recovered his strength. And it's true, you cannot wait, or else you risk attracting the rest of the pack to the easy pickings of your forest.

'Of course. You must rest.' You give him half a smile. 'Not hide here in my stables as though trying not to be found by your wife.'

A flicker of discomfort crosses his face, as though the joke strikes a little too close to the truth. 'Yes, sire.'

'And ensure you speak to my physician before you leave. Perhaps there is something he can give you to speed your re-covery.'

He nods. 'I'd be grateful for it,' he says, and kisses your hands before taking his leave.

You remain in the stables, because it is a relatively secluded place for a king to submit to the maelstrom of his thoughts without being observed by a bevy of servants and hangers-on.

Bisclavret did not seem happy, nor did he look as though marriage agrees with him. It's early days, of course, but such a rapid decline bodes ill. If his wife were not your ward, and you were not certain of her virtues, you might wonder if she poisoned him, for him to fall ill so quickly after their marriage.

A small, cruel part of you is perversely pleased to see him so weakened, and you despise yourself for it. If he were happy, content, it would be a wound and a reminder that he never needed you. If he is unhappy, perhaps she cannot offer him what he was looking for, either.

But you don't want him to suffer. You gave him up so that he would be happy. If it were within a king's power to grant him that happiness, you would do so, but all the jewels in your crown cannot buy you such influence over Fortune.

Instead you send a messenger to his cousin. He is rarely at court, now, taken up with his duties, and Bisclavret's estate thrives in his hands, but when summoned, he rides hard to answer it. He arrives flustered and a little less put-together than usual, and is shown into your presence.

You pour him a cup of weakened wine, because he is still panting from the journey, and while he drinks, you say, 'Bisclavret has a condition.' There is no point beating around the bush. 'Some kind of recurring illness. This is why he was so hesitant when he thought he might be obliged to stay at court, because the strain would worsen it. Following his marriage, he has suffered a bout of this illness, and now returns still suffering the aftermath of it.'

His cousin contemplates this pronouncement for a moment and then says, 'That is more or less the truth of it, my lord.'

'Tell me about the "less",' you say. 'What am I missing?'

'Sire, it is not my place to disclose—'

'I am your king.'

'And he is my kin.' It causes him difficulty to speak thus, you
see that, but nevertheless he sets his jaw and it is plain you will
get nothing from him that he does not wish to tell you. 'Sire,
Bisclavret is a faithful knight to you. Where his limitations
allow it, he'll serve you as faithfully and entirely as any other
man in your service. I will not deny that he has limitations; his
health is not strong. As you may recall, he made this plain to
you from the beginning and I was the one to push him on it. I
did not expect, I will admit, that he would marry; I might have
cautioned him against that, had he sought my advice on the
matter. But he did not, and I have no right to stop him.'

And nor do you, when this is Bisclavret's choice, but if that
choice is hurting him as much as it seems to be ...

'My lord,' says the cousin, 'I'm sorry I can tell you no more.
But either he is your knight, or he is not. If he is your knight,
then he must keep to his oaths and it is your place to challenge
him if he does not. Do not think to spare him that – he would
not wish your pity, however poorly he might feel that day. Has
he failed you in some way?'

'No,' you say immediately. 'No, of course not. He declined to
join the hunt for the sake of his health, and he was quite right
to do so. I should not have asked him in the first place. My
reason was momentarily overcome by my eagerness to give him
his share of glory, but hunting wolves in his state would be far
from wise.'

Are you imagining it, or does his cousin, too, flinch at the
mention of wolves? Perhaps there is some darkness in their
family history that instils such deep fear in them both.

'He is still weak, my lord,' he says. 'He would be better resting. When I realised he had come here instead of going home,

I—' He breaks off, as though he has said more than he meant to.

'He was abroad, then? Away from home, in his illness?'

'It takes him like … like a sleepwalker.' His cousin chews on his lip a moment. 'Deranges him of his senses and sets him walking, wandering in the woods.'

'A dangerous occupation,' you note, 'when there are wolves about. He could have been killed.'

'Yes,' says his cousin miserably. 'When your messengers arrived this morning, I feared that would be the news they brought, though I hadn't heard then of the wolves. There are other dangers, of course, for a man wandering witless. I was relieved to learn that he was here, instead.'

Not madness, but like madness. You are beginning to think Bisclavret was not overstating the matter when he spoke of it in such terms. 'And his wife, she knows of this affliction?' you say, expecting assent, but the expression on his cousin's face says otherwise. 'Why not?'

'Pride? Shame? I couldn't rightly say, sire. I hoped he would tell her before they married, but he would not be persuaded.' His face is drawn with concern, and you wonder how he found himself in this peculiar position of responsibility for his kinsman. They had some youthful friendship, you know that much, but many men are close in childhood without making the other their steward and closest confidant. 'What he hopes to gain by delaying the moment of confession, I can't fathom. And to come here …'

'He sought to delay it still further, I suspect.' You sigh. 'You're right. He should be resting.' You would rest with him, if you had the chance; with this dull weight on your mind and the bitter, dank cold of the rainy day, you'd rather be in bed than hunting wolves, a chase with no feast waiting at the close of it. 'But if you could convey to him my concerns, I would appreciate that.'

'With gladness, sire.' He is certainly more comfortable now that you have stopped asking difficult questions. You respect his concern for his cousin's secrets, but nevertheless resent his silence. You would have the knowledge from him that you cannot obtain from Bisclavret, whether or not he wants you to know.

After a long pause, you say, 'The roof. Is it mended?'

'I beg your pardon?'

'Some weeks ago, Bisclavret told me that there were holes in the roof. Are they patched?'

His expression clears; he has followed your meaning. 'Yes, sire, and the draughts kept out. The house still wants for colour but it's a safe, dry place for an invalid to convalesce, and the servants well able for helping him.'

'Good.' The relief comes with a counterpart of dejection: there is now no reason you might beg Bisclavret to stay a few nights here, and be cared for in the comfort of the castle. 'I suppose you'll see to it that he doesn't overexert himself during his recovery.'

'I plan to do my best.'

And no doubt Bisclavret will make it a challenge. 'Then I will give him into your capable hands. But will you not join the hunt yourself?'

You are not mistaking it: there's fear in his eyes. 'No, sire,' he says, covering his discomfort quickly. 'Unless you object, I intend to return with Bisclavret. I am more use as his steward than as your huntsman.'

There'll be enough of you, anyway, once word has got out. 'If there is anything at all you feel would aid in Bisclavret's recovery, you have but to ask,' you tell him. 'He is my knight; I would have him recovered quickly.'

'Yes, sire.'

'And—' You break off. 'And give him my best wishes.'

It is nothing, but it is all you can give.

23

Him

Three days.

He was gone for three days. His memories of the time spent wolfing are blurred, fragmented into smells and feelings. He doesn't remember hunting the deer, or crossing the boundary that demarcates his woods from the king's forest. He hunted, and he has no memory of doing so, and that terrifies him.

Unless, of course, there's another wolf in the forest. But he would know. He would *know*. Which means it must have been him.

When he first shifted back, he kept vomiting, as though his body was trying to purge itself of poison. A human stomach isn't made for raw meat, and the venison must have been sitting heavily in his belly. Now he's weak and hollowed out, but the thought of food makes bile rise in his throat again. It'll be a while before his appetite returns.

He's never allowed himself to hunt like that. He was going to sleep, to rest, to wait it out – and he failed. How did he fail so badly? Was it because of her touch that he lost his mind as well as his body? Did he leave that crucial part of himself in their bed?

It feels like a punishment for all the risks he has taken, all he's dared to hope for.

He doesn't go to the physician. There's nothing they can tell him that he doesn't already know, and no cure they might offer will balance the humours of the wolf that wears his skin. He's on his way to the armoury instead, in search of boots and a warm cloak to keep out the chill for the journey home, when he finds himself crossing paths with the king's scribe.

'I heard you'd been ill, Bisclavret, but you look more as though you've crawled out of your grave.' He clasps Bisclavret's shoulder, his good humour not hiding his concern. 'Are you well?'

Bisclavret gives him a stoic grimace. 'Well enough, and mending,' he says.

'Hmm. Your wife is here, you know. She came in search of you.'

His wife. He thought at least he would have the ride home to think up some excuse. 'She's here?'

The scrivener gestures vaguely. 'In the chapel.'

His heart sinks. 'Thank you. I should go to her.'

'Like enough you should,' the scribe agrees. 'It's always dangerous when they start praying for you.' His smile is light and irreverent, but there's an edge to his expression as he gives Bisclavret one last clap on the shoulder and then disappears.

Dry-mouthed, Bisclavret makes his way to the chapel. With luck, the chaplain will be there to mediate, to offer intercession between Bisclavret and his lies and his wife – but when he lets himself in, there's only one figure kneeling in front of the altar.

His footsteps are too loud on the flagstones. She looks up, and at the sight of him she drops her psalter and pushes herself to her feet. 'You,' she says, and he can't tell if it's relief or anger that makes her voice shake. 'You're here.'

He swallows. 'I'm here. I'm sorry.'

She seems unsure whether she would prefer to slap him or to embrace him. 'You ran from me.'

'Not from you,' he says, pleading. 'From myself.' He cannot look at the altar without remembering the vigil he should never have kept and the oaths he should never have sworn. He isn't made for knighthood. He isn't made for marriage. But in the eyes of God he is bound to both, and cannot abandon them. 'I came back.'

She reaches out her hand, brushes his tangled hair away from his eyes. He can see the questions in her face, and the pain they bring. He would kiss away those soft creases in her brow if he could, and take from her the worry; he would have her fear nothing. But it would be a peace made of lies, and it already tastes bitter on his tongue.

In the end, she doesn't ask. She looks him in the eyes and says, 'You came back,' in a voice that's soft and doubtful and full of gratitude. 'But you came here instead of home.'

'Perhaps I knew I'd find you here,' he says.

Her small, sad smile shatters his bravado and flirtation: she knows the thought never crossed his mind. 'I came here to pray for your soul when I thought you must be dead,' she says. 'I kept a vigil for you last night, in case you lay unshriven somewhere in the forest with nobody to find you. I stayed until the candles burned out.'

Of all the ideas she might have come up with to explain his absence, he didn't expect his death to be among them. A lump rises in his throat at the thought of her on her knees on the cold stone for his sake. 'You truly believed me dead?'

'I believed you loved me,' she begins.

'I do,' he interrupts.

'And so,' she continues pointedly, 'I believed if you were alive, you would have come back.'

She has faith in him. She looks at him, still, in that way of hers – seeing the whole of Bisclavret-the-man, and none of

187

Bisclavret-the-wolf, the way he has always wanted to be seen. She raises his hand to press a kiss to the inside of his wrist.

That should be his part to play. But he has a mind to let her court him, run ragged and exhausted as he is. 'I would not have left if I felt I had any choice,' he tells her, which is as honest as he can be. 'And I will always come back.'

She kisses his wrist again, and his hand, and finally his lips, and if she notices the sour smell of sickness that haunts him or the iron tang of the blood spilled by the wolf, she doesn't comment on it. 'Then let us go home,' she says.

Bisclavret smiles. 'I have no horse and I'm not dressed for the weather. Let me rectify those faults and then we'll go.'

'I promised the servants I would be home by Nones,' she says; Sext is long past, the winter sun already weakening, and she will be pressed to keep her word. 'Follow after me, then. You ride faster than I do, and might well overtake me on the road.'

He's not ready to be parted from her – he owes her penance, atonement for his failures as a husband. But it will be easier, if he can travel alone and have time to fashion his thoughts into human patterns. 'Very well.'

'And don't tarry,' she says. 'You've been gone long enough.'

'I wouldn't dream of it.'

But when she's gone, he takes a moment, leaning against the wall and waiting for the dizziness to recede. It must be days since he ate a proper meal, food meant for human consumption, and exhaustion thrums in every shaking muscle. Blackness stains the edges of his vision, and he tries to blink it away, but the fatigue is not easily banished.

He's not paying attention to the footsteps approaching him, but he notices when a figure in travel-stained court garb stops in front of him. 'I'm well, I'll be gone in a—' He looks up. His cousin. 'What are you doing here?'

'I was summoned by the king to answer to your condition,' says his cousin stiffly, and Bisclavret feels sick. 'Don't look at me with such alarm. Of course I didn't tell him. Nor have I told your wife, and that, I confess, needles my conscience more.'

'The king summoned you?'

'That is what I said, is it not? Though in any case I might have come to accompany your wife back home in your absence. The roads grow ever more dangerous, and the woods more so. After all, they say there are wolves hunting there these days.' His tone has sharpened.

Bisclavret doesn't know how to respond to this. 'What did you say to the king?'

'That the secrets of my kinsman were not mine to disclose. And that you would be as loyal to him as any man could be, within the limits of your ability.' It ought to be a relief, but it feels like the sort of statement that comes with a sting in its tail. When his cousin speaks again, the barb makes itself known. 'I am beginning, however, to think I overestimated those abilities. How long were you gone this time, Bisclavret?'

Bisclavret is silent, and his cousin crouches down and grips his chin so that he has to meet his eyes. He forces out the words: 'Three days. I was gone for three days.'

'And I suppose you told your wife where it is you went, didn't you? That must be why you are here in the chapel, why I saw her with the chaplain this morning.'

'She thought I was dead. She went to pray for me. She doesn't – I haven't *told* her – I ...'

His cousin lets go of him and pushes upright in disgust. 'Then she is deceived as well as despairing. She deserves better than this, Bisclavret.'

Better than you. 'I know that,' he snaps back. 'Do you think the thought doesn't haunt me?'

'And yet you're not here to seek an annulment, are you? It cannot, then, haunt you so very much.'

'An annulment?' echoes Bisclavret.

'I'm assuming you did not manage a consummation before … this.' The word is accompanied by a gesture – an attempt, it seems, to encompass the whole of Bisclavret's being and all of his failures. 'It would not be without shame for either of you, but that doesn't mean it wouldn't be for the best.'

Coldly, fighting down the wave of dread that threatens to swamp him, Bisclavret says, 'You assume wrong.'

His cousin closes his eyes and takes three slow breaths. 'So she is bound to you,' he says finally, opening them again. 'She might have had her pick of knights, but she chose you, and now she is trapped. In the name of God, Bisclavret, have you considered what might become of your children?'

'How can I not have considered that?' cries Bisclavret in response. 'Of course I have thought of that! I have scarcely stopped thinking of it since she first expressed her willingness to be my wife.'

'And yet that consideration did not change your actions! I have thought you many things, but selfish was never one of them. But in this you have done wrong – you have been selfish and unkind, and you have hurt her. I have failed you and I have failed her by not doing more to stop this. I—'

'You have the manner of a man who would have married her himself,' Bisclavret says, before he can think better of it. The words are meant as a joke, but land as something sharper. His cousin's colour is high, his eyes bright and manic, and the pieces fall into place: 'Is that what it is? You would have married her? You did not say as much, when there was still time. Is that why you seek to take her from me now?'

'No.' The answer is curt and difficult to believe.

'What happened to protecting me?' he asks spitefully.

'I *am* protecting you,' his cousin retaliates, lowering his voice. 'Or do you think the king will take your side if you lose control and kill her? Do you think there will be anyone standing between you and the hunters when that happens? You entered the royal forest. You killed three deer – and do not think to deny it, for I know full well that there are no other wolves in that forest, just as I know that you would not have done that deliberately. Which means you lost control, and might well do so again. It's only a matter of time before somebody finds themselves on the receiving end of your lunacy. When that happens, somebody will need to speak for you. If you continue to ignore my warnings and my attempts to help in order to pursue this pig-headed approach, it will not be me. I will not see her dead by your hand.'

'And so your means of protecting me is to leave me abandoned?'

'When have I ever abandoned you, Bisclavret? I have been faithful to you since we were children. I gave up knighthood to stand at your side; I risked my position at court to present you to the king. And still you accuse me always of meaning you ill.'

'Perhaps you should not have done,' says Bisclavret. 'Perhaps you were better off as a knight. I would arm you again, if that's what you wish.'

'You need me,' says his cousin. 'You need me as your steward. And your wife needs me, to stand between her and the violence of the wolf.'

'I am not *going* to kill her!'

'You cannot know that! Not any more, not after everything that has happened!'

Bisclavret is exhausted and faint, but he struggles to his feet and begins to walk away. His cousin easily keeps pace with him. 'Perhaps I have surrendered some measure of control over the last few days,' he begins, as they leave the chapel, 'but that doesn't mean it will happen again. I was overtired and over-wrought and—'

'And you can guarantee never to be overtired again, can you?'

The worst part is that his cousin is right. The words cut deep because they're the refrain of his own mind – the fear that he'll snap, and hurt her, and that there'll be no coming back from that. Once he loses control of his own mind, he loses every-thing.

'This was your idea,' he spits. 'I tried to retreat, to back out of knighthood. You were the one determined that the king should have his way.'

'There is a difference between being a knight and marrying the king's ward.' His cousin stops dead, folding his arms. Bisclavret tugs him into the relative shelter of the chapel doorway before their conversation can echo around the entire courtyard. 'Before, you were taking risks with your own name. Now, you are taking them with her life. You have denied yourself the safety of your own house as a retreat from scrutiny, and that loss of safety will bring the wolf ever closer to the surface. And your wife—'

'She is not making it worse.'

'You went wolfing on your wedding night and vanished for three full days, returning thin and injured with three ravaged deer in your track. Forgive me if I do not believe you.'

'And I'm supposed to believe this is concern speaking, when you've as good as admitted you're in love with her?'

His cousin's cheeks are flushed. 'What has love to do with any of it? My feelings are of no concern here.'

'No? So it's merely a convenience that if I should repudiate her on the basis of her safety, you will be there to offer her your hand.'

'Well, no one else will now, will they? Would you have her left to starve, the widow of a living man?'

'I would have her be mine.'

'I would have her *alive!*'

Bisclavret turns his face away. He doesn't know how he can possibly respond to that. Of course he wants her safe. He'd cut off his own hands to keep his claws from scratching her. But he's never felt as much himself as he does under her touch; never felt as present in his humanity as when she looks at him. She's safety, belonging, selfhood, and despite his care for her, he cannot bear to surrender that.

Perhaps his cousin is right. Perhaps he is selfish.

He walks on, not looking at his cousin, not speaking; perhaps if he walks fast enough, he can leave this whole argument behind, and with it the knowledge of his failings. He hears footsteps and knows that his cousin has followed, but he doesn't look back. They make it most of the way to the stables in this manner, locked in a fragile silence.

'Bisclavret,' says his cousin eventually, tiring of the stalemate. 'Bisclavret, look at me.'

He doesn't. He says, 'I have never hurt anybody.' It's almost a plea: *you know me, you know what I'm capable of, how can you still think me willing to maul and murder?* He's speaking to himself, to those self-loathing corners of his heart, as much as to his cousin, because it is so easy to forget that fact. He has never hurt anybody. That means something. When it comes down to it, that *must* mean something.

'I know,' says his cousin. 'But you have never before hunted the king's deer, either.'

He's right about that too, damn him. Bisclavret is haunted by the gaps in his memory, the hunt he doesn't remember. If he is so close to losing his reason, there's no telling how much further he might fall. 'I'll be more careful in future. Lay safe-guards, ensure I cannot stray.'

'And if I asked you to tell her, would you do it?'

He turns then, sees his cousin's open, earnest face. Not the expression of a man conniving to steal his kinsman's wife. Just concern, and hope, and something else he can't place. 'Why?'

'She deserves to know. Tell her the truth of it and let her decide. Perhaps she can help you, find a way to ensure you don't wander too far.'

Perhaps she would. Or perhaps, for all her goodness, his wife would turn from him. She knows her own worth too well not to recognise that she deserves better – and his cousin must know this, which makes his suggestion feel vicious and cruel.

'I can't,' he says, almost a whisper.

'I cannot condone you lying to her.'

This is your fault, Bisclavret wants to say. *You would not let me hide at home. You would not let me flee the court. If not for your meddling I'd have stayed alone and exiled and would never have loved her and would never have had to lose her.* 'I don't need your permission for the living of my life.'

His cousin makes a noise of disgust. 'Perhaps you would not have my friendship either, then.'

'Is this friendship?'

'You know that it is.'

They walk on a little further. Bisclavret says, 'Is it only my wife you fear for?'

'What?'

'You think I'm a danger to those around me. Your concern must extend to others who spend time with me – the knights, the king, yourself ...'

'*I* know to be cautious,' says his cousin. 'As for the knights and the king – well, the situations are hardly comparable, unless you are spending rather more time alone with them than I'd realised.' His cousin eyes him warily. 'If you want to convince me you're trustworthy, this is a strange way to go about it. What are you trying to say?'

'You love my wife.' The words come out too harshly, and Bisclavret wishes he could bite them back. But the resentment boils over inside him. There is so little that is his own, and his cousin who is human and safe and has never felt his body un-making itself will not be the one to take this love from him. His cousin who could have any woman in the world, if he wanted. 'Explain to me why I should believe you are not led by your heart on this matter.'

'Of course I am led by my heart,' his cousin snaps in return. 'How can I be otherwise, when I have cared for you for years and that love has not faded? But Bisclavret, you must see that these situations are not the same. The king has guards, other knights, the means to defend himself. Your wife—'

'Is perfectly safe!'

'So you say! And I wish I believed you, but this is *dangerous*.'

'I have always been dangerous,' he spits. 'No more now than ever. Perhaps you should have thought of that *before* you dragged me to court.'

'I have thought of it every day since.'

The confession hangs limply between them, and it says every-thing Bisclavret needed to know. He turns and begins to walk again, faster, knowing the other man will struggle to keep pace with his loping stride.

'Bisclavret, *wait*.'

But the damage has been done.

'You've always been the only person I trusted,' he tells his cousin. 'But you've proven yourself the same as the rest. I'll find another steward, and you may return to knighthood, so that you might not begrudge me the sacrifice of the life you'd rather be living. You will have only the best arms, the finest horse I can offer you. But I want you gone from my lands. I've no need of you.'

'You need me as much as you ever have.'

He needs nothing. He has his wife, his king, the castle, the knights. He's more than a wolf-man, more than a vagabond, more than a pitied cousin living out his years in exile. He has always thought he needed this charity, but that was when it was all he had. And now he has more.

'Perhaps I was mistaken then, too,' he says, and does not look back.

24

You

The hunt is unsuccessful, if success is to be measured in face-to-face encounters with vicious predators. You ride all day, and catch no glimpse of the wolf. The tracks in the forest are muddled, bewildering even the best of your huntsmen, and only the mangled remains of the deer confirm that there was ever a wolf at all. By the time you return to the castle, your whole party is cold and dispirited. Food has been prepared, but you've no appetite. You take a hunk of bread, leave instructions that you're to be left alone, and retreat to your chamber.

You don't remember falling asleep, but you're woken the next morning by the sound of the door opening. 'I gave orders that I wasn't to be disturbed,' you say, propping yourself up on your elbows; your chamber is meant to be inviolable, closed even to your seneschal should you wish it.

'Those instructions don't usually include me,' says a familiar voice.

You let yourself fall back onto the bed. 'One day you'll pass a whole day with no other concern but your books and I'll be so astonished to see you at your scribing that I'll faint dead away. Why are you here?'

Unusual as it is to see him this early in the day, your scrivener looks far more awake than you feel. 'To see if you are well,' he says. 'You went so early to bed and are so late to rise. The knights tell me you didn't train with them this morning.'

What time is it? You'd assumed it was morning, but as you become more alert, you see that the daylight is streaming in. 'How long have I slept?'

'Long enough for people to worry for your health,' he says, then adds, 'They've rung Sext. They'll be long done with the psalms by now.'

Some way past noon, then. You run your hands over your face and sit upright. 'I am quite well,' you say, swallowing the profanity that comes more easily to your lips. 'Only fatigued by yesterday's hunt.'

'Ah, yes. The hunt. No luck, I suppose?'

'No wolves, if that can be called poor luck.' You narrow your eyes at him: 'You didn't come here merely to wake me.'

'No,' he agrees. 'I came to give you this.' He hands you a slim volume, newly bound between wooden boards. The binding is simple, little ornamented but for the corner pieces and the bronze clasp that fastens the codex.

You glance up at him, but his expression gives nothing away. Uncertainly, you open the book, and see his familiar clear script in crisp black ink, initials marked out in red.

'It's the lais,' he says, unnecessarily, for you can see that clearly enough. 'It was always intended as a gift. I'd meant to include another of the romances with it, but in the end I didn't have the time.'

Time. But there should have been no deadline for this collection of stories, this frivolous, precious book. No patron commissioned it and no business rests on its completion.

You hold the small codex in your hands and you say, 'You're leaving.' He cannot leave. Not when you are so alone, and need him more than ever.

He offers a small smile. 'I should have known you'd guess. Yes, I'm leaving.'

Your vision blurs. You close the book hastily. 'Where are you going?'

'A pilgrimage of sorts. It's past time I saw my homeland again. I was travelling overmany years before we met, longer than I'd planned, and I cannot stay away forever. It was kind of you to grant me a place here, but my home is calling me.'

Home. Across the sea, to the land that taught him his story-teller's tongue and gave his precise, pointed script those quirks that so irritate your seneschal. Back to the lies that shroud his past. 'Forever?' you say, sounding like a child. 'That is, do you plan, at all, to return?'

'That depends what I find on my arrival,' he says. His smile is sad. 'I'm sorry. I mislike to leave you, and after only a handful of months at your court. I have greatly valued your friendship and confidences, as I have done since we met. But I must attend to a higher duty.'

You don't want him to go. Impulsively, you reach out, snatch at him, clinging to his wrist. 'When?' you demand. 'When are you leaving?'

'As soon as my effects are in order. I have made arrangements with your seneschal. He, at least, didn't seem sorry to see the back of me.'

For once, you cannot laugh at his joke. 'But I could – I could forbid you to go. I am your king.'

'You could try,' he says. 'But you may find that I am not so tractable. I've never truly been sworn to your service, sire, and there are greater loyalties imposed on me. I must obey those calls as much as yours.'

They are all slipping away from you, water through your

fingers. Soon you will have nothing left. Your voice cracks: 'Please don't leave me.'

He frees his wrist from your grasp, but doesn't let go of your hands. 'You'll have your pick of scribes,' he says, 'if you continue to feast with storytellers and praise the tongues of poets, but there is one among the chaplain's clerks with a mind for stories and a heart for secrets. You would do well to call on him, and he's local enough that his hand will cause the seneschal fewer headaches than mine. He hasn't my experience with binding, but—'

'Forget the books,' you say. 'Forget the records. It's you I'll miss.'

'For a little while,' he says. 'And then you'll move on.' He kisses the inside of your wrist, trailing his lips up towards the soft crease of your elbow. 'You have friends at this court, my lord, though difficult it may be for you to see them. They will be faithful to you if you give them the chance to show it.'

But their unflinching service and wholehearted fealty is nothing compared to his wry smile, his irreverent wit, his commentary on all the absurdities of the court. Their memories of your youth cannot compete with shared exile and the fragile thread of continuity that helps you understand your place in this world. They were not there for you when you were half-formed and abandoned, seeking friends in a hostile land.

'Please,' you say again, but like a priest he kisses your forehead in benediction and offers only an uncomforting promise: 'You won't be lonely forever.'

But you're lonelier now than you thought possible.

You allow him to say his farewell, but his fingers against your skin sting with the thorns of parting, and it robs his kisses of their sweetness. You would hold him, tangled with you, unable to free himself without permission; you would keep him beneath you for as long as it might take to persuade him to stay. You cannot lose him now, when you are so alone, when you have no one else to confide in.

You find yourself crying. He kisses the tears from the corners of your eyes and when his mouth meets yours again his lips are salt with them. 'Don't weep,' he tells you, but it's a useless command, one you can't obey. 'You don't need me.'

But you do.

'I could forbid you to go,' you say again. 'I could have you bound in irons. I could have every ship in every harbour turn you away. I could have you dragged back over the borders every time you tried to cross them.'

'You could,' he agrees.

'I could have you kept here for the rest of your life,' you say, pretending not to notice that you're weeping again.

'You could try,' he says. 'But you won't.'

No, you won't. You hold him, and allow him to hold you, and the day is already fading to evening by the time he clasps your hand one final time and walks away, a small sorrowful smile on his face as he glances back.

And then you are entirely alone.

‡ ✳ ‡

The remainder of the winter passes in a haze. Sometimes Bisclavret is there; sometimes he's not. He's often a little pale, eyes bruised with sleeplessness, but when you spar he wears his old smile and fights with his usual strength, so you don't pry. You treat him as any other knight and he behaves with due deference, and neither of you acknowledges that it was ever otherwise.

But it is impossible to ignore that he has argued with his

cousin and the two are at odds, for the man is no longer his steward. He has sworn himself into service again, his lord's knight once more, though he brings his own fine horse and good armour, which must ease the sting of the interruption. He trains with you briefly, but only for a matter of days; his lord is returning to his estate, and he will go with him. Bisclavret seems relieved rather than saddened by the separation. He will not, however, acknowledge that anything is wrong.

Deprived of distractions, you throw yourself into kingship. The grey fog isn't gone, but the sharp blades of loss have punctured it, cutting away the veil, and through those rents in your mind you glimpse a sort of clarity. You listen attentively to your seneschal's reports and engage with your barons' counsel as you have not done since those first weeks after your coronation. You leave every meeting with an aching head, but at least it is time spent not thinking about anything else.

The promised clerk presents himself to you and he is, of course, a perfectly adequate scribe; even your seneschal finds no fault with his record-keeping. You rarely speak, and that's fine. Occasionally, you call by his chambers to consult some charter or volume, but you don't linger. There's no longer anything for you there.

You're lonely, but what man isn't?

Half a dozen more hunts are mustered, but the wolf is nowhere to be seen, evading all the traps set by the huntsmen. There are few reports of further damage, although occasionally a deer is found, or there will be some other mark of its passing. It leaves too few traces to be living only in your forest, and you wonder where it spends the rest of its time, and what causes it to stray.

You're sparring with Bisclavret one morning when you recall that his own lands must be in as much danger from the wolf as yours. You ask him about it – has he strong enough fences? Are his livestock and people safe?

'Yes, my lord,' he says carefully. 'We've had no trouble from the wolf, and I don't anticipate any. In any case, I have had the cottages secured and the fences strengthened.' His mouth twists with something that might be amusement. 'I imagine the foxes are wondering what cruelty drives us to deny them any hope of access to our chickens, though they cannot be more dismayed than the hens by their enclosure. Renard with all his wiles could not slip through.'

Despite his joke, his manner is stiff, uncertain, and his divided attention allows you to disarm him.

'But you never ride with us on the hunts,' you say. It's not that you mean to press him, but you're curious. 'You're recovered now, are you not?' He still looks too thin, but he's lost the unhealthy pallor that followed his earlier bout of sickness, and he doesn't fight like a man who should be confined to his sickbed. 'You're such a skilled hunter; we miss you on the chase.'

'I'm sure you do.' His smile is more of a grimace. 'But I have no taste for hunting wolves, sire.'

Is it fear, or a softness for them? You had thought the former, but for the first time you wonder about the latter. 'In the north, they let them roam untouched.'

'So I've heard,' he says.

'They speak of garwolves. You've heard the stories?'

He stiffens. 'Garwolves?'

'Men who walk and hunt as wolves, but return to their own skin when the moon is right, or when their bloodlust fades, or by some other mechanism, I know not what.'

You've always suspected a certain heterodoxy from Bisclavret, but you have no sense of how he might react to such blatant superstition, better suited to a peasant than a king. You watch him carefully, but his expression is still and controlled.

'If such men exist,' he says at last, choosing his words with care, 'then they must bear some frightful curse, and I pity them. And it seems to me as good a reason as any to let the wolves alone. This one seems to run with no pack, and certainly does not appear to mean harm to you or your people.'

'You speak as though it's rational,' you say with a small laugh. 'What does it mean, for an animal to mean harm? Are they not incapable of such reasoning?'

At that, he laughs. It does little to diffuse the tension in his shoulders, but you welcome it anyway; it is a long time since you heard his laugh. 'If I did not already know you for a king, that would be the statement that marked you as never having worked the land. Animals know malice as well as any man, sire, as you would be aware if you'd ever earned the enmity of a watch-goose.'

The idea makes you smile. 'I will grant that geese seem fierce in their likes and dislikes.'

'And fierce in acting upon them,' he agrees. 'My lord, my land overlaps with the forest, and I have seen little sign that the wolf is a menace to you – if it's there at all. Perhaps it's time to abandon these hunts.'

'Perhaps,' you say, but you find yourself eyeing him thoughtfully as the bout resumes, wondering why he speaks for the wolf when your other knights are calling for its blood.

25

Him

It is a fragile peace and cannot last.

Bisclavret considers himself fortunate if he only loses one night each week. Most often it's more. Two days, three days; he can't remember the last time he lived one Sabbath to the next in the same skin. The wolf drags him away more often than ever, and each time it's a little harder to come back. He leaves his clothes neatly folded near the border of his estate, somewhere he can always find them, and still the shift threatens to tear him apart again even while he dresses.

Human, he tells himself, over and over, fumbling his tunic over his head. *You are human. Stay here. Stay like this.* But the wolf is growing stronger, and he's afraid.

He conjures excuses that he knows his wife doesn't believe. No knight is called away by the king so often, and if she chose to ask at the castle, she'd know he never sleeps there, nor does he have business enough to take him afield so many nights each moon. But he brings her gifts, when he can – bright cloth, soft ribbons, delicate pastries, the first flowers of the spring. Anything to make it up to her. Anything to assure her that she isn't the reason he strays.

If she didn't know he was lying in the spring, she must know it by summer, and by autumn it's undeniable. But she doesn't ask. Not yet. Not as long as he always returns to her, speaks softly to her, lets her touch keep him human in the long cold nights. And when she looks at him, he never sees fear in her face, or disgust. Above all else, she still sees him as human.

When he's with her, he can pretend that's true.

The pretence is a mask he finds himself wearing more and more. In his exile, it was easy enough to manage with one or two servants, leaving comparatively few witnesses to his eccentricities, but that's impossible now. His wife builds a bustling household around him, and his days of isolation are over, banished by guests and visitors. Their feasts may not rival those at the castle, but the storytellers come nonetheless, and the musicians, and they bring songs of love and tales of glory and a smile to the lips of the lady, so they are welcome. The knight in green comes visiting with his own wife, and before the day is done, the two women are exchanging knowing glances and promising to send over this recipe or that yarn. Even a man like Bisclavret, with little knowledge of women, can grasp that they will be discussing more than householding when they are alone together. But it makes her happy, to visit and be visited, and once upon a time, it was what he wanted too.

The house is transformed after its years of neglect: the roof mended, new hangings on the walls and dust swept from corners left abandoned since his father's death. The overgrown herb garden has been tamed and coaxed to new life, and sometimes he finds time to walk there with his wife, as once they did in the kitchen gardens of the castle.

But still the cracks are beginning to show. Bisclavret strays further afield, unable to limit his transformations to his own estate because the risk of being seen is too high. He finds an old ruin, a forgotten chapel of one of the old orders – abandoned when the new monastery was built – and hides his clothes there, instead of among the trees. Each time he comes back to himself in that leaf-strewn house of God and walks the two miles home on human feet. Each time his wife is waiting for him, with her careful lack of questions, and a smile that grows more brittle by the day.

This truce is an impossible bargain. Every day is something he has stolen from the jaws of the wolf, and every night it comes feels like a battle for territory he refuses to cede, but he is losing ground, day by day, night by night, and he fears, too, that he is losing her.

She is not yet with child. It's been long enough now that this is occasioning rumour at the court, in the guise of concerned enquiries, though Bisclavret himself isn't sure if he's concerned or relieved not to have to test, yet, whether monstrosity lives in the blood. It weighs heavily on her, though; every time her blood comes she is quiet, withdrawn, and no matter how often he assures her that he doesn't blame her, it is clear that she blames herself, and finds his promises less and less convincing.

'We have time,' he tells her, over and over again. 'I am content with this.'

But as the season turns and the winter encroaches and her blood comes as regular as church bells, his assurances offer scant comfort, and finally, finally, she says, 'Content? How can you claim to be content, when it is so abundantly clear that you are not?'

'If I have led you to believe otherwise ...'

Her laugh is sharp and bitter. 'Everybody believes otherwise, Bisclavret. They know that you are gone from me near half the week. They can't decide what's more likely – that you're flee-ing a harpy's tongue or that you've got yourself a lover at some remove and are riding out to her in secret. But that you never take your horse, I would assume the latter too.'

He flinches. He should have foreseen that she would perceive a connection between his ever more frequent absences and their lack of a child, as though he married her only for an heir and not for the light and the love that she brings into his life. 'Of course there is no lover.'

'*Of course*,' she echoes. 'As though such questions are unwarranted. You do me insult, husband, to speak that way, when well you know that you have kept secrets from me. Long I have wanted to ask you for this truth, and long I have been afraid that you would be angry with me for asking, and so I have held my tongue.'

'I would never be angry with you for asking anything.'

'How can I believe that, when I have seen your temper for myself?'

A year ago he would have claimed no temper, but the strain of keeping the wolf at bay has robbed him of patience and sharpened his tongue. A pointed remark from a fellow knight or a small problem on the estate has been known to draw great rage from him, the wolf's fury seething in his blood, and less and less can he hide his true mood behind a courtly mask. He has never turned that anger on her – that much he can claim, at least – but he suspects that is little comfort.

'I will not be angry with you,' he says again, though his heart is in his throat. He cannot tell her the truth: it will ruin him, ruin this, unmake the life that they have built.

'Then let me ask the question I have swallowed for so long. If not to a lover, where is it that you go, when you are lost to me?'

And there it is.

It would be a softer cruelty to let her continue believing he goes to another woman's bed, but he cannot do her that dishonour. Not when it isn't true, and could never be true, because the only woman he has ever trusted with his heart is her. And he has told her enough lies; all the pretty gifts in the kingdom could never make up for that.

He's still wrestling with what to say when she adds, 'I'm afraid, every time you leave, that you won't come back. That one day I will lose you.'

He lets out a bitter laugh. 'I'm afraid of the same thing,' he says, which does nothing to mollify her. 'By God, wife, if I could tell you, I would. You know that I would. But I fear I have too much to lose. I am what I have always been: a coward.'

'You are not a coward,' she says. 'I would not have married a coward. But you are a fool, if it hasn't occurred to you that I have more to lose than you. What becomes of me, without you? This land is not mine. We have no children to lay claim to it. I am not your heir. I would be as much an orphan as before, exiled or once again in the care of the king. Perhaps I will never be able to give you a child, but I am owed answers.'

He suspects, in his heart of hearts, that she is not the reason they have no children. 'I would give you anything but this,' he says. 'Any answer but this one.'

'This is the one I have asked you for.'

And he owes it to her to answer honestly. She's allowed him to keep this secret for far longer than he deserves, and what else has she asked of him but this? His cousin would have told her by now, if he had let the man stay. *He* should have told her by now. It was wrong of him to keep this hidden, and let her believe herself unloved, unwanted, second to some other desire.

The words stick in his throat, and he chokes on them, but then they're out, falling heavily to the ground between them.

'I become a wolf.'

Her silence is a wall. Perhaps she thinks he speaks in jest or riddles. Perhaps she's waiting for him to dig deeper into his own grave. He swallows, mouth dry, and tries to pull together further explanations, but can think of none. What else is there to say? *The deer that were found dead in the king's forest, that was me. I am a monster. I have always been a monster.*

He says instead, 'I go into the forest. I try not to stray too far from home, so that I can find my way back.'

She meets his gaze. 'You are a garwolf.' Her careful, even tone frightens him; it is as impossible to interpret as her expression.

'If that is what you call it when a man loses his skin but not his mind,' he says. 'I ... I know myself, usually. But yes. I suppose that is the word for it.'

He sees her swallow. Her throat is so pale and fragile. He understands too well what it means to be afraid of him, of the wolf, and he hates that she now shares that fear, and that he cannot relieve it. He knows that, in this moment, it means nothing that she has slept by his side for a year and always woken unhurt, because the man she thought she was sleeping beside is not the one who has revealed himself to her.

She says, 'Clothed?'

He cannot help himself: he frowns. 'What?'

'Do you go clothed, when you are a wolf?'

'No,' he admits. Somehow there's shame in that confession, though he'd never expect his hounds and beasts to wear garments. 'I go naked.'

She considers this. Perhaps these practical questions are a way to avoid the horror of it all, keeping it at arm's length, or perhaps she doesn't believe him, thinks this a figment of an imbalanced mind, and probes him only to see how far the story goes.

'What do you do with your clothes,' she asks at last, 'when you ... change?'

'I leave them somewhere I can find them again,' he says. 'I—' He breaks off. He has never had to explain this before;

his cousin knew him in his youth and understood his condition before he had the language to describe it. Now that he must articulate it aloud, he struggles to shape it into phrases that make sense. 'I need my clothes to stay human,' he confesses. 'Without them, I might not be able to come back.'

Her expression doesn't change, but when she says, 'Oh,' there's an odd note in her voice, as though she is beginning to understand him.

'Yes.' He sounds pitiful. He almost pities himself, and he hates it, that desolate helplessness in his tone – *yes, I hide them in the woods so that I might dig them up later like the dog I am.* 'There is ... a chapel, a little way off the road, where I am able to leave them and know that they will be undisturbed.' He creeps in there with his skin still shifting and seeks absolution and humanity at the same time, dressing himself before the altar and the eyes of God.

'You must struggle,' she says carefully, 'without somebody to help you.'

For a moment, he imagines her going out to the edge of the woods to clothe him as he stumbles home, still half a beast. Her hands fastening his garments, sewing his sleeves, binding him into his skin. A little too late, he realises that this is another way to ask if he has trusted some other with his secret, in place of her.

'My cousin has helped, in the past. He is the only one who knows. Otherwise I must manage for myself.'

He cannot interpret the look on her face. He feels as if he has lost the right to understand her, after so many months of lies and masks. He waits for her to push him away, or to run screaming from the house, but she doesn't.

'But if your clothes were taken ...' she begins.

'I might come back.' Or he might not. Or he might come

back only for his bones to twist and warp on him again, inverting him even when he thought he was safe. He might spend days and nights shifting back and forth, his organs remade over and over until there was nothing left of them and nothing left of him. Perhaps it would kill him, eventually. Perhaps it would drive out his sense and condemn him to madness. 'I think I would struggle to stay. It's my greatest fear, you know. Not being able to stay.'

'You want to come back.'

'Always,' he tells her, voice low and hungry. 'Were it my choice, I would never leave you. You must know that.'

There's a long pause during which he expects her to refute it – *how can I know that, when you have lied to me for so long?* – but at last she smiles and says, 'I know that.'

He doesn't dare lean forward to kiss her. He's terrified, however irrationally, that she'll recoil despite her gentle words. 'I'm sorry,' he says instead. 'I should have told you. I couldn't find the words.'

She nods. She hasn't forgiven him, but maybe she understands his sin a little better now that she has the truth of it. 'Your cousin is the only one who knows?'

'Since my mother died, yes. I have always kept it secret.'

'So you have not told the king.'

'No, and were it my choice, I would that it would stay that way. I don't intend to give him any cause to regret knighting me, but if the truth were to become known, no doubt many would think he shouldn't have done so. Perhaps they're right.'

'You are a good knight,' she says, though fear is still thrumming through her, her body tense and taut with it. She's working so hard to stay at his side, though her heart is telling her to run; her love is as pure and painful as a blade through his ribs. 'One of the king's best fighters, and one of his best hunters, too.'

Then her expression tightens: 'The deer, the wolf in the royal forest, was that ...?'

'Yes.' It is the hardest confession so far. 'I ... I don't remember those nights as well as I usually recall the wolf's hours. I try hard not to hunt, and to leave no trace of my passing. But sometimes the wolf is ... hungry.'

'Hungry,' she repeats faintly. 'And you have – killed.'

'Not people. Never people.'

'The stories of garwolves say—'

'The stories are wrong.' The words burst out of him, harsh and fierce, and she flinches. He didn't mean to snap at her. He didn't mean to turn his rage on her. But the words to apologise elude him. 'The stories are just stories. I am not ... I am not a killer.' Yet. He hopes. Only of deer and dumb beasts, like any hunter.

'Is it because of this that you sent your cousin away?'

'Largely,' he admits. 'He opposed our marriage, and the arguments that followed broke the trust between us.' He does not tell her that his cousin loves her. Perhaps she already knows – perhaps he proposed his suit before Bisclavret ever came to court, and she turned him down. Perhaps she has no idea, in which case he would not give her more reasons to regret marrying the wrong kinsman.

'He opposed our marriage?' she echoes, apparently caught by surprise.

'After our wedding night, when I ...'

'You transformed,' she finishes, only now drawing the connection between his headlong flight and this confession. 'That's why you fled from me. I ... I wondered.'

Of course she wondered. Of course she must have thought it was her own fault, no matter how many times he assured her that it wasn't – must have thought something about her behaviour or form drove him away. He regrets the pain that misapprehension must have caused her.

'My cousin feared for your safety,' he says. 'He would have had me repudiate you then, and perhaps I should have listened to him. But I couldn't bear the thought, when I have found with you such peace as I have never known before and might never know again. He was right, however, that I should have told you. I'm ashamed that I did not. I've wronged you with my lies.'

'I understand,' she says, a little unsteadily, 'why you would not.' Because of course this wasn't something she wanted to hear; because of course she is horrified and disgusted by this revelation. How could he expect anything else?

'I must know,' he says finally, more begging than commanding, 'what you are thinking.'

She's silent for so long he fears she won't answer him. At last she says, 'I am thinking that next time you turn, I will know to watch for you coming back.'

It is everything he has ever wanted to hear, and still the words taste of loss, taste of grief. He would not have her know him as a wolf. He would not have her see him in those moments of change.

'For as long as I am able,' he promises, 'I will come back to you. On this you have my word.'

When he kisses her, both their lips are bitter with lies and salt with tears.

26

Him/Other

a day, two days, to bear the human brunt
of confession, to watch for fear and see her flinch
like prey and then contain herself, love
like a shield and a restraint. but after that wolfing
comes easily, lost skin and a fractured mind –
she knows – still the rituals, the chapel, the woods
a sacred space and a holy of unholies –
what does it mean for me that she knows? –
the same as any other day or any other loss,
all the colours and the scents of a world changed
and a night spent in sleep and hunger and absence
until the morning sun burns the wolf away
like mist – *let me come back let me go home* –

And he is human, momentarily, hands rough – cut – bleeding from the impact against the bark of the tree. He fell. No time to catch himself. Not enough legs. Too many hands. But dear God, he has hands again. Bisclavret lifts them to his face, trembling, ecstatic, and then—

the cold shakes free the wolf from the man –
I am just wolf I am just wolf –

unclothed and unremembering of how it feels
to be human – *perhaps if I had my clothes*
I would remember – abandoned and feral –
I left them at the chapel I must get back to the chapel and

—he opens the door with human fingers, bare feet like a pilgrim's pale against the stones of the nave. Nobody comes here. It's long abandoned, the monks who once sang psalms within its walls long since left for living orders: grass and tree roots have made a home of its paving, and weeds curl around the font. But there, near the old altar – now chipped and puddled with rain from the leaking roof – is a dry space, a quiet corner where he keeps his clothes. There's hardly a glimmer of moonlight creeping through the overgrown windows, but he can find his way there as easily by touch as by sight.

He crouches to pick up his clothes, and his hands close on nothing. The carefully folded garments that he left there, where are they? Perhaps they've fallen further back. Perhaps the wind – the draught is fierce – has swept them out of reach. His fingers twist and shatter into something curled like claws as he scrabbles at the ground, looking for them – *no* – but once he finds them he'll be able to settle back into his human skin. And they must be here. He always leaves them here.

But the wolf is waiting to heave itself out of his skin, to shed him like dead leaves, and he cannot find them, he cannot find them – but they were here. He always leaves them here. Extravagant though it is, he had a tunic made just so that he could hide it here for the nights when he loses himself suddenly, without warning, so that there is always something to find his way back to. How, then, can there be nothing?

And he is—

falling again

—barely human. Momentarily unmade. He snaps back into his own body with the ricochet of a broken spine locking into place and knows he doesn't have long before the shift comes again, this time for longer. If he cannot dress, if he cannot find his clothes, he will—

stay like this I cannot stay like this
I need to know that I can always come back
because if not I am nothing I can only

—stagger forward. He gasps and steadies himself. The clothes are gone. He's naked beneath the Heavens and his body threatens to dissolve into beast at any moment, and there's nothing he can do to stop it. The chapel that was once a refuge becomes a cage, the damp grey stones imposing enclosure around him when what he craves is space. To run—

—but that is the wolf's heart in him. Like he didn't come all the way back this time.

He makes a small, frightened sound in the back of his throat, somewhere between a man's keening and a hound's whine, and then—

why does it have to feel so much like being ripped apart

—he is gone and back and gone and back and—

like falling like being unmade
like losing everything all over again
it is too much like despair

217

the wolf eats my heart from the inside out
consumes everything about me that is real and good and

—his clothes are still gone and he cannot remember how to stay human. He tries to fix his mind on it, on what it means to feel present in his own skin. He tries to remember words, to snatch at prayers; he clutches the altar as though Eucharistic stone will bind his skin in place, but the only holy water in this chapel is the rain seeping in, washing away the sacraments and ritual. There are birds nesting in the walls, mice curled up in the corners, and—

a wolf in front of the altar, shuddering and violent
with the effort of trying not to become

—it has the air of an abandoned thing, that cloying desolation that chokes the surrendered, leaving behind—

despair – *that's it that's the taste*
in the back of my mouth – is a little like bloodlust
and a little like rage.
full of emptiness. made of loss

—nothing to hold him, nothing to keep him real, and in the end—

I slip out of my skin one last time
leave the man crumpled by the altar
invisible and unremarked except to ghosts
but I know he's there I saw him fall
and I am just wolf and I cannot undo the shattering of my bones
and I cannot repair the sundering of my flesh

I am just wolf even if I remember being something else

—it feels like grief, being wolf – it is so much like grief, so much like loss, so much like kneeling abandoned beside the body of something destroyed—

I am just wolf just grief just wolf just grief
all lost

27

You

Bisclavret is missing.

At first you think nothing of it. It's not uncommon for him to be gone for a short while, though few tales ever reach you of his time errant and you're still unsure where it is that he travels. Your concern grows as the days stretch into a week and then further, but still you keep it to yourself. No doubt he has told his friends where he has gone and why.

He should have told you too, of course. It is unlike him to neglect such a courtesy. But he will have had his reasons, and you try to put it from your mind. It's only when the other knights comment on his absence that you realise there may be some genuine cause for concern.

'He hasn't been seen in days,' says one.

'Longer than that,' says another. 'My wife sent word to his, but she had little news to offer, except that his steward has recalled his cousin to act in his stead. Bisclavret is away from home. Nobody knows when he left or where he went, and nobody knows when he is coming back.'

'Oh, his *steward* recalled the cousin, did he,' says your red-haired knight, sharp-tongued and inclined to rumour. 'That's not entirely the tale I heard.'

'What did you hear?' you ask, and they turn to you in surprise:

normally you refrain from contributing to their discussions until your input is requested.

'It's small-minded tattle,' says your knight in green. 'Pay it no mind, my lord.'

His wife is good friends with Bisclavret's; perhaps that's why he's hesitant to give credence to whatever unkind whispers are spreading. But you would hear them anyway. You turn to the others, and one, at last, answers: 'The rumour is that his wife mourns him as though he is dead.'

'That's only half the rumour,' says your red-haired knight, and though it's sharp it's not vindictive, for he's not so crude a man as that. 'The other half is that his cousin is ... comforting her in her grief. That he's been recalled because he's Bisclavret's heir. That she'll marry him rather than leave her home.'

As though he is dead. But he cannot be dead. What danger would Bisclavret have met that would have killed him, when he has sought no battles and mustered no hunts? He meets no danger in his own lands that he's not more than capable of facing down. Unless ...

You turn away, striding to the stables and calling for a horse. You would speak with his wife before the rumours have a chance to grow wilder. You find it hard to believe that she would bestow upon his cousin any affection beyond that of a kinswoman, when she has always been so devoted to her husband and when you know her to be of good character. And as for the rest ...

As though he is dead. Bisclavret has been gone too long. He has never stayed away like this before.

You take an indirect path to his home, out through the forest to the point where your hunting ground becomes his, approaching his estate from the east rather than by the cart road. There's little to mark the boundary, but that your own forest is more carefully managed, while he has left the flowers to mind their own growth – even now, so early in the year, hints of yellow amidst the green leaves promise the coming of primroses, and spring with them.

You can see the edge of the forest from here, deceptively close without leaves to conceal the light or block your view, and you're riding hard for it when your horse startles, almost throwing you from her back as she rears. Only your saddle keeps you from falling, and even as you murmur reassurances to ease her fear, you look around wildly to see what it is that provoked such a reaction.

A heartbeat, then two, and then you see it, almost invisible against the grey-brown of the bare trees and the thick mud. The wolf.

The only danger Bisclavret might face here against which he has never proven himself.

Your heart beats against your ribcage as though trying to break bone, and the wolf holds you steadily in that baleful glare, ceding no ground. You spur your horse, but she will go no closer, panicked by the scent of the beast. Cursing, you slip down from her back, freeing your sword from its scabbard as you do, but before you've taken more than a step through the mud, the wolf turns tail and flees, loping away through the trees so quickly you can't hope to pursue it.

No man could outrun that creature. No man could escape it.

No. You knew the wolf was here in this forest. You have known this for months, and never before have you lost a man to him, and never yet, for Bisclavret is too strong a knight to have been bested by a creature like this. You will not let despair overwhelm you without firm proof to support it. You will not let the dread build, though relentless its assault upon your confidence.

Determined, you remount, and urge your horse onwards

until you emerge from the forest and come within sight of Bisclavret's home.

His wife, when you arrive, seems a little unsettled, but perhaps that's only the natural anxiety of having a king for an unexpected visitor. Bisclavret's cousin is there, too, giving the rumours weight you wish they didn't have.

'Where is he?' you demand, before they can fall over themselves to offer hospitality.

'My lord, something to drink—'

'Where is Bisclavret?'

Gradually, their story emerges: Bisclavret went out late one night. He was inclined towards taking long strolls in the moonlight, but sometimes he would grow lost or distracted – well, you would know of that, of course. Here they pause and look to you for agreement, which you give, for you remember well his cousin telling you of Bisclavret's wandering. Is that what they suggest is happening now? That he is simply ... away?

His wife shakes her head. She's weeping now, such that you've never seen her weep, and you almost know what the bundle in her hands will be before she brings it forward. Bisclavret's clothes, torn and bloody. You recognise the woven ornament on the sleeves. You recognise the lacing of it.

You wish that you did not.

'The wolf,' you say heavily. 'I saw it, in the forest.'

'You saw it?' says his cousin, startled. 'Did you – did you give chase?'

You shake your head, running a finger over the muddied garment his wife has presented to you. Surely a man mauled by a wolf would leave behind more than this ribboned cloth? Surely there would be ... remnants? You would have seen them. You are sure you would have seen them. You would have *known*.

224

'Perhaps he freed himself from the wolf's grip by shedding his clothes,' you suggest.

'Perhaps,' agrees his cousin, doubtfully. 'We hope for some miracle of this sort – hope always that he will return. We have been watching for him, but there has been no sign. With every day that passes we have less faith in his safe return.'

'If he is in the forest,' adds his wife; she seems entirely over-come, unable to manage the words, 'how is he surviving? What is he eating? We cannot believe he will find enough to endure there for long. Not in the midst of winter.'

You swallow. 'You believe him dead, then.'

'We fear as much,' says the cousin. 'Whatever chance remains of his return, it grows more slender by the day.'

'And you did not tell me?' you say. 'He's been missing for days. We could have mounted a search, scoured the forest for him.'

'Sire,' says his cousin, with perfect humility, 'we had no wish to trouble you with what we hoped was a mundane matter. When he first wandered away, there was nothing to suggest it was anything other than his usual behaviour. By the time I arrived to help in his absence, the wolf had been sighted, and we feared there was little you could do.'

Strange to summon him at all, without knowing for sure if Bisclavret were dead. You would ask if his wife or his steward made that decision, but that you fear giving credence to rumours better forgotten.

But there must be something they aren't telling you, something that will make sense of this. Their story is bitterly plausible, you cannot deny that: the wolf has been quiet recently, but winter would drive its hunger, and it might well be on the prowl again. And if Bisclavret were absent and unknowing, in the grip of his almost-madness, then a beast that encountered him at his going astray would face no real challenge. His usual skill with a blade would do him no good if he lacked the wit to call upon it.

You cannot, however, accept that he is dead, plausible or not. Bisclavret cannot be dead.

You hardly remember mounting your horse and riding away; the world is fogged with your disbelief. You remember a little better the long ride that follows, scouring the forest as though you might hunt the wolf singlehanded, but it has found for itself some secret den and defies your searching. When you arrive home, mud-splattered and tearstained, you can scarcely manage the words to explain.

Your chamber is empty, lacking in answers. The hall echoes with absence. You let your feet take you where they will, and find yourself in a room where the very air is redolent with the scent of parchment and of ink; you run your fingers along the lid of a book-chest before you have consciously registered the absence of a candle or a familiar figure at his workbench.

He's gone. Of course he's gone; he's been gone for weeks. And his replacement spends less time holed away in this chamber, copying stories for his own delight, so there is nobody to see your grief. You slump down to the floor in the same corner where once you were kissed and hug your knees to your chest, a pose more befitting a child, abandoned and lost, than a king. You don't feel much like a king. You bury your face in your knees and try not to weep.

You fail. If Bisclavret is gone, then you're more alone than ever. To think you imagined him lost when he was married! That was a mockery of grief. You were a child, naive, not to understand how much more profoundly it would cut to have him entirely gone. No longer his smile at your feasts, no longer his melodic voice raised in song, no longer the curious magnetism of his loping stride, no longer his blade meeting yours and his amused gasp of exertion when you manage to catch him out while sparring.

Married, Bisclavret wasn't lost to you. Not like this. His life pervaded yours in a dozen ways, and you were a fool not to see it. Now the heart has been ripped from the world, and all you can do is curl up in this lonely corner and weep.

Nobody disturbs you. Perhaps they don't hear, or perhaps they assume your tears are those of some exhausted page, too lowly to matter. You're left uninterrupted and uncomforted, sobbing until you are hollowed out. When they find his body – *if* they find his body – you'll grieve as befits a king on the loss of one of his knights. But for now you mourn as a man mourns the loss of an intimate friend.

And you mourn, too, that you face this loss alone, without the one man who might have understood you. The room is bitterly empty, the books locked in their chests like bones in a coffin. None of them may help you. None contains prayers to heal a broken heart, or spells to repair a body torn apart by a wolf's teeth, or the secret of the flowers that weasels know, which bear within their petals the power to return the dead to life.

He cannot be gone. You refuse to be living in a world bereft of him. And yet the enormity of loss will not be held back; it's a wave crashing down on you, implacable and furious. It feels like the truth, as unyielding as the challenge in the eyes of the wolf. It feels like you'll never see him again.

You cannot be sure how long you stay there. Grief renders time meaningless, marked only by the dryness of your throat and the stinging of your eyes. Eventually you can cry no more, and your cheeks are wet and raw with salt. You remain curled in the corner for as long as you can bear, and then you haul yourself to your feet and stumble from the room. Part of you hopes to encounter somebody who will recognise your sorrow and offer you some balm for it, and part of you wishes only to return to your chamber unnoticed, to wash your face and surrender to the healing solitude of sleep.

The hall is empty, but you've put only one foot on the stair to your chamber when you meet an interruption in the form of the chaplain.

He's taken your Confession too many times not to recognise your distress. You try to brush past him with some platitude, but he holds you firm by the arm. 'Tell me.'

So you bring him into your chamber with you, and you tell him that Bisclavret is dead.

You aren't sure what response you expect from him. Perhaps some commentary on the immortal nature of the soul and the reassurance that your knight is in paradise. What reason to mourn a man who is with God, freed from the burden of mortal strain and toil? It will be no comfort at all, but it is the way of priests, to seek their answers in the intangible and forget the pain of mortal bodies.

He doesn't say that. He says, 'I am so sorry,' and then he holds you, and if you had any tears left you would weep them now, in the assurance of his embrace. Instead you can only keen softly, your breath catching in your throat as his arms encircle you.

He makes no suggestions. Does not ask what you'll do next. Does not suggest seeking comfort in any one person or activity; does not prescribe distractions. He simply holds you while you mourn.

Eventually, you become aware that he is praying. It was so soft and unobtrusive that you can't be sure when he started; perhaps he has always been murmuring the familiar words. His prayers are simple, humble, and he seems to expect nothing from you, but you follow him in reciting them anyway. *Subvenite sancti dei*

occurrite angeli domini suscipientes animam eius offerentes eam in
conspectus altissimi. Assist, saints of God; hurry, angels of the Lord,
to receive his soul and bring it before the sight of the Most High ...

Will it help Bisclavret's soul, to speak these words for him?
Will something of the love you felt for him be diffused in these
prayers, to dissipate and speed him on his journey through torment to paradise? At least then it would not remain a hard rock
in your chest, impotent and unbearable.

Your throat is dry from weeping and from praying. The
chaplain fetches you a drink and stays with you until finally you
tell him you'd prefer to be alone, to seek solace in sleep. He
retires with promises to keep a vigil for Bisclavret's soul, and to
pray for you too.

You don't need his prayers. You're not the one who is dead;
it's not your soul that has fled unshriven under the onslaught of a
wolf's claws. Dear God, the horror of it – no confession, no absolution, and after such bodily torment, what manner of suffering
must Bisclavret now endure? Perhaps his half-mad wanderings
make him child-like, his innocence granting him clemency. You
mislike to believe in any God that would condemn him to suffer,
but all must wait for Judgment, and bear the answer.

You spend most of the night on your knees. If your prayers
could cleanse him, his soul would be washed clean by your tears
by now. Your candles burn themselves to stubs and you turn
away the servants who come to replace them. Morning imposes
itself unwelcome on your mourning, and you're forced to wash
and dress yourself to face the world. But when the night comes
again, you wander phantom to the chapel and let yourself in
through the unlatched door to kneel on the cold stone and
whisper words that burn your lips and sting your heart.

The prayers are no comfort to you, but perhaps they bring
him warmth, wherever he is now.

28

Other

✦ ✳ ✦

this has always been a story about lying.
about running and pretending to run
in order to avoid the bigger lie:
that there is anywhere left to run to.
the grief – *I thought she would leave*
she said that she loves me but I am not me
and to leave is her right
but this
this theft this death this violence she has done me
surely she wouldn't
she said she loves me – is endless,
incomprehensible as death.
lies feed each other, smallest into biggest,
until they grow as epics do,
with the weight of blood.

she was my home
she has taken my home

in an epic, home is something left
something lost embattled remembered yearned for
– a mistake only a mistake surely it is a mistake –

and running only takes you as far as your strength
but collapse can be forestalled, held off, kept at bay
as long as the sun doesn't rise to burn the shadows from the
story.
and in the end they're human shadows
because to a wolf forever is a night and a forest
is the world and we run –
perhaps tomorrow
tomorrow it will be over
nightmares are pledged to end with morning

tomorrow is a human word,
a linguistic concept, a lie of language.
I have a human grief –
and a wolf's voice under a wintry moon,
bright and cold, stripping bare the trees
and creatures in its light, thoughts shattering
in its pale glow, silver-struck,
lunar-caught, half mad and howling.

to go back is to know
it is not a mistake it is not my mistake
they are gone and she took them
I am gone and she drove me away

it is a moon for leaving
– maybe I will run until my feet are bloody –
and in the north they say there are garwolves,
men who know how to be caught between two skins
– maybe they will teach me to make peace with it –
there's little peace in wolfing but there's a violence

that can be taught – *then teach me*
to have a taste for blood.

many things are easier with a hunger
but some hungers should not be fed.

I cannot go home
she was my home she has taken my home
if I return I will only hurt her
my grief births my rage my violence fed by loss
better to stay trapped in the chapel walls
better to pound on the stones and beg for freedom

this is already a gaol of a kind
– *dear God will I never be free* –
already haunted, always living
at arm's length from ourselves.
always I am hiding.

confession is a painful path
and a bitter penance
– *who can forgive me this?* –
forgiveness, like love,
is a process of negotiation.

can I be loved?
do I need to love my own skin before another will love it?
do I need to be present before I can start to live?
I am tired of dying
always I am tired of falling away from myself
always I am tired –
sleep brings a little of death's kindness

233

– to sleep isn't safe
when I sleep the wolf will be free –
nothing is safe
– I am never safe –
not here not like this

always I am tired of running

29

You

The winter ends, as winters always do.

Spring brings shorter nights and shorter vigils. You sleep sometimes. On your knees in the chapel. Curled up on the floor in amongst the documents and books, soothed by the familiar smell of vellum and ink, even with the aftertaste of absence. In your bed, in the middle of the afternoon, or in the early hours when the chaplain finds you dozing at your prayers and raises you gently by the elbow to lead you there. Still your eyes are bruised and bloodshot, and your pallor provokes the court to rumour. Your servants try to keep it from you, but you know what they're saying. That you're mad. That you lost your mind when Bisclavret disappeared.

You didn't lose your mind. But sometimes it feels as though he took your heart with him, and left you barely alive, your blood sluggish in your veins and your breath thin in your lungs.

You don't fail to notice when his wife marries his cousin and heir. It's natural enough: he has some kinsman's duty to look after her now that her husband is gone, and she could do worse than to marry him and keep her home. But it takes some effort to push the uncharitable rumours from your mind and wish them both the happiness you've lost, and you do not invite his cousin to court to take Bisclavret's place as a knight.

You withdraw from your councillors and advisors, leave your seneschal to handle the business of ruling, and let mourning dictate the rhythms of your life.

You would spend a year and a day in Masses for his soul, if only it would help. *Nunc suscipe, terra, fovendum, gremioque hunc concipe molli. Take him, earth, for cherishing, to thy tender breast receive him.* Except that you have no body to bring, not even a ruin; no bones to settle in the soil to be planted with flowers where they sleep. Perhaps if you did, you would not feel quite so much as though you failed him.

Your knights and nobles try to draw you from your penitential self-enclosure. They beg you to spar with them, to hunt with them, to ride out to tournaments with them – but you've lost your stomach for the kill, or even the pretence of it. You hunt once, and when you see the deer struggling in a pool of its own blood as the hounds slaver and growl, all you can picture is Bisclavret, pinned to the ground by the wolf. The agony of those final moments. It sickens you; you turn back, and leave the rest to complete the hunt alone.

It will pass. You've been told this – that the grief will ease. You aren't sure how that can be true, when Bisclavret will never stop being gone and the world will never be any less empty of him. But perhaps it comforts others to claim that it will grow easier. Perhaps they find solace in those lies. Sometimes, you're even capable of pretending that you believe them, mustering a smile and thanking them for their kind words and thoughts.

They cannot bring him back. You want them gone from you until they can.

It doesn't pass. But you grow numb to it, as the weeks wear on. Your mind hardens against the agony of remembering, as a body does to an old wound. *Bisclavret is dead* ceases to be a fiery lance of pain every time you brush against it by mistake, and becomes a dull ache, a gnawing emptiness. One day it will be nothing but a scar, inured to sensation.

As spring wears on and the weather grows warmer, you go less often to the chapel. You speak prayers for him morning and night, but you trust the chaplain and his clerks to speak the Masses. You commission a fine psalter. You donate gold to a monastery, that they will pray for his soul. You begin once more to take care of your hair and clothes, to look a little more like a king.

Finally, with the hardships of Lent forgotten amidst Easter revelry, you put on your crown and sword and you play the king again.

The first few times you train with your knights, they're careful with you, treading around your feelings and rusted combat skills as though you're made of precious glass. You would resent it, but these months of inactivity have weakened you, your body half-starved from long nights of desperate piety and endless fasting, so all you feel is gratitude.

Gradually, as your mask improves and so does your strength, they begin to treat you again as they once did, making jokes when you fail to parry an obvious strike and poking fun at simple errors. They invite you to drink with them, and to your surprise, you agree, though melancholy creeps back as the wine chases the cold from your veins.

'We miss him too, you know,' says your knight in green, an uncharacteristic sincerity in his voice. 'He was our brother, and we loved him as such.'

Yes, they miss him too. And no matter how much you wish to tell them that they cannot possibly understand your mourning, you know that would do them a disservice. Of course they understand your grief – especially this knight, who took Bisclavret under his wing and treated him as a brother. You could have wept together, all this time, if you were not too proud to come to them with your agony.

'He was taken too soon,' you say, which isn't anything they don't already know, but they raise their cups in salute and drink to honour the remark, because it's true enough to be worth toasting. He was taken far too soon.

You're deep in your cups, all of you, by the time the conversation comes around to Bisclavret again; none of you have the courage to talk about him sober, too afraid of your own grief. 'Will you avenge him?' one asks you. 'Find the wolf who took him and have it skinned?'

You've thought of this often, remembering the implacable gaze of the wolf, the pitiless glint of those eyes. Would it help at all, to know that his killer is gone? Perhaps, but the thought of it exhausts you. Your previous wolf-hunts have borne no fruit, and to pin your hopes of closure upon its death is to condemn yourself to heartache.

I have no taste for hunting wolves, he told you once, and you have come to know how he feels.

'It won't bring him back,' you say instead, which isn't a real answer, but they take it as one and don't press you.

Except for one. 'Nothing will bring him back.' Your knight in green, again. His tongue is sharp with truth and has an edge honed by years of friendship. He has known you since you were beardless and green as new branches, and once you trusted him with your joys and griefs and foolishness. There's no malice in his words now, but they still cut like axe-heads. 'Grief will not bring him back. Nor will laughter. Seeking comfort in others or secluding yourself to mourn – it makes no difference. He's gone regardless.'

'What,' you say with difficulty, 'would you have me do?'

'Live, my lord,' he says. 'And I think I knew Bisclavret well enough to wager he'd say the same if you asked him. You're no use to anyone withered into an early grave and a crown left spinning in your absence.'

You're no use to anyone anyway.

But he's right. You cannot live in a world with Bisclavret in it – a cruel truth – and you cannot unmake yourself or change the past. But your people need a king who cares enough to rule them, not a man who locks himself away in his chambers and leaves the decisions to others, consumed by his own desires and his own grief. Your father did not send you away that you might hide when the time came to use the lessons of your exile – and if you did not learn the bloodthirstiness that he hoped for, what of it, when your kingdom is at peace? You learned to do better than this.

You *will* do better than this.

Neglect has grown like moss over your understanding of politics and your grasp of the sharp rocks in the currents of your nobles' petty disputes and longstanding grievances. You are fortunate that your seneschal is a true and honest man, unready to take advantage, but you are perpetually aware that he honed his acumen in your father's service. If he has practice at ruling the kingdom, that is only another sign of your father's failure, and you will not perpetuate the injustice of his self-serving rule.

But you are not too proud to learn from such a vassal as this, and the seneschal guides you readily through the weeds of inheritance laws and unpaid taxes, the conflicts over the drawing of borders and the struggle of a failed crop or three fishing boats lost to the sea. Gradually, you become canny, and start to see again the pieces of the game. You begin to understand the reports from your treasury, and no longer need explained to you every careful column of figures. Your father may have hosted great feasts and hunts with little care for how they would be paid for, but he left you with debts. Frivolity, charity, and necessity all must be diligently budgeted, expenditure recorded with care in the castle's ledgers. If you wish to summon musicians and poets to chase the mourning from the shadows of the hall, you will need coin to pay them with, and food to feast them with, and a merrier court to hear their stories.

You throw yourself headfirst into the complications of kingship, your mind so full of figures and names that you've no time to sink into the mire of grief that held you captive before. The grey fog that has always haunted you nips at your heels, persistent as ever, but where you might have expected grief to feed it, instead it has diminished it, made farcical the weight. What emptiness was that, what loss, compared to this? Your mind is clear, lanced by pain.

But some moments serve only to remind you of what you're trying to forget. Bisclavret's cousin and steward, now his heir, comes to you with a petition for help. His land is not flourishing: they've lost more than a dozen animals to wolves, and the winter is not yet returned. You send him away with half a promise of help, but before long, the families who work his land come to you begging to be allowed to move elsewhere, to find another lord less afflicted by poor luck. Every plea is a reminder of what else – who else – has been lost to you.

'A hunt, sire,' say your knights, when you mention it to them. 'The wolves cannot hide forever. We know they're in those woods; we'll find them if we search long enough. And your people will thank you for it.'

Still you refuse, though by now you've lost all sense of your reasoning. Are northern superstitions so catching, that you've attributed to the wolves a supernatural significance, and in doing so, given them a new power over you?

When you confess to the chaplain your fears of irrationality, he only gives you a soft sad smile. 'It is not irrational,' he says, 'to fear confronting the beast that killed your dear friend. For if the wolf is indeed only a beast and can be vanquished with a hunt, then there will be no true relief in the revenge – only the knowledge that Bisclavret fell against an animal, and not some untouchable foe.'

The words sting. You have long accepted the bitter truth: that Bisclavret was taken by misfortune, not amidst a heroic struggle or in a blaze of chivalric glory. It's the crushing banality of it that pains you. Still, the chaplain may not be wholly incorrect. Once the beast is slain, there'll be nothing left to imagine, no comfort you can bring yourself. It will be over, and Bisclavret will be entirely gone.

You are not ready to let go of him yet.

The wheel of the year turns, and your grief ceases to be an overwhelming, all-powerful force, but it doesn't fade. It clings to you like a shadow, ever-present, and still you keep walking forward: keep ruling, keep fighting, attend to every business to which a king might be expected to attend, applying yourself to solving problems others may not have dared to tackle.

If you don't stop working, then you never have to think. If you are always busy, then you need never be alone with your grief.

Your kingdom may have survived your distraction, as it survived your father's neglect, but now, slowly, it begins to thrive. You remember your exile, the scholars and abbots with whom you kept company, and you extend an invitation to them. You consult them about agriculture, religion, literature, the arts. You learn of the debates happening across Christendom and beyond, and have books copied that you might read of them yourself. When scholars and scribes present themselves to you at court, your heart lifts with the hope of glimpsing a familiar face. But he is never among them, nor do any of them bring word of your story-spinner, book-master, scribe and friend. You swallow your disappointment and lose yourself in the new ideas and tales they bring you, but at night you return to your small volume of lais and trace the spiked letters with your fingertips, remembering the hand that wrote them. They speak of a world more magical than your own, where knights may fly as birds or find a wife from a world of fairies, and sometimes, when all else feels impossible, you imagine slipping between the lines and being made strange yourself by the enchantments of the storytellers.

But always you wake in the real world, and after the first bitter moment of loss when you open your eyes in the morning, you push aside the marvels to attend to your people, your land, and all that you owe them.

You initiate reforms. You levy taxes to rebuild villages devastated by past war; train men to defend them; have priests sent to minister to them. You take the focus you've always dedicated to the sword and experiment with what happens when you commit it to the pen. After weeks of conversation and study, you pick up your own quill and begin to write what will become the first of many letters going back and forth to great minds across the land – to the friends of your exile and to their friends and to those abbots you have heard tell of and more besides.

What news, what scandal, what heresy, what wisdom? You beg for it all and the edges of your world expand with every letter that returns, stretching far beyond the borders of your own kingdom.

And sometimes, when one of your barons questions a decision or your seneschal raises his eyebrow at a judgment, you doubt yourself, until you remember the knight who advocated for the life of the wolf that would kill him, and then you pick up your pen again. There is brotherhood in this, a spiritual friendship, a connection that goes beyond the body. These men understand your desire for more than your father's wars and skirmishes. They do not think you weak. They do not think you lacking.

'I want to be a king of peace,' you tell the chaplain, first, like a confession. 'Not only of not-war. Of something bolder and brighter than that.'

Peace is a hard-won thing; respect is earned more slowly through farms and roads than through bloody victories. But farms need tending and roads need repairing nonetheless, and though there's no glory in the work of building, each stone laid strengthens the foundations of your kingdom. Trade flourishes, goods more easily moved from the coast to the markets inland. Farmers thrive. Day by day, the land begins to blossom, and your reputation spreads. *That young king, the peace-weaver, the road-builder, the letter-writer.* No longer your father's inadequate only son, the dismal heir. Now, the king of peace.

And as your reputation grows, so does that of your kingdom. For so long a rustic backwater to be ignored, it soon demands the attention of rulers who once saw it as beneath their notice. They send missives and envoys and merchants and thieves, and all of them have designs on you.

But strangest of all is the fact that these are not the only bargains they're trying to strike with you – for now that you're known as a careful king and a thoughtful man, they've set their sights higher.

They have started to send their daughters to pay you court.

30

Other

✴ ✷ ✴

the mind of a man is difficult to lose:
it whispers *human*, whispers *I*,
first person, self-absorbed, tangled up
with the gut instinct that pinpoints revenge.
farm animals are a small casualty
and the cousin (human again, remembering family)
deserves worse than the loss, but the wolf
pushes aside those parts of the mind that recall
– *hands* – lacing a shoe, a tunic, a mantle,
and in their place a simpler need:
RUN
no room left for abstract, no time for wondering.

but even now there are echoes
– *I will be like this forever I think* –
of a human kind of dread.

sometimes I cannot bear it

knowledge of forever is a dark thing,
drives a wolf into the shadowed forest
to howl heartbreak at the ancient trees

(if they hear it, the depth of longing,
they have no tongues to answer)
but it's a freedom, too, from the temporary,
from the loss of change,
and when there's nothing left to be mourned
maybe there's a peace in that.
maybe there's a surrender.

but it hurts
it tastes like betrayal
my clothes stolen my life stolen my wife stolen
I was made wolf by them on purpose
abandoned to live feral in the forest like I'm nothing
but I loved her

love is another human lie and close kin
to hate, easily sharpened to a ruinous edge.

I see her sometimes on the edge of the forest
she looks afraid as if she knows I'm watching

guilt makes prey of a hunter, makes haunted a ruin
— I would be the ghost that trails her —
it steals her softness, gives edges to her beauty
until like rock the cruelty becomes apparent.

I wonder what she told the king
whether he knows that I am wolf
how can I know when he hunts so rarely
but if he thought I was wolf he would he would he would —
what would he do, Bisclavret?

THE WOLF AND HIS KING

(see I still have my name)
(this is how I know I am more than this)

can the king move mountains?
upturn the natural order?
remake worlds in a kinder image?
more likely a quick death,
a head mounted like a trophy on the wall,
if he bothers at all.

I do not believe that

then once again this is a story about lying

lies are better than
HUNT
and
RUN
and
SLEEP
when I have hunted and run and slept
for what feels like a thousand years

even a wolf has a sense of its prey.
this is just wandering, just wild, just chasing moonlight
– I'll know it when I see it –
what is 'it' but 'something other than this'
– in the end that's all I want –
more time lurking on the boundary-lines,
more time watching from a distance.

more time to live
more time to laugh
more time to watch the king grow
from an exiled prince into a king who knows his people
who cares for them

his grief has aged him already.
see him emerge, gwyllt, wild, half-dead and shattered with it.
if the saints would stop tormenting him they might make a king
— they say he is a good ruler —
they say a lot of things
— a wife
they're looking to find him a wife —
no rumour spreads as fast as one of love.
the kingdom burns with it, the taste of the story
on the wind and on the wing.
the daughters of kings and counts, the hope
of a kingdom and its people.

perhaps I should be happy for him.
if a wolf can feel that kind of happiness.
at the very least I wish them the best of luck.
a sly remark and no mistake.

I suspect they don't know the king the way I do
but perhaps I'm wrong about him
perhaps I have misunderstood him
I am only a wolf after all and what do wolves know of these things

31

You

* ✳ *

There's a young man standing in front of you.

He's handsome enough, a few years younger than yourself but with the bearing of a grown man and a strong fighter. His expression is pleasant, and he shows no signs of resentment or discomfort as he is presented to you, though the muttering from the rest of the court is difficult to ignore.

'Sire, I fear this is some trick of the count's,' says your seneschal, low and urgent in your ear. 'He intends to cause you dishonour, or to provoke rumour, but—'

You glance at him, and then the young man. 'Dishonour?' you echo, beginning to understand the commotion. 'Is that the motivation you lay on this particular envoy?'

The seneschal flushes red. 'For what other reason would he send his son, my lord?'

You can't help it: a smile tugs at the corner of your mouth. 'Perhaps he seeks knighthood,' you suggest. 'How unlike you to leap to conclusions.' You know, even as you say it, that this young man is not here to swear himself into your service – not in that way, in any case. No, the count has seen the endless parade of daughters sent to court you, and minded their lack of success; now he tries another tack. No wonder the court is so uncomfortable.

The young man's gaze is steady as he meets yours, and he allows you to appraise him without once fidgeting. He's as demure and personable as any of the young women who have been presented to you this week, and you wonder whether this was his father's idea or his own.

'Tell me,' you say more loudly, directing the remark at the visitor himself. 'By your own account, are you here for knighthood or to cause me dishonour?'

To his credit, he doesn't flinch or bluster. 'Neither, my lord,' he says. 'If my presence here is not pleasing to you, I'll leave immediately, and there will be no difficulties between our households following this. I give you my most solemn word.'

You already knew you had nothing to fear from political reprisals if you sent him away – you've been paying close attention to these matters lately, and though his father's powerful enough, he doesn't have enough allies to cause you trouble. But it's intriguing to hear it from the young man himself, and to know that he's not relying on fear to provoke you into action. Nor, you think, is he particularly keen to leave.

It is unwise, perhaps, but for the first time in months, you have a mind to see where this might go.

'And if not dishonour,' you say, your tone still hard, 'what did your father mean by sending you, and not your sister? You do have a sister, don't you?' you add, as though uncertain of it, when you know well that she's a beauty courted by many, and witty besides.

For the first time, the young man looks nervous, glancing at the seneschal as though seeking permission. Your advisors, you sense, would love to tell you that this is improper and shouldn't be countenanced or obliged even as a matter of curiosity, but they don't dare, unless you yourself express enough discomfort to assure them of their right to say as much.

The young man says, 'My father noticed that no lady had yet won your hand, and had the idea that you might respond favourably to an alternative approach.'

Tactfully worded, but bold, nonetheless. You raise your eyebrow. 'Your father has taken it into his head that I only get into bed with other men,' you say baldly. 'And has sent you in the hope that I'll prove him right and confirm all his suspicions about our kingdom.' Ever the rumour has circled that your people are minded to seek the pleasures of adolescence even as adults, and neglect the begetting of heirs, and that your priests turn a blind eye to the practice. You think if this were really such a rural backwater or deviant borderland, untroubled by the censure of homilists, your father would not have been so disappointed by you, and would not have sent you away – his reasons were no secret, even if they were never uttered aloud.

Evidently exile was insufficient to cleanse your name of those whispers, if still they follow you.

But the young man says, 'No,' so firmly that it draws looks of disgust from the manners-minded courtiers. 'My lord, no scheming of my father's would draw me here if I thought he intended you harm. I'm here because I asked leave of him to come.'

You eye him again in this new light. There is no fear or shame in him. He has never known exile, never been cast out. 'Give us the room, please,' you instruct, and when the hall is empty of all save yourself, your guest, and your seneschal, you say, 'Elaborate.'

'When word reached us that you were being courted, my mother's instinct was that my sister should be among those paying you suit. You met her once, though some years ago now, and seemed to show her favour, though I'd not presume that you remember such an occasion—'

'I remember,' you interrupt, though you were both only

youths at the time, her beauty still unformed and you awkward and ungainly. 'I've heard that she has flowered and flourished in the years that have passed.'

'Sire,' he acknowledges, with a small bow of the head. 'My mother's thought was that she would have as much chance of winning your hand as any other, but the question was raised as to whether that were any real chance at all. Your failure to find a bride thus far cannot be due to the unsuitability of the candidates who have presented themselves, so we thought perhaps your interests lay elsewhere.'

You suppose it was inevitable, that people across the kingdom and beyond it should speculate about your tastes, but it still feels strange to hear it presented so honestly. No doubt others think the same, but would not voice it, and still more of them fear you'll cloister yourself eventually and leave the throne open to any capable of seizing it, since your father made it clear enough he expected that sort of thing. And that's assuming good intent and genuine concern, and not ill-feeling towards your kingdom and its stubborn refusal to become part of their great empires and speak their tongues and conform to their liturgy.

You might have hoped they would expect more from you than the neglect of your kingdom for the sake of your own desires, after these past months working to prove that you have a greater sense of duty than your father. Perhaps they do you the courtesy of assuming you intend to name an heir another way, but you fear you have not yet won their trust.

'And so you asked to be sent instead,' you say. It's not a question, but he makes a noise of assent anyway. Your next inquiry's half a mockery, a note of mischief creeping into your voice: 'And I suppose that was out of concern for your household's future, was it, and the status that might be earned should you succeed in winning my favour?'

He takes a breath. Looks at the seneschal. Looks back at you. And says, 'No, sire.' Then, halfway to mischief himself, adds, 'My father is a count. I do not lack for status.'

Interesting.

Despite yourself, your attention's been caught by the young man. You can't keep him in your household for long, you know that – it wouldn't benefit either of you. But he is unabashed and uninhibited in a way that you find intriguing, and it seems a shame to send him away without exploring that at least a little more.

Your seneschal will disapprove. You try not to resent that, for he has been your saviour these past months, and his disapproval is grounded in a politic mind and a canny sense for the winds of favour, but you wish his sense of duty did not cost him his sense of sport.

You glance at him – he is trying hard not to frown, and not entirely succeeding – and then fix your gaze again on the young man. 'You'll stay here tonight, then? You've travelled far; you must be tired. There's a feast planned for the end of this week, and ...' You're forgetting something, some other plan for these next few days.

Before you can admit defeat and ask him, the seneschal says, 'The hunt, sire. There is also the hunt.'

The last before Michaelmas, the end of the season for roebuck. You have missed so much of the hunting this year, your stomach still easily turned by the chase, but you have promised your men this mustering and you will not fail them. You smile at the young man and say, 'Well, of course you must join us for the hunt.'

It's not preferential treatment. All of the young women have been housed and feasted, before being sent away with gifts to ease the sting of rejection. You'll do the same for him – and in the meantime, you may as well ride out together. Perhaps the sweetness of a new companion by your side will ease the unsettled chill in your stomach that still haunts all thoughts of hunting.

You have servants find him a place to sleep, clothes, food. You inform the stables that he'll be riding with you on the hunt, and that they should ensure his horse is made ready. Then you look again at the mount – a quality beast, but better suited to travel than hunting – and tell them to prepare instead one of your own coursers for his use. You do everything properly, as though he were any visiting nobleman, and you treat him with all the kindness and distance with which you treated all those daughters.

But not one of those daughters was bold enough to leave their bed in the dead of night and mount the stairs to your chamber, knocking so softly on the door that at first you're unsure what woke you. None of them stood bashful on your threshold, skin pale against the open neck of their undertunic.

None of them said, in a voice so low as to be hardly audible, 'Send me away, and I'll go.'

And if they had, perhaps you'd have done exactly that. But you don't send him away. You remain where you are, propped up in bed, with your bedcoverings and hair disarrayed by uneasy sleep, and hold his gaze until he takes a few hesitant steps across the room. And then a few more. And then, finally, after what seems like an age, he's standing in front of you.

He looks younger like this, away from the formal trappings of petition. Or perhaps it's only that he's nervous: you see him twisting his fingers into the fabric of his tunic, and the frantic way he swallows.

You say, 'Do you want to go?'

He shakes his head. No, he doesn't, does he? He came to

you, this bold count's son, and he must have known that his quest was doomed from the beginning – that as king, whatever your own inclinations, you could not make a husband of him. And yet he thought it worth trying, if only so that it might bring him here, half-dressed, to your bed.

He has the advantage of height on you, when you sit there in your bed and he stands before you. But he kneels, and places his head in your lap. *Fealty.* For as long as you want it, and whatever you require of him. You run your fingers through his hair, startled by its softness, and feel the gentle warmth of him. You have had little time in recent months for simple intimacies, and the warmth of slow touch and quiet company.

You take him by the hand and pull him up so that he's sitting beside you on the bed. You trace his shaking palms with your fingertips. You say, 'Do you know what it is that you want?'

He's wide-eyed, more innocent than you expected from his confidence earlier, and you have the sense of having caught him with his guard down. Perhaps he never anticipated coming so far. Perhaps he thought you'd turn him away at the door.

He says, 'No.' Then he swallows again, his gaze drifting to your lips and back up to meet your eyes, and says, 'Yes. I would like to kiss you.'

His lips are warm. It's no kiss of peace – it's filled with fire, setting you alight, and you shudder under his touch as he runs his hands along your arms, as though marvelling that he's allowed to touch you at all.

You break apart, and he says, 'Am I ... may I ... sire, I don't want ...'

'Am I wearing a crown?' you ask him, words soft as feathers. He shakes his head. 'Then tonight I am not your king.' And then you kiss him again, to remind him, and feel his warmth diffusing through your cold, grief-laden bones. He cannot fill the hollows inside you, but he can close them off for a moment, because he's *there*, real and solid and burning in your hands.

You press yourself a little closer and he gasps into the kiss, and you know then that you could have him, in whatever way you wanted him, in all the ways you could never have had Bisclavret. *Fealty.* This man will give everything of himself to you.

It's been so long since you wanted any of that. But his touch wakes something in you that has been long asleep, some hunger that yearns to be fed, and you find yourself helping him to remove the last of his clothes, the warm skin of his torso against yours the most exquisite sensation, your hands moving against his back in ways that make his breathing catch and stutter.

And you allow him to press you down into the bed. Allow yourself to want him. Allow yourself to pull him closer, to put down the walls you've built these last few months, to be held – allow yourself, for once, to be known.

32

Other

✦ ✳ ✦

the woods breed hunters like decay
but this time the rot's not distant,
baying of the hounds made phantom by remove;
this time the impact of the horses' hooves
shakes the world, crumbling earth
into trembling pieces; this time the circle
closes like a trap, sprung unknowing.

they don't know I'm here

the months have woven a new tapestry
from the colours of the forest,
trees shifting orange to skeletal to new growth
as the flowers keep time, scents and shoots
a wolf's only calendar. but change
has been an external thing, a forgotten thing.

I thought I had nothing to be afraid of
now that the worst has happened
but there are hunters in these woods

not being afraid is a luxury
but riches ever fade
— if they knew it was me would they still hunt me —
and there's a royal bloodlust to be slaked.

he is not a king who thirsts for blood
he is bright prince sword swinging laughter
he is king with heavy crown and banked fire and yearning
it is a peaceful man who is lost to me

stories scavenged from the edge of the forest
cannot slake the thirst of loneliness,
but there's a sanity to be found in them.
at least the half-lost sanity of a memory of a man
scattered and incoherent in a wolf's body.

RUN

I don't have to run
I could stay here and let him find me —
poetic, really, for a king to kill his knight,
unmake the one he made,
unname the one he named.

I remember that first hunt
how he watched me
how I pretended I was lost to it
and to the thrill of being a predator
no novelty in that except the human taste of it

THE WOLF AND HIS KING

I wasn't lost
I let him watch me
I dared him to do anything but watch me

sometimes others are a better mirror
  – I want him to watch me again
but I am not me I cannot even watch myself –
and the wolf's a bitter armour

  he believes I killed me –
so the stories say, in their way, a classic tragedy:
a man wandering, half-mad, stolen by a wolf's teeth
  – perhaps it's true
I lost my wits and my skin together
it was a wolf who stole me from my wife
  and from my home

and for a king to wage war on a wolf
is as much the stuff of stories as the rest,
  an ill-fitting vengeance.

  let him
  what good am I alive
  what life is this that I lead
  RUN
  not this time
  I will face him like a man
  I will make them face me
I will make them look me in the eyes when they kill me
  see that a thinking creature wears this skin
  they will live with that knowledge
  HUNT

I will not hunt the king
he has my oath he has my life
but this is the way of things the way it always is
he is man and I am beast
that is ever the difference between us

RUN

not any more

33

You

✦ ✳ ✦

You are tired for hunting and lacking in bloodlust, but the sight of the count's son riding out to meet the rest of the group at least sparks some enthusiasm for the sport. His hunting clothes, though borrowed, fit him well; he has well-turned calves and strong shoulders and a shy smile that he offers you, a little uncertainly. You nod to him in return, the expected response, and see his relief. Perhaps he thought you would hold his boldness against him. How uncharitable that would be, when you have tasted the sweet nectar of his kisses and felt the warmth of his skin against yours and allowed his touch to drive away your melancholy, even if only for a moment.

You find yourself falling back until you ride beside him, trusting those ahead not to stray from the trail. 'Do you hunt often, in your father's lands?' you ask him, though it's a banal question and well you might guess the answer.

'Often enough,' he says, predictably. 'Rarely in woods that carry rumours of wolves, however.'

Perhaps that's the cause of his hesitance, and not some lingering regret for the previous night. You hope as much; such concerns are easier to assuage. 'Our chances of meeting a wolf are slim, if it pleases the Almighty to preserve us,' you assure him. 'With luck we'll meet only deer. Do you prefer to hunt par force, or are you a man for falconry?'

He shoots you a sharp look, as though reading euphemism into your honest enquiry, but whatever he sees in your expression softens his response.

'It's the hounds I favour, for the most part,' he says, 'though our kennels can't hope to match yours.'

Yours reflect your father's concerns more than your own, but it's true, the hounds are fine and spirited and ready for the chase. Fearless, too, even in the face of deadly quarry, capable of staring down boar as though they might take the kill themselves.

The memory recalls Bisclavret to your mind, and you feel again the ache of missing him. You want him here *now*, riding out with you, unflinching in the teeth of danger. The count's son beside you does little to ease the absence: all you can think about is the fact that he isn't the man you wish him to be.

Grief disarrays your mind again, scattering your attention, and you would sooner be at home than here in the woods. But a cry goes up – tracks found, prey sighted – and you spur your horse forward to join them, disguising your sudden melancholy as a surge of enthusiasm. The count's son follows, ignorant of his failure to be somebody else.

'A wolf,' comes the word. 'There's a wolf in the forest. The wolf is here.'

A wolf.

The wolf.

The wolf who took Bisclavret.

The wolf who escaped you once before.

Suddenly your enthusiasm is real, spurred by rage. He should be here to make the kill, but in his absence, you must do it for him, offer up vengeance for a life taken too early and with such indignity. You forget your peace and the softer tones of your grief in favour of the red fury of facing your enemy, ignoring the cautions of your nobles and the count's son to ride out to the front, weapons ready.

When you don't look back at them, Bisclavret might be beside you.

'Sire,' calls your knight in green, and it's almost a reprimand.

You can't pretend that's his voice. He'd not have spoken with that echo of reproach or hint of impatience; the same word from his lips would have been a softer utterance. Where the others would have heard deference, you'd have heard secrets in the aching familiarity of the syllable. The rustling leaves of these sepulchral woods are falling ash, smothering you, and for a moment your breath catches on the airlessness of absence.

No matter the distance you put between yourself and death, the shadow of grief never stops haunting you.

All you can hope to do is outrun it. You spur your horse and ride ahead, forcing them to follow you. You will find the wolf and make it pay for its sins against the both of you. Nobody will take that victory from you, or claim its pelt when it's yours to skin.

You've caught the trail yourself, now, despair-clouded eyes sharpened once again by hatred. The wolf was here, and recently. It will not escape you this time.

It's not running. Perhaps it hasn't caught the scent of you yet, or perhaps it means to rip you from your horse and fight to the end.

'Sire,' says your knight again, more urgently. To be a king is to have no name, only this title, this reminder that you're supposed to lead, not wander astray.

Not chase a ghost through the forest.

'It's here,' you tell them, voice desperate, deranged. 'The wolf is here. This time I will catch it.' This time it will not evade you, flitting away between the trees before it can be made to pay. This time you'll see its blood steam red on the ground, its skin ragged like the scraps of Bisclavret's torn clothing.

Your knight in green tries one last time to warn you: the woods are too dark, too deep, and already you've strayed too far from the usual paths. The hunt must circle round and find another track or risk losing its way.

You turn to look at him for the first time. At all of them.

You say, 'Please.'

You are a king. You should beg for nothing. But you'd crawl on your knees if it would reclaim him from whatever shadow has swallowed him, and damn the mud on your crown. If you cannot unbury him, then you'll offer blood sacrifices on the grave he never had, feed his shade with the entrails of his murderer.

They let you go. They could never have stopped you.

You ride on until you find yourself crashing through the undergrowth and then out into a clearing and—

Your horse rears so suddenly there's no time to calm her. You're thrown from her back, a tumult of falling and fear and impact, softened by mud but hard enough to bruise and bewilder.

You hear somebody call out, and then they falter into silence, and as your vision clears you see what they've seen.

The wolf.

It's the same beast you saw before, that awful day when you learned of Bisclavret's death – you'd swear it, solid as an oath. Huge, implacable, utterly unafraid of you. Something in its face that isn't wolflike, something knowing.

Your horse has abandoned you. Your men can come no closer or their own beasts will panic. Some of the huntsmen are archers, and you hear the creak of their bows as they prepare their arrows, but they hesitate to loose them.

Why do they hesitate?

You push yourself up from the mud, and the wolf keeps its uncanny eyes fixed on you. Is there time to reach for your sword? Could you still have a chance of victory, if you—

The wolf moves.

Blindingly fast. Directly towards you.

You think: *I'm going to die.* You think: *this is what Bisclavret saw before it took him.* You think: *my sword my sword where is my sword why don't they shoot am I to fall here alone are they to abandon me is this the end—*

And it stops, so close you feel the heat of its breath. You're frozen to the spot as the creature carefully, deliberately, places its heavy paws on your lap and presses its nose against your hands like a courtier swearing fealty.

Your breath catches. The wolf's teeth are a hair's breadth from your hands, but it makes no attempt to bite. It looks up at you again with that too-human stare and then repeats the gesture.

Fealty.

Shaking, you push yourself to your knees, and then your feet. The wolf prostrates itself before you and then, standing, makes the same gesture for a third time, before it waits, head bowed, for your response.

If it were human – *it's not human, it's a wolf, outlaw, murderer, forest-wild* – you would have thought this loyalty. Subservience. The wolf has put itself under your protection and bared itself to your retribution. If you pulled free a blade now, you could take your revenge so easily, without breaking a sweat, and yet your hand doesn't stray to your sword. You're transfixed by its strange expression, and the impossible gentleness of the way it placed its paws on you.

'Sire,' says a shaking voice – one of the huntsmen, an arrow trained on the beast. 'We cannot shoot without hitting you.'

We cannot save you. But you don't think, somehow, that you need saving – not from this.

You glance up in time to see your knight in green cross himself, all the wry wit drained from his expression. 'That wolf,' he says, 'has the mind of a man.'

The mind of a man.

Can it be possible? Is this a garwolf?

If so, the stories do them discredit to paint them as witless beasts. This creature is no monster: it pledges itself to you as its king as though it were your knight, defeated in battle, though dressed in furs instead of armour.

'Put down your weapons,' you say. Your voice shakes, and they hesitate. You're not used to needing to repeat yourself. You take your eyes off the wolf for just long enough to fix them in a firm stare: 'I said put them down.'

They lower their arrows, let the strings of their bows go slack. They know, as you do, that if you're wrong and the beast means you harm, this is the kind of mistake you won't survive.

You swallow.

The wolf raises its head and looks up at you. It is so very large, you think, inanely. It would be the work of seconds for it to maul you – a quick death, at least – and your knights' hands are twitching towards their blades. But they obey their instructions, and keep their swords sheathed; the huntsmen's arrows remain in their quivers.

You reach out a hand, and wait to feel the wolf's teeth close around your wrist. Nothing. Only the surprising softness of its fur as you bury your fingers in it, the creature leaning into the touch. It's been run ragged, burrs and mud matting its pelt, but that can't disguise the thick pile of it, the warmth of its skin underneath. The beast remains utterly still and allows you to pet it like a hound.

You hear the soft exhalation of a dozen nobles releasing a held breath. The count's son says, 'Why, the beast is practically tame.'

'Not tame,' you say – there's something feral in the creature's eyes. This isn't a domestic calm, an absence of threat; this is teeth withheld and violence curbed. 'But safe, I think.'

A defeated enemy, placing himself in your hands. A subject, swearing fealty. A lonely creature, desperate for the momentary relief of touch.

But what now? Can you leave the animal in the woods and go home? Will you try to explain to the court that you've found the wolf they've feared all these months, and wish for it to be left alone? It's difficult to believe that this can be the same monster, and yet you know it, have seen it before, have hunted it. Do you now intend to pass a decree that forbids such a thing?

I have no taste for hunting wolves. Bisclavret would not have resented such a ruling, you suspect. Something about the animal reminds you of him: his loping grace in its movements, his quiet intelligence in its eyes, his poise and restraint in its readiness. Maybe he saw that familiarity too; maybe that was why he treated the beasts as kinsmen rather than enemies, coexisting in the same forest.

You take a few steps, as though to walk away, and the wolf follows.

'Do you intend to follow me all the way home?' you ask it softly, in the tone one might use for a wayward kitten. 'The forest is a more fitting home for a wolf than the court.'

The wolf is undeterred. Its expression clearly conveys that it cares nothing for what is fitting, and will follow you wherever you choose to go. *Fealty.* This was no mere mimicry or imitation. This was an oath, and one the wolf meant wholeheartedly.

Perhaps it does have the mind of a man after all. Perhaps

some unknowable part of the creature is loyal to you. Or perhaps you're a naive dreamer, easily fooled by figments, and will find yourself attacked the first time you turn your back on the wolf.

You turn your back anyway, waiting for the claws to fall on you, but the wolf keeps padding softly at your side.

'Sire,' says one of your barons, some nervousness in his tone. 'You cannot bring the wolf back to the castle with you – there'll be panic, and—'

'I cannot?' you say, soft and dangerous. 'Is that so?'

He swallows, realising too late his overstep. 'I beg your pardon, I only meant—'

'I know what you meant,' you say, cutting him off before he can stammer an apology. 'But the beast is intent on following, and I choose not to be the one to drive it away.'

You wait for them to counsel that you should have the creature killed before it's too late, but although you hear that advice in their silence, they have more sense than to speak the words aloud. Your knight in green crosses himself again – any other day, you would marvel at such piety from a man who has always flirted with heresy and irreverence, but today there are greater wonders.

And you have become one of them, walking out of the forest like this: weapons unbloodied, one hand buried in the wolf's fur. It walks steadily beside you, no humbled predator but a loyal retainer, and when you come to the court and people recoil in fear, you allow them to see that you're fearless, that there's nothing about the wolf that should concern them, that it means you no harm.

You think you believe that. You are, at least, able to pretend enough to convince them. And behind that mask of courage, you walk inside, and the wolf follows.

34
Other

✦ ✷ ✦

predator turned sentinel: a wolf
curled at the king's door like a hound
– he has brought me home –
and a king who smells of distraction.
hard to say how much of this
wolf-suspicion, predator-wariness,
is the beast's heart and how much
is the man's, but the boy that's with him
has a smile like a secret, softening
the barbs of the king's thoughts.

he brings the young man inside with him
he is surprised too I think but if my king wants it
if my king thinks it is safe
then I will let him pass

'do you plan to stay there all night?'
to a wolf, wordless, the question is parsed
like sunlight through trees, dappled with meaning.

he's asking if I will guard him
his smile is soft and sad –

his smiles are often sad these days,
painted with misunderstood grief.
but the wolf waits at the door,
keeps out the draught and the blade and the bad dreams
and in the morning when the young man sleeps
the king slips from his bed to the stairwell,
quiet as a wraith, and the wolf follows.

PACK
some loyalties run blood-deep
FOLLOW
a stone courtyard is unlike the woods
but the path is clear enough,
bed to chapel, sleep to prayer.
here no ivy tangles around the altar-stone,
no leaves crunch in the nave.
in his pale nightshirt the king is a ghost,
cold as the stones, but his candle
holds the force of a star. he kneels
 — he must be cold —
and begins to whisper prayers.
they are unknowable,
layered in human-sense, no wolf-sense to them,
a soft chant of syllables.

I will stay by him anyway
I am at least warm in this cold place
I will keep him from freezing at his vigil

the candle burns low, guttering
with every exhalation. it flickers,

270

and as the flame goes out the priest emerges,
well-timed and hesitant.

I recognise him
I remember this man he was kind to me

stories of the wolf have spread.
rumours are as swift as prayers.
he stops to speak to the king and—
'bisclavret'
– my name
he says my name this priest he says my name
I hear it as clear as if I were human –
these men of god and remembrance
can summon phantoms with their words.

why does he say my name

perhaps he speaks of loss. the king's answer
is a whisper, faint and non-committal,
like the beast to his skin.
he shakes his head. says
'the mind of a man'
quoting, it seems, his knight.
the words hang uneasily in the air.

this priest he must know I'm no thing of nature
only a monstrous aberration
and he
he must see the devil's work in me
and yet he steps away

a burning star – another candle, sheltered
from the draughts of the chapel – a clasped shoulder,
a murmured prayer, and then the priest
is gone and the king resumes his vigil,
and the wolf resumes his waiting.

I cannot go home
I can never go home
I will never have my own skin
my body has forgotten how to be human
even despite the dreams of it

this place is not home but half a tomb,
cold stone and candle wax,
but still the dust is a breath of life,
still the pale dawn of candlelight is homecoming,
away from the forest and starvation and desperate bloody survival.
not home but a resting place,
a moment's grace
– *for as long as he will have me here* –
'bisclavret'

he remembers my name
he speaks it when he's praying
perhaps I am not lost after all

35

You

＊ ✳ ＊

You send the count's son away, eventually. You have to – it isn't fair to use him to keep your loneliness at bay, nor to encourage his family's hopes of favour, though where they think this will end, you can't imagine. Rumours are already beginning to spread that you've no interest in encouraging: it is any king's right to invite his favourites to share his bed, but it will cause tension if you're thought to show a preference for a foreign count over one of your own barons, and you have admitted so few into your intimacies since your coronation.

When he's gone your bed is cold and far too large and you rise too early for prayers from fractured sleep. The wolf is curled outside your door, less disreputable after having been washed and groomed by the keepers of the castle hounds. It – *he*, there's too much intelligence in those eyes to think of him like any other animal – looks up at you with placid loyalty, and follows you to the chapel.

It's always cold there, on your knees, but the warmth of the wolf beside you chases away some of the chill. When your prayers are uttered, you twist your cold fingers into his fur and feel the heat that radiates from his body. He doesn't seem to mind. He nudges you gently, as though encouraging you to come closer.

But the chaplain made it clear that he is not enthused about the presence of a wolf in his chapel, so you don't linger, returning to your chamber. The wolf's about to lie down in front of the door when some soft instinct prompts you to say, 'No, come inside.' As if he can understand you.

Maybe he can. Certainly he follows you, and curls up beside your bed like a guard. There's space enough for him in the bed itself, in place of the friends you don't have, but perhaps the floor suits him better; lying on the edge of the endless bed, you can still reach out and touch him, and his presence is comforting. It's easier than usual to slip back into dreamless sleep until the morning comes properly to wake you again.

The first time the servants find him there, they're startled, but it becomes a familiar sight: the large wolf beside you as you sleep, protecting you from harm. Perhaps it's as well that you never acquired the habit of inviting your barons to share your chambers and gain a little honour that way, though it would be a fine test of their mettle to know if they'd dare to lie down beside the wolf and close their eyes. If nothing else, you know you need fear no assassin or spy, for the wolf growls fiercely at any who come unannounced to wake you.

Gradually, the court lose their fear of the animal. It helps that he shows no inclination towards violence; after months of quiet companionship and protection, even those initially timid have grown fond of him, and will spare a morsel from their plates or offer him a scratch behind the ears. But you take care not to let stories of his docility spread beyond the castle walls. It can be useful, sometimes, to have him stare down petitioners when they become too strident and demanding; they are suddenly minded to curb their tongue.

You've always talked to the wolf, in the way that anyone talks to their hounds or their horses – small murmurs of reassurance, basic instructions – but as weeks stretch into months, you find yourself confiding in him. Especially at night, alone in your bed, when you curl up against the beast for his warmth. It is less lonely than talking to yourself, and lacks the bitter sting.

At first you speak of little. Your tiredness, maybe, or a hard day, one where an issue brought before you is more difficult to resolve than most and you cannot be sure you made a fair judgment. You talk about your knights and their foibles and quests, recounting a joke told at a feast or a story brought home from a tournament. You have no real sense that the beast understands you – despite his intelligent eyes, he makes no response to these tales that suggests anything more than recognition of the rhythm of your voice. But somehow it helps to tell him. You confess your fear of the growing unrest on the eastern horizon, the threat of war that comes ever closer in the reports of your advisors and the epistles of your correspondents: *this may be my last letter for a while*, one writes, *for once the fighting reaches the river, there will be no safe path for messengers* ...

You don't know what you will do when it arrives, and you don't dare tell anybody else that, either.

One night, you tell him about Bisclavret. The reminiscence slips out, unprompted: you think of him daily, keep him in your prayers, but usually, these days, you spend less of your time lost in nostalgia and grief, and are not minded to speak of him. You aren't sure what nudged the words loose.

Perhaps it's because it's the anniversary of Bisclavret's wedding, unmarked and uncelebrated.

Once you start, it's difficult to stem the flow of memories. You talk of him late into the night – half recollections, half confessions, everything you should have said and didn't, all the things you think he knew but wouldn't acknowledge. Briefly, you voice a fear you've never spoken aloud before: that he's not dead but hiding, having fled your court and your affections when he became unable to bear your gaze.

The wolf makes a low growling noise – outraged either on your behalf, or because you dared even think Bisclavret capable of such disloyalty. But it helps to have said it aloud. Until now, you hadn't truly dared admit it to yourself: *I fear I drove him away. That he chose to leave.*

Having discussed Bisclavret once, it becomes natural to do so again, and again, until it's a familiar part of your nightly routine.

'I wish he were here,' you say to the wolf one evening, both of you curled in front of the fire. 'He would know what to do about the war.' He'd have an answer that would cut through all the fussing of your advisors.

It is not your war. That much you've known from the beginning. It's another kingdom's dispute, allies betraying allies and succession crises raging, and it should have nothing to do with you, except that they hope to enrich themselves and their cause by annexing you and bidding your nobles to fight for them. You've watched the threat of it grow like a shadow, but you've no more sense now of how to avoid it than you did when word of the struggle first reached your ear.

The latest letter from one of your correspondents at another court was not encouraging. *Better to live as a subject than die for a principle you have not the men and arms to defend. You'll lose little – the name of king, perhaps, but what harm to rule a duchy instead, and know there's a greater land to call upon should you need them in turn?*

Is he right? Is it better to surrender and swear your fealty to a stronger king, that he might use you to vanquish his enemies? Perhaps – but the idea tastes bitter. Why should your people die for another man's cause? Why should you send your nobles and their sons into battle for a struggle that means nothing to you?

You think of the count's son, and wonder whose part he has taken, and whether he will survive to rue his choice. You imagine him dragged from his horse, trampled in the mud with his shy smile slaughtered, and it seems unconscionable to wish such a thing on any man. Your father was right: you don't have the stomach for war, or the heart for it, and even exile couldn't hammer it into you or give you a taste for blood.

'Bisclavret would know what to do,' you say, but you know it's a lie. Bisclavret was a gifted hunter and a skilled swordsman, but he was no politician. You've latched onto the memory of an imagined man, put him on a pedestal no human could live up to, and you do your knight a disservice by not remembering him as he was. 'I wish he were here,' you say again, because that part, at least, is true.

The wolf doesn't answer. He curls close to you, docile as a puppy tired out by play, and you rest your hand on his back and try to push the war from your mind. If you allow yourself to dwell on it, you'll never sleep.

Your mind wanders instead to your once-scrivener, whose departure left as many questions as answers. There has been no news of him since he left. He promised to send word, didn't he? You can't remember. You can't even be sure whether he said he'd ever return. But it strikes you now that *he* is the kind of man who would know what to do about this war. He'd have stories to tell, tales that feel half-real and half-magic, flitting from the battlefield to the heavens in moments, and hidden amidst his stories would be the truth of what you should do. But when you accused him of playing advisor, he would only smile and say that he was nothing but a scribe, and refuse your attempts to contradict him.

277

You miss him. Not in the same aching, abstract way that you miss Bisclavret, but with similar intensity. You are lost without the softly sarcastic affection that permeated his advice.

'Why does everybody have to leave?' you ask the wolf. He will stay, at least. He has a hound's loyalty, faithful and true, guarding you from loneliness. He is the only thing preventing you from retreating entirely and hiding in your chamber like a wraith, for you must move yourself to ensure he's fed and exercised, tasks you hesitate to inflict on a nervous page boy.

If not for the wolf, perhaps you would have kept the count's son here a little longer, allowing your fear of solitude to override your consideration for what is politic and polite. Instead you sent him home with gifts and gratitude, taking care that neither was too effusive, and hoped he's been brought no disgrace by the whole affair.

If he has, well, war will give him a chance to clear his name, redeem himself through martial strength or die a martyr in his father's eyes. But if it were up to you, you would not send him to war. Not if there were any other way.

I want to be a king of peace.

You tell your barons as much the next day: that you will not involve yourself in the squabbles of counts and kings of other lands, nor will you surrender and allow them to drag you into it that way. Your kingdom has endured for generations, insulated by its size and its refusal to leap into every war or skirmish that offers the potential for riches, and you will not have it become another piece in their territorial games. They dream, it seems, of rebuilding the empires of old until their names are known the world over, but you have no interest in that. Your crown has enough weight to it already.

'We will not fight,' you say. 'Not unless they invade and it is our only choice. There is no value in courting trouble.'

'But sire—' Some of them are still young men, still desperate for glory and young enough to think they'll find it in blood – of course they argue with you. In your weariness you feel abruptly aged. *What good is glory to the dead?* you want to ask them. *What good is fame to a corpse?*

You would never have made a very good hero.

'Your father had an agreement—' begins your seneschal.

You quell him with a look. 'I am not my father,' you say, 'disappointing though that may be to all involved.' They flinch. They did not, then, expect you to notice. As though you could ever have stopped noticing, when that disappointment has followed you all your life, when it is what drove you into exile in the first place. Here it is, the test of your father's fears, and they have been proven: you are unwarlike and unmanly, and they resent you for it.

Your father, though, was wrong to see these things as your weakness. You will prove that to them, one way or another, just as you have been proving it to them with every road and every letter that has laid the foundations of your kingship so far.

'There is a right part here,' says the seneschal weakly.

'Perhaps there is,' you say. 'In which case God will see fit to favour the man who should be king and grant him the crown, whether or not I send my men to help him, for that should be well within His power.' You are letting impatience make acerbic your tongue; you should be mindful. 'Joining this war will not end the dispute, only perpetuate it. There will be a second war, a third, a dozen – all to maintain the sovereignty of a man without the strength to take it in the first place. And these men do not see us as true allies, only a prize to be won. They've been looking for an excuse to invade, and our involvement would offer it, make us an enemy to be eliminated before we can further complicate things. I will not invite that end.'

Your barons seem taken aback by this pronouncement. Perhaps they thought you didn't grasp the politics of the situation, as though your letter-writing has taught you nothing of foreign courts and powers.

'You think they will leave us be if we remain neutral?' asks your seneschal hesitantly.

'I think we should pray for as much,' you say, 'and prepare in case those prayers are not answered in a way we would like.'

There are murmurs at this, but they see enough sense in your decision not to object aloud, though you know they mislike it. They've never had time for your peace-weaving, and the way you seek books and scholars and ideas in place of war, glory, more land. Sometimes you think the chaplain is the only one who respects you for it. But your kingdom thrives in peaceful hands, and why should you throw that away, to satisfy the cravings of greedy men? Your first duty is to protect those who depend on you, to repay the fealty your subjects have offered you. Any path other than peace would be a betrayal of their trust.

'And by prepare,' says the quavering voice of one of your oldest advisors, 'you mean to ready a force? For if there is a need to defend ourselves we risk being unarmed and helpless.'

You purse your lips. To raise an army, equip them to fight, and expect them to be satisfied with the peace you pray for is a dangerous thing, for a hunger roused is a hunger that must be fed. Dangerous enough that your knights are restless and spoiling for a fight, that your wolf's teeth are as sharp as ever and his hunter's heart untamed by his time at your side.

But the man is right, nonetheless: you owe it to your people to have the forces to protect them if an invasion comes, just as you owe it to them not to seek the conflict.

'Yes,' you say reluctantly. 'Let each lord raise ten men, and have them equipped and trained in the use of arms. Recruit only those of an age to know the risks, not the green youths who dream of a glorious death. Understand?'

Agreement, grudgingly, is reached. That will have to be enough. You have done all you can.

36

Other

＊ ✳ ＊

war tastes like metal.
metal and sweat and new men in the king's livery,
swinging swords with little grace.
it is storm-wild and snow-sharp and the king says
'do not call it war'
but it's not peace, this thing, strange and new;
it brings no life.

if I were there on the field if I were me
I could teach them better than that
maybe I could teach them to survive

the men he's chosen are prey-scared,
waiting to be hunted, pretending otherwise,
and all the while the king braces himself for the loss,
a sacrifice he's too bright and good to make.

I don't know why he bothers with it at all
I will protect him I will protect him I will protect him –
but his kingdom is bigger than that,
bigger than his kind heart and loyalties,

and the man's mind knows that. the wolf
only longs to prove itself with claw and tooth.

I will protect him

at night the king's fears escape him,
slip and skitter like falling leaves,
language dissolving, too human for the wolf.
he says
'bisclavret'
and then corrects himself, catches himself,
as though he never said it at all.
he tries to avoid it
– I wish he wouldn't –
his shame stealing words from his lips.

*I am more me when he says my name
like he gives me back the pieces of myself*

his gaze that shears through men
sees only the wolf, a partial truth.

*I am the worst of me
still he keeps me by him in my monstrosity
how can it be that I am allowed this
I am only wolf*

he speaks of his people, a king's love
in every word. his fear, his inadequacy, the failure
of giving them everything that he is.

THE WOLF AND HIS KING

I would tell him otherwise
if I had the tongue or the teeth for words
instead I only listen

'if they invade we are lost we cannot fight their armies'
he says and
'I am arming these men for their graves'
and
'I will be remembered as a hero when I should be named a
failure'
'better to surrender and hope for mercy than be slaughtered
where we stand'
'I am a fool to have agreed to this'

he is no fool to me –
but a wolf's heart will always want to fight,
always want to stand teeth bared on the margins of the kingdom.

it doesn't matter anyway
I cannot tell him

there's reassurance in presence
– the king knots his fingers through my fur –
he pretends he isn't weeping

I don't know why he pretends
he need not hide his tears from me
I am only a wolf and a wolf cannot judge a king

37
You

The war threatens endlessly like summer thunder, heavy in the air but never breaking. You see only scattered showers of rain – small skirmishes in the borderlands, little more than the usual disputes. You send knights out to scout the marches and count them as they ride back home, relieved whenever they return unharmed and sorrowful when they don't.

You lose two, in total – one young and beardless, with a singing voice to shame an angel but only when he's in his cups, and the other a tried and tested warrior whose loss will be keenly felt by all who knew him. On the battlefields to the north, your neighbouring kingdoms are losing a generation of warriors to siege and slaughter, and this is a small bereavement by comparison, but still those two deaths grieve you, bitter and painful.

You might well have retreated to carry your grief alone, but your knights have learned from past mistakes, and will not allow it. Your knight in green is their leader, you know, but all of them take up the task of persuading you to each feast and bout and ride. You toast the departed with them, and as days pass and the sting of sadness fades, your men return to their joking – but occasionally you see their wistful looks, as though they're caught by a memory or an idea of what their lost comrades might have said, were they here to say it.

It should bring you comfort, to have company in your mourning, but if anything it only intensifies the weight.

I had their oaths, I held their lives, I owed them protection, I have failed them – and ever the threat of greater failure draws closer.

Your knights may understand your grief, but they do not understand your inactivity. They are men bred for war and restless with the urge to join and end the violence. They would have you sell your books, send letters seeking military aid instead of intellectual stimulation, teach the kingdom's youth the handling of a weapon instead of their alphabet – and each night on your knees in the chapel you wonder if they're right, if you have doomed them all with this hunger for peace. If it is even peace you want, and not merely to keep your own hands clean of blood. Your father's voice echoes in your ears, decrying your inadequacy, and you know – you think you know – you are sure that he was wrong, but it becomes harder to believe with each day that passes.

The wolf is your sole point of stability, your truest ally, the only one who demands nothing from you that you cannot give. Much as you might like to, you cannot hide from the world while your kingdom is in danger, so you have started to allow him to follow you to meet with your barons and knights: at least you will have the comfort of his warmth.

He's there the day the messengers arrive, begging for relief to help them withstand the bitter siege that has become the centrepiece of the struggle – for supplies if not men, food if nothing more than that. How they think you might offer such aid when the whole place is surrounded, you aren't sure, but your barons would have you answer the plea anyway. You're tempted, nagging guilt weakening your resolve. Supplies are not weapons – food is not joining the fight. But it might as well be, in the eyes of your enemies. If you enter the war like this, it will not end with aid to the starving. Not once you have declared allegiance.

With gentle violence, you tell the messenger of your decision.

It is not received gracefully. The messenger ducks his head to hide his disappointment and steps away in peace, but your barons – oh, they're angry, furious at your refusal to heed their counsel, to do even this small thing. The argument grows until you think for a moment that your seneschal might strike you – but the wolf steps between the two of you and growls low and dangerous in his throat, bringing you both back to your senses.

A few days later, a small number of knights, sworn to one of the lords who opposed you, take it upon themselves to answer the call you've been ignoring. They ride out at dawn and cross the border before nightfall, but news of their departure only reaches you two days later, when your barons use it against you.

'The people are ready and willing to fight,' says one. 'This enforced neutrality is unpopular.'

'What concern of mine is popularity?' you ask mildly, when inside you are seething and grieving, afraid for the men and furious with them. You are afraid for yourself, too. You know well enough that a knight given no enemies may go looking for them, and that they are not trained for peace. 'I had thought it was by divine will that I found myself with a crown on my head, and that the word of the Almighty still carried some weight among His faithful.' *Divine will.* If this is the will of God, then let it be over soon. Let nobody else die for this. *Kyrie, eléison.* Lord have mercy, for men have none.

'If they have a will to fight, sire, what harm can it do to send them?'

'Ask me again when they come back,' you say, and walk from the room.

You don't have long to wait. Within a fortnight the young

men's bodies are returned, stripped of armour and valuables. One is missing, presumed lost rather than survived.

They're laid out on biers, and you walk between them. Most were your own age, or near enough, and you weep as you look at their still faces. You did not know them, but any young life wasted is a life to be mourned. They weren't gone long enough to have made it to the main battlegrounds, or come close to the sieged castle; they must have fallen at the hands of border guards and deserters.

You linger longest on the last body in the row, the youngest of the fallen, scarcely a wisp of beard on the young man's face and a youthful body not yet hardened into full manhood. He would have thought it an adventure, to ride out like this in search of glory, hero of his own song, and what has it brought him? No immortal fame. No joy or riches.

Boys like this will always leap to answer the call of any who might summon them. Perhaps his lord promised him a future, as a churchman might promise absolution for those who wash their sins in blood in the Holy Land. Such violent and self-serving lies sicken you; you cannot blame the youth, but you will not readily forgive the man who led him.

You raise your gaze to look on him, there at the front of the hall where he waits, ashen and unarmed. 'What have you to say for yourself?' you ask, in the mildest tone you can manage.

He kneels. He grovels. He begs you for mercy. He kisses your feet. His excuses are many and his apologies florid, but none of them justify this waste, or explain it.

You permit his self-abasement a little longer, and then you say, 'Did you order them to go?'

Did you disobey my orders? Did you send these men to their deaths? Or are you so poor a lord that you cannot expect even the obedience of your own sworn men?

You already know the answer. But you would hear it from him.

'Sire,' he says. 'I thought ... I believed ...'

You regard him for a long moment. You know him. He was not precisely a favourite of your father's, but he was close enough, and knew something of his friendship. Perhaps that memory of preference fed his arrogance. 'You have killed these men,' you tell him. 'You have betrayed your king. You have invited danger into your kingdom. You have violated your oaths and my trust and your honour.'

'My lord ...'

'Do you deny it?'

His tears are many, and will not save him. 'No, sire.'

You gesture to the seneschal to have him taken away. You will not have him here, disrupting the dead. You will not look on him again until the moment of his death.

Perhaps some expect you to be kind, and grant him clemency as once you showed mercy to poachers and thieves, but what would be the worth of that kindness when a dozen mothers' sons are lying dead because of his actions? Because of his disobedience? He was sworn to serve you, and they him, and every choice you have made has been to keep youths like these from harm, but he dishonours your judgment with his own.

There can be no clemency for a man who betrays his king and his own men in this way.

If the chaplain disapproves – and well he might, cleric that he is, forbidden the wearing of arms or the using of them – he doesn't say as much, when he finds you faltering at your prayers.

'Is this peace?' you ask him, eventually. 'You would tell me, surely, if I am making a poor judgment.'

He is tired and worn from his vigils and his prayers, the masses he has spoken for the dead. Perhaps that is why he takes a long moment to think before he says, simply, 'It is the law, and the king's seal that makes it so.'

Scant comfort, to know that if you act thus, you do so supported by your father's judgment and his father's before him. But there is nothing else you can do, when already your perceived weakness emboldens nobles to ignore your orders. If this man lives, more will follow his example, and you will walk among the dead again and again until there is nothing left of your kingdom.

The chaplain clasps your shoulder. 'You are the king,' he says, 'and a good man. You will do what you feel you must.'

Of course you will. You have sworn oaths too. You have your duties, and your obligations, and your service.

The lord's death, when it comes, is swift. Swifter than he'd have got in battle. It turns your stomach and steals your appetite – *Coward*, says your father's voice – but you stand as witness and do not look away, because he was yours. For the sake of his oaths, violated as they were, you have an obligation to him.

He will be buried as a traitor, but you will add his name to your prayers.

He is the last of your people to die for this war. A few hundred miles away, a man besieged to starvation raises a flag of surrender, and an army falls. It is not long then until the war comes to an end, without ever encroaching further on your marches. Letters begin to arrive again, of counsel and of comfort, and you know that you are, for now, safe.

It should be a relief. But you're simply tired, still aching from the betrayal and the loss, uncertain of your choices. There must have been a path you could have taken, you think, where nobody would have had to die, a path where you might have saved lives, rather than leaving them to starve in a distant siege – but you could not see it. This is hardly victory for a peace-weaver, to avoid a war instead of end it and to kill a man for joining it, and though the chaplain will order no fasts or penance, you feel the stain of the act on your hands regardless.

Perhaps a king and a wolf have this in common: they are killers both, however carefully curbed their violence.

38

You

Doubt and melancholy are prone to linger, but your seneschal has other ideas. He informs you in no uncertain terms that, with the war behind you, the ordinary festivals must be observed once more, and that the harvest feast is fast approaching and will require your attention.

The harvest feast. Always quite the celebration, at least in years when the weather has been kind and the crops fine – and this year there will be relief as well as gratitude in the harvesting of them, for they have been spared the devastation of war and the burning that would likely come with invasion. It would ill become you not to acknowledge that relief, or celebrate the flourishing of fields under the new systems you introduced, or mark the death of summer with all the joy that is needed to bid farewell to the light while still staving off the darkness a little longer.

You assure the seneschal that you'll deal with it, and push aside your gloom to focus on the practicalities. It will need to be quite the gathering, after the hardships of the last few months, and after weeks with feasts and celebrations suspended to fund the arming of men. Your barons will have to be summoned, of course, even those holed up in castles on the far-flung coasts. There are men sworn to you that you have not seen since your coronation feast, and not missed them, either, but they will expect to be hosted.

You cannot think of your coronation feast without re-membering Bisclavret. It is unlikely that the harvest festival will bring you such an interesting companion again, and any who appeared would find themselves compared unfavourably to their forerunner – an unfair behaviour, you know, but you cannot help yourself. Still, perhaps there shall at least be some distraction. And you will have the wolf's company, of course, providing both comfort and enough threat to keep strident guests away.

When the feast day comes, you're melancholy again, your mood greyed; you'd rather spend the time in your chamber with the wolf, half-slumbering in front of the hearth. But this, too, is duty; this, too, is kingship. You allow yourself to be dressed in all the silks they can drape about you, and then you process to the front gate with the wolf to greet your barons as they arrive.

They come in all their finery, their horses bedecked with ribbons and cloth almost as bright as their own clothes. They have nothing but smiles for you, even those who resent your taxes and condemn your failure to join the war, and though you see the falsehood in their masks you have locked your own thoughts firmly behind your own, and have only smiles for them in return. At the gate they dismount, and you embrace them, and render a private prayer of thanks that the seneschal schooled you in their heraldry and names these last days so that you might greet them with enquiries about their land, their wives, their children.

Some have castles and palaces grander than your own – they might well think their power near equal to yours, though they're too well-trained ever to speak it aloud. Perhaps that might change, were the wolf not at your side, ready to challenge any who make a nuisance of themselves, and even with your bestial guard, there are some who have yet to learn the art of keeping their opinions to themselves.

'It's a pity, really,' says a young man, not much older than yourself, with the emblem of a raven on his shield. 'The war, you know.'

'War is often a pitiable thing,' you say, carefully, burying one hand in the wolf's ruff as though it might lend you patience.

'I've men enough eager for a good fight, and they had so hoped it would be their chance. Not enough land for them at home, you know, they would have liked the opportunity to win their fee the old way—' He breaks off, so perhaps your mask is not as well-fixed as you might have liked, your courtesy failing you. 'But of course,' he says, catching himself. 'No doubt you made a wise judgment, and spared us much grief.'

'No doubt,' you say, in the most pleasant tone you can manage, and are relieved when the seneschal appears to whisk the man inside and allow the next to approach you.

Many, it seems, have brought their sons – interchangeable young men, most of them aspiring to knighthood of a brighter sort than any they might find in their father's service, but some, perhaps, seeking something else. You greet them all the same. You're introduced to a fair few young ladies, as well; attempts to persuade you into marriage have not yet desisted. Most are models of courtesy, and were your mood brighter you might have found some pleasure in colloquy with them; one, however, has an interest in the beast so careless and claustrophobic that the creature growls and shifts with an impatience you've never seen before. You ask her to step back, for you fear the consequences if she doesn't – and this, of course, only incites her interest further. A *dangerous* beast is an exciting one, a story to take home.

You encourage her to leave with her story before it becomes a scar, and turn your attention to calming the wolf.

'Are there many more expected?' you ask the seneschal at last, for the air has an autumnal chill and you are growing tired of your position here at the gate.

'Some,' he admits, but on catching your expression, adds, 'It would be perfectly courtly to receive them inside, should you wish it.'

Of course it would be courtly: you on your throne, they on their best behaviour. But greeting them here, before they have had time to arrange themselves after their journey, with all the strains of travel chipping away at their edges, gives you a more honest understanding of them. Some have been months away from court, for you recall them only when you must, and they have no mind to offer service that is not ordered. Their kisses taste of duty, and their words teach you much about them.

'I will stay,' you say, 'though if you might have a cup of wine fetched, I—'

The wolf snarls, furious. You turn, startled by the noise, to see his teeth bared and his hackles raised, and when you follow the beast's gaze you see a lone man approaching.

It takes you a moment to recognise him. His dress is a little more sober than the rest, and he is mounted on a serviceable courser with an ordinary riding saddle, free of ribbons and bells. His heraldry, though ...

The wolf growls again, and the man stops, slightly further away than is truly polite, as though unwilling to bring the horse closer to the beast.

'My lord,' he begins, as soon as he is within earshot, 'I am honoured—'

You will never learn what has honoured him, for the wolf is a blur of movement, an arrow from a taut bowstring released, and before you have truly registered that he's left your side, his teeth have closed around the man's tunic and are dragging him from his horse, stealing his words along with his breath. The baron lets out a strangled yelp of shock and fumbles for his sword, but the wolf bats at his hand, his claws drawing blood, and the panicked horse is rearing, trying to escape, and the man falls, hitting the ground hard.

The man. Bisclavret's cousin.

When last he came to you at a feast it was to bring you the sweetest of gifts, his kinsman, an offering for which you are still grateful no matter the grief you have borne. But now he is flat on the muddy ground, the wolf's teeth inches from his throat, paws on his chest. You have never seen the wolf like this before, his wildest self: predator, hunter, killer. For the first time, you might believe that he killed Bisclavret.

That thought breaks the spell of immobility that holds you. You're on your feet, snatching a spear from one of the guards at the gate, using the wood of it to drive the beast back. He growls and snarls at you with uncharacteristic fury, but doesn't bite, and you push him away. You glance over your shoulder at his target: he's bleeding, but from the way he scrambles backwards and heaves himself to his feet, you think he'll live.

The seneschal has called for help before you might think to do it yourself. Your knights come running, swords drawn. 'Get rope,' you spit in their direction, and in the moment of your distraction, the wolf tries to dart past you. He has the scent of his enemy now, and will not let it drop. 'Leave him, damn you!' You block his path, gripping his ruff as hard as you dare. You have no fear for yourself – you may never have seen the wolf as wild as this, but he would not hurt you.

Would he?

Somebody has brought a coil of rope. You have the wolf

muzzled and restrained while a servant catches the baron's flee-ing horse and another brushes the mud from the man's clothes.

'I wonder what he did,' says a voice. Your knight in green, you see, turning your head a little.

Still stunned, and shaking now with the aftermath of violence, you manage, 'What?'

'The baron. For the wolf to attack him in that way.'

Perhaps it's the shock of the attack that deprives his words of sense. 'He is a wolf,' you say, numbly. 'It is … it is his nature.'

'He's lived here the best part of a year,' says your knight. 'I have never seen him snap at anyone – much less try to bite. And yet within moments of this man's arrival, he's been torn from the saddle? This looks to me like revenge, my lord. Some unknowable grudge of the creature's.'

You regard the wolf as though you'll find the answers just by looking at him, but he seems more animal than ever. Bisclavret's cousin lives close to the forest; perhaps the beast has seen him there. Could the baron have tried before to hunt this wolf, thinking him his cousin's killer? Does the wolf seek vengeance now for the insult and the injury?

'The baron is my guest,' you say finally, 'and he has been at-tacked in my presence. I must – I must compensate him for this insult. Excuse me.'

You take the wolf, for you would not leave any of your serv-ants with the enraged creature. He is still muzzled, still furious, growling deep in his throat at the injustice of a hunt denied. As you cross the courtyard, he tugs so hard at the rope in your grip that he almost tears free, straining like a hunting hound on the leash, and you must exert all of your strength to haul him back. The baron – Bisclavret's cousin – flinches where he is walking to the keep, and the servant leading him to the physician does too.

'Be calm!' you tell the creature, but you have never learned to settle him, because you have never needed to. 'He is my guest. You will treat him as such.'

The wolf's hackles remain raised, but the rope in your hand slackens a little, and you gesture for the baron and the servant to make haste. Then you take the wolf to your own chamber, and close the door firmly behind you.

'What is this?' you ask him, as though he might answer. 'Will you provoke my barons into rebellion with your teeth? You will stay here, tonight,' you add. 'I cannot bring you to the feast if you intend to bite my guests.' And you will have to seat the baron at your side and offer him some favour if you hope to win back his friendship. Perhaps a gift. His clothes and horse suggest his lands are not flourishing; maybe you might relieve his troubles, and receive his forgiveness that way ...

The wolf whines, pitiful.

'Beg all you like,' you tell him. 'You have made trouble for me. I have no choice.' You will have to lock your chamber fast, and leave him scratching at the door. You cannot have him taken to the kennels, for in this mood, there's no telling what menace he might visit upon the hounds.

But it is not easy, when the time comes, to bid him farewell, and descend to the feast alone. To hear the whispers alone. To know that word has spread already: the king's wild beast attacked somebody; he is as dangerous as they always said; it is clear proof that you are unfit to rule; you have brought this violence into your castle and allowed him to hurt the very men who serve you.

Bisclavret's cousin, the scratches on his hand neatly bandaged, is not greatly mollified by his position of honour, and the intended joy of the feast has been replaced by whispers and speculation. The musicians are cowed and quiet; the storytellers lose the thread of their tales, darting nervous glances at you as though you, like the wolf, might at any moment attack them. Only the jugglers keep their nerve, but then, they are men of daring, tossing knives from hand to hand as though they fear not the blade's edge.

When the candles have burned down and the entertainments have ceased, the baron at your side stands. 'My lord,' he says, 'I bear no grudge and seek no restitution, but I will take my leave of you. Good night.'

'Stay,' you begin, half-heartedly, but he has already walked away.

Amidst uneasy murmurs, others follow suit, each lord and knight bidding you farewell, until at last there is nothing for it but to stand and take your leave, and let those who dare to remain in the castle make their beds and seek their rest.

Inside your chamber, the muzzled wolf waits, plaintive and unhappy.

You unbind the ropes, each loosened knot a whispered apology. 'I wish,' you say softly, 'that I knew what you were thinking.'

39
Other

✦ ✸ ✦

there's nothing left but
HUNT
the target found, the monster named
– he is the traitor who helped her steal my skin
I know this the way I know so little –
each day a little more is lost,
the man's mind mutable and muted.
sometimes there is only wolf
and all I know is
HUNT
but I know him and I know my fury

the hunter's back, long dormant;
not quite the king's dog after all,
though the mistake's easily made.
– I let him feed me
I listen to him talk of his sorrows
sometimes I even understand –
and other times there's no language
but the rhythm of it, like a river – yes,
the castle has seen it, the court knows it.

sometimes he says my name
he gives me back the fragments of myself
but now
HUNT HUNT HUNT

few instincts are stronger than violence,
few bloodier than vengeance

they are pulling me back
why would they take this from me –
a wolf's revenge can look like savagery to a man
– why won't they let me
HUNT

if I cannot be human
let me at least be wolf

40

You

It's no surprise that your servants are nervous around the wolf after that; what's more remarkable is that your knights aren't. They come as close to him as they ever did, offering him a comradely pat, with no apparent fear of his teeth.

'The way I see it,' says your red-haired knight, proud and honest, 'we have had a year of the wolf's company and we know him to be peaceful. If he can on occasion be provoked to violence – well, I've seen enough of my comrades at their worst to know that no being should be judged on that.'

This is followed by laughter, and a few ribald suggestions as to what various knights' 'worst' has looked like.

'I can't deny there are men I'd fight as soon as look at them,' adds your knight in green. 'I've always heard it said that wolves are canny creatures, and this one has more wit than most wild beasts. If he has the mind of a man, perhaps he has the enmities of one, too.'

You agree with that, but why Bisclavret's soft-spoken steward of a cousin? 'You've heard nothing of the baron to explain such enmity, I suppose?' you ask him.

His brow creases in confusion. 'No. I have no particular knowledge of the man.'

'Your wife,' you say uncertainly, wondering if you've

misremembered. 'I thought once she had a friendship with Bisclavret's wife, and that they might yet talk.'

His bewilderment passes, but he seems no less troubled. 'I'm afraid their friendship did not long survive Bisclavret's loss, my lord.'

'I'm sorry to hear that.'

His shrug is uncomfortable, uncertain. 'No doubt it is my fault. It was our companionship that brought them together, and there was little to keep matters so once that was gone. But there was ...' He hesitates. 'I'll confess it, though I mislike to do so when she was your ward once. My wife was not comfortable with how quickly his lady sought refuge in his cousin's arms. She thought there was more to it than practicality and inheritance – that perhaps there had always been something more to it. They quarrelled about the matter, and time has not yet mended the rift.'

Such a disagreement could ruin even the fastest of friendships. You spare a thought for how isolated Bisclavret's widow must be, bereft of friends and associates. Your obligation to her ended on the day of her marriage, but for the sake of the care you once showed her, you might have thought of her before now. It was cruel of you to forget her in your grief, but it is also too late to repair that damage.

Life resumes, a little muted, still ringing with the echoes of the war and of the wolf's violence. You allow the beast to guard you in your sleep as you ever have, although you know that if he attacks you while you slumber, you stand no hope of surviving it. He's had ample opportunity to maul you, these past months, and never taken it. Every morning you wake unharmed and every morning you know it's not because the wolf is incapable, nor is he afraid.

Fealty. The beast is sworn to you.

His loyalty is proven, so you feel no compunction about allowing him to lope alongside you when you ride out for the first full hunt after the war's end. His long limbs let him keep pace easily, and your horses have become accustomed to his presence, though a few of your lords have mounts less habituated to the creature, and they're skittish and afraid.

It's perhaps the biggest hunt the wolf has accompanied you on: lords and knights in their finery, looking to impress; huntsmen turned out in great numbers; eager hounds racing ahead; the din of horns and beaters and hooves ... You're briefly worried it will all be too much for a beast who relies so heavily on his own senses, but he seems unconcerned by the fuss.

It wasn't planned, led as you are by the tracks of the doe you're pursuing, but the route takes you back through the clearing where you found him. It's changed little in the past year, and you wonder if he recognises it. Certainly, there's a new wariness in his posture, ears alert for danger. Something has set him on edge – a sound? A scent? Some other beast that wanders these woods?

There's the faintest rustle of leaves, and the wolf's head snaps up.

'Be calm,' you mutter to him. You've no wish to spark panic if the creature goes hurtling after a squirrel, and if there's game here then you wouldn't rob your people of their sport by allowing the wolf to make the kill. But he's growling, low in his throat, in a way that has you reaching for your sword.

The figure who emerges from among the trees is neither an animal nor an enemy, however. It's a woman.

She's dressed in finery – an intricately embroidered silk bliaut with trailing, impractical sleeves, her hair braided beneath a veil of thin silk, a circlet holding it in place. Strange garb for a walk alone in a forest, and a few moments pass before you recognise her.

Bisclavret's wife. Your ward.

You haven't seen her since she remarried. She looks well with it, which eases the faint sense of guilt you feel for neglecting her; she has not been without comforts. But your thoughts are cut off abruptly, because the wolf snarls, vicious and slavering. You throw your leg over your horse and drop to the ground, burying your hands in his ruff to hold him, restrain him. If he chooses to break free, you've no hope of holding him like this, but he knows to obey you, to stay where you wish him ...

At the sight of him, she blanches. She has in her hands some small item or gift, and it's clear she sought to cross the path of the hunt deliberately – she should know better than that, she should know the danger she was placing herself in – but she did not, it seems, anticipate the presence of the wolf. Perhaps she thought you would have had the creature removed or locked away after he attacked her husband.

'Don't be afraid,' you call to her, without stepping forward or letting go of the beast. 'He means you no harm.'

It's hard even for you to believe that, when you can feel the wolf testing your grip, tugging gently as though to let you know it's only out of respect for you that he hasn't already shot forward towards her.

'Sire,' she says, 'I bring—' But she breaks off, staring at the wolf, and her next words come out in a flurry of panic and fear: 'I cannot, I cannot, please bid him away from you, I must—'

'Good woman,' you say, as gently as you can, 'calm yourself!'

'That beast killed my husband!'

A growl – a roar – rips from the throat of the wolf at your side, and before you have a chance to tighten your grip, he's torn free, paws crashing against the ground with every bounding leap across the clearing. You hear weapons being unsheathed, but nobody dashes forward to intercept him. Like you, they're rooted to the ground, unable to do anything but wait. Watch. Witness the moment the animal collides with the lady, slamming her into the uneven ground, and closes his teeth around her face.

She screams – tries to scream – it's a gurgle, really, a sound drowned in blood, her breath stolen by pain.

Perhaps he would have killed her. For a moment you think he already has, the scene a blur as your knights leap from their horses and drag the wolf back from her with ropes. You were wrong, you think; this is Bisclavret's killer after all. The cousin's small injuries were nothing compared to the mess of her face, the gaping wound where her nose should be, the sodden gasps of her attempts to breathe.

The wolf heaves and wrestles against the strength of the knights, but they've spent a year training themselves to sharpness and he's spent that time as your pet. They bind and restrain him, and one even succeeds in muzzling those fearsome teeth.

Her screams subside into sobs. You remember yourself enough to walk over to her, kneel by her fallen body, and press a clean cloth to her face to try to stem the bleeding. Somebody else calls for servants to fetch water, a physician, bandages. What a shame, you find yourself thinking, that the lovely embroidery on her clothes is ruined, for it must have taken months – and then you catch yourself in the thought. How can you think of the needlework at a time like this, when her nose is ruined – gone – and your wolf is the culprit?

A strange, unreal calm fogs your thoughts. How could you have been so wrong about him?

'This wolf,' says your knight in green to the lady, 'did not kill your husband.'

You look at him. His tone is certain, rock-solid, and there's no animosity in his expression, but now is hardly the time for the distribution of blame – it will not comfort the mauled woman in her agony. 'Leave it,' you say, a warning in your voice. 'There'll be time for that later.'

'This wolf did not kill her husband because her husband is not dead,' he snaps.

You stare at him.

For a moment, you think he means the cousin. You know well that he is not dead – he left your feast with a bandaged hand and his head held high, hale and haughty. But your knight stares straight back, a defiant certainty shining in his eyes, and you realise he is not talking about the cousin after all.

Not dead.

How can Bisclavret not be dead? He's been missing for the better part of two years; his clothes they found mauled and bloody. You've mourned him, been cut through by the keen loss of him, and now this knight thinks to suggest that Bisclavret isn't dead?

'Sire,' he says urgently. 'I should have seen it sooner, but only now has it become clear to me. From the day we encountered him, I told you that this wolf has the mind of a man – you've seen yourself how he feels loyalty and hatred the way a man feels them.'

'What is your point?' you ask. The blood has begun to saturate the cloth in your hands; it's sticky against your skin.

'My point is that he has shown nothing but gentleness and protection towards us all since the moment you brought him home. There is nothing violent in his temperament. And yet we have seen him just these past days inflict violence upon two individuals, as though he harbours some grudge against them. But what grudge would a wolf have towards Bisclavret's cousin and his wife?'

You look across to the wolf, still pulling at the ropes holding him back, refusing to be calmed. His usually placid eyes are filled with murderous intention as he looks at the woman in front of you. Very few people could look on such a creature and believe there is *nothing violent* in its nature.

'Because they live near the forest?' you suggest, already knowing it's the wrong answer. 'Because they have come against him in the past?'

The lady makes some remark through her sobs, inaudible because of the cloth pressed against her face. She pulls it aside and manages to repeat: 'He *is* dead. The wolf – the wolf has a hatred for our household. He killed Bisclavret and now he will kill me and my husband. He has already tried.'

You have no desire to believe her – it grieves you to think you've found companionship in the beast that killed a man you held so dear. But how else are you to make sense of this?

Your knight in green shakes his head vigorously. 'It isn't so,' he insists, and he's so earnest you're inclined to listen, despite the wildness of his claims. You want him – need him – to be right. The idea that Bisclavret might have survived ignites in you a desperation you thought had long since faded into the dull acceptance of grief. 'This isn't the violence of a wild animal. This is the vengeance of a wronged man.'

It's true that you've remarked on the wolf's curious intelligence, the hints of a rational mind beneath the animal skin, but that doesn't mean you intended for such utterances to be taken as truth. And yet—

You look from the wolf to the injured woman and then to the knight: 'Explain.'

'The wolf is not Bisclavret's killer,' he says, eyes bright with conviction. 'The wolf is Bisclavret.'

41

Other

✦ ✷ ✦

there is nothing left in me but rage

her blood tastes like rot, love made hate by decay,
by loss, and every minute spent wandering, wolfing, lost.

they hold me back with ropes
restraints
like some kind of madman –
this is the truest sanity: anger
burning away the dreams,
the promises, the sweet nothings.

all that I am comes back to me
I remember her I remember the way she pretended to care
I remember how she used her gentleness against me

fury makes a hound a threat;
the king's sweat tastes of fear.
surely he can see I'm justified in this –
he sees only the wolf

I can smell her lies from here
(they will not let me closer)

he hears them too. he listens
to his knight in green, trusted tongue,
who tells a different story

I always felt he saw something real in me

what he sees is hard to know,
but the way they stare – it loosens the wolf-skin and
for a swift second of something that tastes like hope
my body almost remembers who I am but
perhaps the hunt still singing in our blood
is what keeps us wolf, binds us wolf.

if I can feel this aching wrongness and not change
then I am bound to be wolf forever
bound to this skin this form this grief
and I want to
HOWL
the desolate rage of it at the sky

the bonds are tied too tightly for that,
muzzled like an animal
– I bit her I tore her nose from her face
HUNT
what manner of monster am I? –
a hunter who could not face the kill.

she deserves that death
if I were myself I would know that

and the knight says
'the wolf is bisclavret'
with clear eyes that cleave through illusion,
tear away cobwebs of lies.
his gaze is as sharp as his tongue
but the king just looks,
searching for the signs.

please find them
please see me
please just see me
I have been here all along
it has been me all along please just

see

me

HOWL
I do not think he sees me
I think he sees only the wolf

his eyes are wide, glittering like a river
after a thaw, ice-cold and almost weeping.
he turns back to the knight:
'no'
at least I think that's what he says
'it's impossible'
except his knight in green disagrees,
repeats his claim, gestures to the lady:
'if anyone will know it's her'

and all I want to do is howl and run
and flee the fragile hope inside me

it's too human for this skin it doesn't fit
it feels like something I shouldn't be capable of feeling

wolves are canny beasts but hope,
hope is a human lie, and with it loss and grief and love
and after all
I
am
just
wolf
it's hard to think a man's mind could last this long
without language or longing or life

if I had it in me to be anything else I'd have changed by now
all I feel is the wrongness in my ribcage and in my bones
marrow-deep and unbearable

the king looks again. still searching.
shaping a name in his mouth that he doesn't voice
but which lingers, humming, on his tongue,
like the haunting of a kiss or the ghost of untold stories
– *everything I should have been to him and wasn't* –
'bisclavret'

say it I dare you
say it
make it real
whisper it like all those prayers you have let brand you
'the wolf is bisclavret'
make it true

42

You

You aren't cruel to her. You won't have them say that you were. You won't have them call it torture, not when you order the physician fetched to attend her, and your knights to bring her to her own home, where there might be fewer witnesses to her disfigurement. Not when you're the one to hold that cloth and staunch the bleeding although blood soaks into the beds of your nails and you think you'll never get it out. You cared for her once. You would not hurt her further.

But perhaps ... perhaps you're not gentle in how you speak to her. Perhaps you press her with questions, even while they're still stitching up the ruins of her face and bandaging the wound. You have to know. You ask her again and again and again and perhaps – maybe – you imply that if she doesn't answer you, you'll have the muzzle removed from the wolf.

It's not a threat. Nothing so explicit. But she goes pale as milk beneath the blood, and you know then that it's true, even before she admits it in a trembling voice: 'Yes. The wolf is Bisclavret.'

The wolf is Bisclavret.

It is as though the stars themselves move above you, the heavens refiguring themselves to paint this knowledge into their constellations. The wolf is Bisclavret, because he isn't dead, only changed, made other by some curse or inborn nature. All this time you have kept him close to you. You have told him of your grief, your affection for the man who is gone, all the useless impotent love you've felt like a burden weighing on your heart since he died because with him gone there was nowhere you could lay it to rest. You don't know how much the wolf has understood, but you've found solace in speaking to him anyway, his presence staving off the loneliness and the poor decisions that come with it.

And the wolf is Bisclavret.

Has always been Bisclavret.

He has been there all along.

Hope thrums into life, dark wings beating violently inside your heart. *Bisclavret is alive.* With it comes rage, that the woman should have known this, and kept it from you. How could she, of all people, be capable of such cruelty?

'Can he be changed back?' you demand of her. 'What manner of curse is it that you've laid upon him? Some potion, some spell?'

'The curse that's on him is no work of mine,' she snaps, anger breaking through her pain and fear. Her voice shakes, and her expression's drawn with the agony of her ravaged face, but she manages to spit out her defence: 'He was born with a shifting skin and a wolf's heart and there's no fault on me for that. I married him unknowing, he a trickster who did not confess to me until too late for an annulment, and as God is my witness I think no woman would have done different to me upon the learning of it. We were both of us lied to, my lord, for it's not you he told, either.'

You cannot forgive her for her actions yet, when Bisclavret himself has not. 'And yet you did not come to me with the knowledge,' you say carefully. 'I am your king. I held your protection. He was my knight. Surely this was my judgment to pass.' You cannot fathom what you would have done, if she had told you. You cannot fathom what you would have done if he had, either.

'Would you have taken my part?' she says, with a bitterness to her tears. 'He was favoured, favourite, knight and friend. I am a woman, not to be trusted.'

'You were my ward,' you say, but the past tense lands heavily. *Were.* Until she was given to him, and then she was Bisclavret's, and she is right: you would have weighed her word lightly against his. You close your eyes for a moment, to better carry the burden of this knowledge, and then you look on her again. 'Very well. He hid this from you, and you kept it from me. But while the curse may not be your work, still it must be you who entrapped him. For he who was ever-shifting and human enough to be knighted has remained a wolf now for two years, and I must think it was you and his cousin who made it so.'

The physician has almost finished with her face. She'll be badly scarred, all her gentle beauty lost, and for a moment you are filled with pity and with grief for that. And then you recall the wolf vagrant in the forest for a year until you found him, the creature sleeping at the foot of your bed, fealty above and beyond his oaths even after he lost the skin he swore them in, and you cannot pity her.

She doesn't want to answer you. She must know that if he's made human again, Bisclavret will denounce her for whatever it is she did to him – but you will have the secret of his changing from her, one way or another.

She says, at last, 'His clothes.' Her words are muffled by the bandages, and you have to ask her to repeat herself. 'He told me that his clothes help him to stay human. I asked him where he left them when he changed and he confessed to me the place he used, and then we stole them.' *We.* So the cousin was a participant, not merely an accessory after the fact. Was it the desire for inheritance that motivated him, or for her hand? 'I was afraid,' she continues, and she looks at you like a penitent seeking intercession. 'Look upon me now and tell me I was wrong to be afraid.'

You look upon her. Her face is a bloody ruin, the violence she wrought on her husband now inflicted on her in turn. It is a grotesque wound, and a painful one, and if she survives without it festering, she'll carry it the rest of her life, unrecognisable as her former self. You cannot say that she was right – but neither can you say that she was wrong, when the evidence for the wolf's capacity for harm is there in front of you.

Fear is a cunning thing, that makes of the most loving wives a traitor.

You push away the question of blame and repeat, 'His clothes.' It doesn't seem enough. 'What do you mean by that – specific garments?' If it's merely clothes he needs, you could have clothed him a thousand times, draping him in the finest cloth and ornament.

She shakes her head, tears running tracks through the blood on her face. 'I don't know. I don't think so. But they need to be his.'

Your heart sinks. For a moment you're filled with visions of Bisclavret made wolf forever, until it occurs to you to ask: 'Have you any of his garments still?'

'I ...' How dare she hesitate? There are lies rising in her throat and you want to rip them from her, all the violence of the wolf's fury curling your hands into fists at your sides. You take a breath, remind yourself that it's not in your nature to hurt her, wait for her to voice some excuse or answer.

She doesn't. You repeat the question. 'Have you any of his garments?'

'No,' she says hesitantly, and you might have predicted as much – why waste good cloth on a man who wasn't coming back? Of course they would be gone, long since remade into other clothes, and your heart and hopes cut into pieces with them. You try to think of workarounds, loopholes. Perhaps livery, armour, anything—

But she hasn't finished speaking. 'I have none,' she says. 'But his mother's estate, where he lived for so long ... there will be clothes of his there yet, for he did not bring them when you made him a knight.'

His exile. Never did you think it might be his redemption, too. You remember well the clothes she means, patched things, unfashionable, but they were the truth of him for so long. Can it be true? Do they exist still?

'Will you swear to it?' you demand. 'This is not some falsehood?'

'I swear to it,' she says, and the winged hope in your heart begins to beat again.

* ✳ *

You have her give the messengers instructions and then you send them on their errand; you'd have sent her, if she were well enough to travel, but the messengers will be faster, anyway. When they're gone, you leave her to rest and return to the castle, but even a hard ride home, testing your horse's speed, cannot relieve you of the impatience that soon has you wearing grooves in the stone floors of the keep with the force of your pacing.

It will be some days before they return, even riding fast and changing horses whenever they can. Until then the wolf is locked in a hastily-emptied stable block, the horses temporarily rehomed so that the scent of him will not startle them. You should go to him, speak to him, but – but you cannot look the creature in the eyes knowing that somewhere in there, possibly, is a man. You're too haunted by all the ways this hope might be destroyed to risk allowing the flame to burn any brighter. Perhaps there's nothing left of him now. Perhaps he'll not be able to turn back. Perhaps, perhaps, perhaps ...

You're a coward, is the truth of it. You don't know what to say to him. How do you speak to a knight who has been so wronged and remained so loyal? How do you face him after confessing all the darkest truths of your heart? He has sat witness to your confessions, to your nightly vigils, to utterances that ought by rights to have been between you and God. You can't be sure what portion of your words he has comprehended – does he have language, sapience, the rationality to understand your prayers? You're both known and unknown, exposed and protected, and the uncertainty of that vulnerability is somehow worse than the simple fact of it.

And so you pace. And wait. And try not to allow yourself hope, because there's no weapon more cruel than the destruction of momentary belief in some better world where the man you love is alive and well and beside you.

Finally, a servant comes to fetch you. The messengers have returned.

You meet them in the hall, where the wolf – uncomprehending – has been brought by two of the knights, and now lies wary but docile at your feet. You take from them the garments they've brought, and your lingering doubts about the veracity of his wife's words fade. These are Bisclavret's clothes, shabby though they are: you recognise them from that very first feast. It's a wonder that his cousin did not burn them for the sake of appearances; still more strange that they have remained intact, and not remade, but that there's little good cloth here to make anything much.

If his wife knew they existed, then his cousin must have done. They could have destroyed them, one or both of them, and rid themselves of the possibility of his return – but perhaps they weren't ready to forsake him entirely. Perhaps some small part of his wife regrets what she did, and wanted to leave herself a ladder back to grace.

Now that you have the clothes in your hands, you know not what to do. You feel foolish as you kneel in front of the wolf, hold them out. He sniffs them and something in his posture changes, but he's no more human than before. Just a wolf, circling the assorted clothing of a dead man and the king who kneels beside it.

You wait. The wolf nudges the clothes with his snout and then noses at your hands, but there's no sign of shifting skin. The truth is bitter: it's not going to work. You cannot bring him back, if he's even there at all.

Still on your knees, you bury your face in your hands and try not to weep in front of the messengers.

The wolf, who has seen you cry more times than you care to recall, nuzzles close to you, as though trying to wipe away the tears. He curls himself into your side, a warm and comforting bulk familiar from a dozen nights spent murmuring your sorrows.

You thought – you believed – you allowed yourself, for a moment, to hope that this would work, and now you've been proved a fool. 'Fetch the woman,' you manage, voice hoarse. 'The cousin too, if you can find him.' You'll demand answers from them, demand that they fix this.

One of the servants makes for the door, but your knight in green steps forward. You don't want to look at him. He started this, dared to tell you that Bisclavret lived, and now you've made a fool of yourself in front of half the court.

'Sire,' he begins.

'Stop.' You've no stomach for his advice. If this wolf is Bisclavret, then *why is he not yet a man?* Perhaps it's merely a wild beast after all. Perhaps the lady's first story was true.

The knight ignores you. 'Sire, with respect, if the beast really has a man's rationality, do you think he'll shift here, in front of so many people?'

'And you're an expert on such things, are you?' you snap, your grief making you sharp.

'You are not alone in your love for old stories,' he responds, almost as sharply, 'nor the only one who knew Bisclavret as a man.' His tone softens. 'He kept his secret close-hidden, my lord; how can you think he would endure the shame of an audience when he changed? Better to take him to some place quiet and leave him there with his clothes, so that he might assume his own form again in private and not face his human nakedness in front of the court.'

It's impossible to believe that the wolf beside you could have such human sensibilities, but you'll try anything. You gather the clothing into your arms and stand. There's no place truly private in the castle other than your own chamber, but that will do well enough: the wolf knows it, knows that it is safe, will not feel uncomfortable there.

You place the clothing on the bed, and find yourself at a loss for what to do next. You have gained an audience – the messengers and servants and knights grow in number, catching the scent of a story – but they have the courtesy to wait outside. You suppose you should join them, and give Bisclavret this space apart. But it feels absurd, shutting a wolf in with a pile of garments and expecting to return to find a man in his place.

You wish you had some promise to make him. *Whatever form you wear when I return, I will not flee from you.* If only you could keep such oaths – but you cannot let a wolf remain in the castle after so vicious an attack on one of your subjects, on a lady. Your people would not stand for it. So if he doesn't change—

He'll change. He has to change. You'll not lose him a second time.

You say to him, 'Bisclavret.' It's not enough, but it's all you can give him: his name. 'You are Bisclavret.'

And then you leave the room, and close the door.

43

Other/Him

my clothes
here in the place where I have been wolf
a place where I've never been human
here they are my clothes
and here in the king's mouth my name
'bisclavret'
as though it has always been my name
as though I've not been nameless through these winters
and I am remembering myself
I am feeling the pieces of myself drag themselves
back together loose stitches torn thread unravelling
'you are bisclavret'
he says and some part of me hears the words
which has heard nothing for so long
some part of me that wakes up now after endless months and I am

—shaking, skin peeling, back arching as his spine reshapes itself, his body trying to remember how to shift. He shudders and reaches out, snatching at the clothes with one clawed hand (a *hand*); he clings to it but—

the wolf will not let go so easily
it's bound itself deeply into my veins
it will always pull me back out of myself
but I had hands for a moment
I remember what it was to have hands
I remember I remember I remember and

—he shudders as he fumbles for the undertunic, feels the worn linen against his skin, and all he can think is: *skin*. He hardly has the capacity to recognise that this is a tunic, to remember how to put it on; he's still half-wolf, body warping beneath him, but he remembers this from the old days in the forest when he'd drag himself to his hidden clothing and dress between spasms of change. He needs to convince his body that it knows its own shape.

But he's worn another shape for so long, and his mind still runs the tracks of the wolf's, thoughts cacophonous and rapid, past collapsing into present and other into self, and—

perhaps I don't have a man's mind anymore
perhaps I cannot remember that

—even clothed some things are stronger: wolflike wolfself wolfbeing, all present and hunt and rage and teeth—

perhaps I'll never truly be bisclavret again
but I want to be dear god I want to be
I saw the look on his face when he left me here
I heard the tone of his voice as he murmured my name
he wants me here
his wanting grounds me it is a tether I can use to come back
'you are bisclavret'

328

he said but what I heard was
'please be bisclavret'
and
'come back come back come back'

wanting is a rope thrown to a drowning man
or else to a stolen one, dragging himself
through the oozing sludge of a wolfing mind
– I remember his grief –
the way he mourned, a sorrow unending,
vigils for an unshriven soul, lit by yearning
– I remember his confessions –
secrets are less bitter shared,
until the sharing shows its teeth.

I remember the shape of me as a knight
created by his words
a memory I hardly have remade by him
I remember myself because he remembers me
I remember how to

—gasp with human lungs, and for a moment everything is
still. His body, calm – too calm, heart paused between beats,
a momentary suspension into immortality, but no immediate
collapse into his animal skin. He allows himself to exist in a
moment of nothingness, and then his heart thunders into life
and the breath comes rushing out of him and he's alive.

And human.

His hands – God above, he has hands, the shape of them so
alien and welcome – shake as he struggles with the braies, and
then untwists the undertunic, easier now he has the shape of it
and a little more sense of himself. Better that the clothes are

old, simple, no laces to baffle his unsteady fingers. The woollen tunic next, red like blood. With every layer his skin fits a little better.

Human.

Human and clothed and real, bound into himself by the garments around his body, reminded of all that he is by the warp and weft of the cloth. He thought he'd never be human again. He thought he'd never have hands again, and he can't stop staring at them. He thinks his mind will burst with the saturation of the world, the colours vivid and many-hued.

He's exhausted, the bone-deep exhaustion of remaking one-self. He should stand, cross the room, open the door and tell them that he's a man again, but he cannot move. Instead he curls up on the bed he's known only as a wolf. He is unsettled in his new-old body, unsure how to fit in this space he thought he knew. This room has been his home for a year and now it is made strange.

Except that the bed is the same as ever, and he's the one who has changed.

He crawls under the heavy blankets, too weary to concern himself with manners. The king will understand, he thinks. He'll understand that being reborn is tiring. That it takes more energy than any duel to build yourself a new body – new blood and bones and skin, new lips, new teeth, new hands.

Hands. He has missed having hands. He's still running the fingertips of his left hand over the marvels that are the knuckles of his right when his eyes begin to drift closed, the weight of his fatigue dragging him down.

And there, in the king's bed, Bisclavret sleeps.

44
You

$*$ ✳ $*$

How long should you wait? Longer, probably. You sit pressed against the door. The wood's hard against your back, the only thing holding you upright. You want to be inside that room, and at the same time you never want them to open the door, because once they open it, you'll have to live with the truth you find on the other side. Maybe Bisclavret is there – maybe you don't have to be alone anymore.

And maybe not.

Or maybe he's there, and human, but all the strange intimacy of the past year will dissipate along with his curse, and he'll be nothing more to you than what he always was – a pledged knight only, the closeness of his wolf months lost along with his claws. It would almost be worse that way, though you loathe the part of you that dares to think a Bisclavret who is alive and happy without you might be something to be mourned.

You wait until you can bear it no longer, and then you stand. But you can't go alone. You take two knights with you – your knight in green with his clear judgment and clearer eyes and your flame-haired knight with the wicked tongue – and you open the door more timidly than any king should open the door of his own bedchamber.

It takes an age to swing open wide enough to enter, and your heart is in your throat, choking you with hope that sobs and soars with every ragged breath.

You cannot look – you cannot know – you cannot bear …

'Sire,' says your knight in green, his tone hushed and reverent, and you open your eyes.

There's a moment before you see him when all you notice is the absence of the wolf, and then your gaze catches on the figure burrowed deep beneath the coverlet. His hair is long and tangled, an unruly dark mane around his thin face with its knife-sharp cheekbones. His eyebrows are a severe slice across his exhausted, sleeping face.

Bisclavret.

His sleep is deep: he doesn't stir as a small noise escapes you, the choking catch of a sob in your throat as you cover your mouth with your hands. Tears threaten to spill as you stare at him. It can't be real. Surely he's a mirage, a ghost, an enchantment – you must have imagined him enough times, and what is there to mark this as something apart from your fantasies? He's so still he might be the portrait of a man.

You stumble towards him, still expecting the scene to vanish and for you to find yourself alone with clothes strewn on the bed in front of you, made a fool by hope once again.

'Bisclavret,' you say, involuntarily. You didn't mean to speak. But now that you've said his name once, you can't stop yourself repeating it, over and over, as faithful a litany as any of your prayers for his soul. You approach your own bed as nervous as a maiden, your hands resting on the coverlet for a moment before you snatch them back, afraid to be caught doing something forbidden. It cannot be permitted for Bisclavret to be here, sleeping, human, alive. It's too much of a miracle to have been worked without the hand of a saint, and there are no holy relics within these stone walls.

He opens his eyes.

For a moment there's a hint of wolf, of wildness, but it fades as his expression sharpens into alertness and he sees you.

You freeze, waiting for the moment he recalls where he is and backs away, shuttering himself behind a mask of decorum. This loyal knight of yours was unwavering in his service and unflinching with a sword, but cautious with his counsel and his affections – and now he knows everything, has the truth of you clear as confession, and all he does is lie there and look at you.

And then he smiles.

It's the hesitant, unpractised smile of a man who hasn't long had a mouth to smile with. It spreads slowly across his face, unselfconscious joy diffusing gradually but without restraint. Tears threaten at the sight of it, and you take his hands and kiss them, swearing your fealty to him, returning to him a hundredfold the oaths he swore to you. You turn his hands over and press a dozen small kisses to his palms. The soft skin beneath your lips is a marvel. You still half-expect him to melt away beneath your touch, but his hands in yours are real, his breath mingling with yours is real, his lips under yours are real and warm and unhesitating, even as you hold back, uncertain, ready to withdraw the moment he spurns your affections.

He pulls one hand free of your grip and raises it to tangle in your hair, pulling you closer. You let out a soft groan of surprise and allow yourself to be led by him, the miracle of his resurrection made ever more marvellous as your fingers trace his collarbones, his neck, the contours of the face you thought you'd never see again. *Real.* What right has this impossibility to be so real? You kiss his temples, his cheekbones, the hollow of his neck just below his jaw; follow the blue veins beneath the pale skin with your tongue and your lips.

The soft thud of the door closing jolts you back to reality, and you recall your knights, bearing witness to this reunion. Their tactful retreat would once have sent shame burning through you, or fear, that you should be discovered in such a state of desperation, but in this moment all you feel is relief, because they've left you here alone with Bisclavret.

'Bisclavret,' you whisper, lips almost touching his ear, speaking the name not in mourning or remembrance but to bear witness to the living man. 'Bisclavret.'

His breath catches. When he speaks, his words are uncertain, shaped with great care: 'Am I real?'

It's the first time in two years that he has spoken, and his voice is hoarse with the remaking.

'Real enough,' you say, pressing another kiss to his neck, hands creeping down to his waist, feeling the warmth of him. 'And if this is some vision, I've no wish to wake from it.'

'Nor I,' he says, and his smile is familiar and new all at once. His hands are hesitant as they trail across your skin, but it's not uncertainty: it's wonder. Bisclavret has been so long robbed of his hands.

The thought makes you interlace your fingers with his, lifting your joined hands to kiss his wrist.

You say, 'I missed you.'

And he who was there says, 'I know.'

He knows everything about you. You've never been laid so bare. 'I mourned you,' you tell him, even though he knows. 'I grieved. I was lost in it. I thought the loss of you would never stop hurting.'

'I'm here now.' He's all angles, worn thin with all that the wolf stole from him. His bones press through his skin, fierce enough to cut you open, but you'd gladly bleed on that altar if it were the cost of holding him.

'Will you leave again?' you ask.

He stills. 'Perhaps,' he says at last. There's tension in his body that wasn't there before, and you regret asking. But he has more to say. 'The wolf,' he confesses, 'is not banished for good, but ... but I think I will be able to come back.'

You press yourself close against him, trying to dispel the thought of it. 'I'll be here when you do,' you say, and it's the most solemn oath you've ever sworn. He will never wander exiled in the forest again.

He kisses you so carefully, his lips gentle as butterfly wings against your neck. In that kiss is all the softness of a man who was shaped for teeth and claws against his own nature.

You say, 'If I undress you, will you lose yourself?'

His answer is a long time coming. When he eventually speaks, his lips are so close to your skin that you can feel them, trailing feather-light across your neck as he shapes the words with warm breath. 'Not like this,' he says, 'not with you here to remember me.'

You remember him. You've already committed every plane of his body to memory. But you'll remind yourself of them again and again until he is branded indelibly into your mind. You'll whisper his nature to him, shape his name in kisses, bring him back with your touch over and over again.

You help him tug his clothes over his head, press kisses to his skin, resting your lips over his heart as though you can taste the beating of it. His ribs, his stomach, the ongoing miracle that is Bisclavret, alive, *here*, your mouth on his skin. You take your time, unfastening his braies, kissing the crook of his knee, his thighs, marking and memorising every inch of him with all the devotion of a pilgrim. And he is a saint, something holy in this, prayers manifest in living form. It is a sacrament you have been starving for.

His hands are in your hair again, tangling there, pulling you close; he drags his fingers across your scalp and around your neck. 'If I undress you,' he says, very softly, 'will you lose your-self?'

You close your eyes. Feel only his touch and the heat of him against you.

You say: 'Willingly.'

And you let him unmake you, touch by touch, and all you can say is his name, first as a murmur and then as a gasp.

Bisclavret.

And he is so human, and so alive.

Epilogue

Him

＊✳＊

Bisclavret is human.

Every morning he wakes and thinks: this is it. Today will be the day he loses himself again. The dread of the change haunts him, no matter how often the king reminds him that he's safe, his lands restored to him and his wife and cousin banished to an even more distant exile than that which once kept him from the world. They cannot hurt him further, and he will not be cast out for what he is.

Nothing, his king promises, can change this.

This: waking in the king's bed. *This:* soft kisses that feel like promises, that knit together all the small wounds left weeping after his two years away from himself. *This:* being held, being known, being loved.

These days, when the king's gaze shears through his mask and down to the truth of him, he doesn't shudder away from it, for he has been witnessed in his monstrosity and still – *still* this man whispers his name with love, unafraid of the worst of him. Bisclavret isn't sure when he stopped hiding, or when that affection ceased to be something to shy from. Maybe when he saw the king on his knees, praying for his soul. It's not the same as the love his wife gave to him, to Bisclavret-the-man; this is a love that knows he is always already Bisclavret-the-wolf, somewhere beneath his skin. His king sees him for who and what he is, and has not walked away.

He's done nothing to deserve this. But he'll cling to it anyway with both hands and he will not let it go.

Over time, he comes to think that perhaps the wolf in him is exorcised after all. Perhaps he has finally done his penance and freed himself of the curse, those long months a scourge cleansing him of sin. Perhaps the king is blessed with a healing touch. It's been so long since he felt the wolf stir in his blood, it's almost as though he's human. Human, and no longer alone.

When the change comes, it rips through him so violently he hardly has time to catch his breath.

He remembers little of the night. It's hard to recall how he got out of the castle, but he must have done, for he finds himself in the king's forest shortly after dawn, wracked by spasms with the threat of the shift ever-present, naked and unstable. His breath gathers in sobs in his throat. He is still wolf. Still lost.

Of course none of this could last.

And his clothes – he has no clothes here. Those he was wearing yesterday must be rags by now, torn when his body threw him out of his skin so fast he had no chance to undress. He senses the chains of wolf-form tightening around him, threatening to steal him for a season, a year, the rest of his life, and he wants to scream with the unfairness of it. He thought this was over. He thought he was cured. Why isn't he cured?

He staggers to the edge of the forest without knowing how he'll get home, naked as he is, and stops short when he sees the figure standing there.

The king.

His king.

He doesn't look surprised to see Bisclavret. He has a bundle in his arms: clothes. Bisclavret is unfairly reminded of another

338

man who once brought him garments when he was lost among the trees, and the pang of remembering his cousin's betrayal is an unwelcome bitterness too slowly pushed aside by relief at his rescue. It is a hurt he has not healed from.

The king steps forward, unafraid, and says, 'I brought you these.'

Bisclavret reaches out to take them, but his shaking hands send them tumbling to the earth, and he's clumsy and slow as he bends to gather them. The king kneels and picks them up, gently brushing away the dirt, and then he helps Bisclavret to dress with careful tenderness.

His bones settle with every touch, the cloth and the king's fingers like thread stitching him back together. *Human.*

The wolf inside him subsides – neither dead nor gone, but sleeping, for now.

Soon Bisclavret is clothed, and the shaking lessens, his trembling limbs stilled.

'I told you I'd be here when you came back,' says the king. 'But that was wrong of me. I should have told you that I'd come and find you.' His lips are soft and taste of truth. 'I will always come and find you.'

He interlaces their fingers, the miracle of hands as astounding as ever, the miracle of affection more so. Bisclavret looks down at them and feels the hot sting of tears, a tightness in his chest born of some unnameable emotion no wolf has ever been capable of feeling. It washes through him in a wave, as bright as hope and as deep as grief.

He says, 'I am already found.'

Because he is human, for now, and he is loved, regardless, and that is enough.

Acknowledgments

I will be eternally grateful to my agent, Jessica Hare, who didn't flinch when, after signing me for a YA thriller with sparse third person present narration and zero romance, she found this in her inbox. Nor did she discourage me when I proposed rewriting sections of it in verse, though many would have done. I'm very thankful for that trust, and the perseverance it took for this book to find its home. Enormous thanks are, of course, owed to Bethan Morgan for *giving* this book its home, and doing it so enthusiastically, and with so much patience for my endless explanatory comments. A lesser editor might well have given up there and then upon seeing the essays I wrote in the margins of this novel, but Bethan was as much into the romance (medieval) of this novel as the romance (modern) – or at least good at pretending she was. Further thanks to the whole of the rest of the team at Gollancz, and to Tom Roberts for the fabulous cover illustration.

This book would not be the book that it is without the contributions of its first reader, Emmet, who not only watched me write parts of the first draft, but was also invaluable to the research process. Eleanor, my heresy reader, played an essential role in weeding out accidental Protestantism and contributing a 'sexy little antiphon' here and there; I relied heavily on her help with the Latin, as I have none of my own (any mistakes are, of course, mine). I am also exceedingly grateful to my other early readers: Brigid, who correctly deduced that there was something odd going on with the scribe; Cristin, who has long inspired me to get weird with verse; Caspian, my most long-suffering reader who is always down to yell about things; and Emily, the designated non-medievalist who helped ensure I didn't stray so far down academic paths that the book became incomprehensible.

It's a strange thing to write a novel so intimately connected to your academic research, and I owe thanks to a number of academic colleagues and teachers. First of all, *The Wolf and His King* would likely not exist without Blake Gutt, who set me an essay on queer readings of Marie de France when I was an undergrad taking a medieval French literature paper. Are the lais of Marie de France 'essentially queer'? I don't know what I would write if I were to tackle such an essay now, but I know I've a reading of Bisclavret to contribute, and several years of work in the fields of queer and gender theory that I can attribute to that starting point. I am grateful also to Bill Burgwinkle, another of my supervisors for that paper, whose work on queer approaches to medieval French literature sparked many of the connections in my own readings, and to Miranda Griffin, whose lectures on bodies, boundaries, and breaking-points in medieval French literature were the highlight of the first year of my PhD. My understandings of knighthood, masculinity, and monstrosity have been indelibly shaped by Jeffrey Jerome Cohen, although we have never met; the threads of his work no doubt run through this novel, some more obvious than others.

I also owe a debt to all who have supported my more in-depth study of medieval *Irish* literature, my true specialism: Máire Ní Mhaonaigh, Kevin Murray, Mark Williams, Emma

Nic Cárthaigh, Caitríona Ó Dochartaigh, John Carey, and others. Aspects of this book were heavily influenced by the palaeography and codicology course I took with Caitríona during my MA, and the attention lavished on the king's scribe can be attributed to the fact that I rewrote this book when I was supposed to be revising for an exam on manuscript production. (I'm devastated to report that the exam involved fewer sexy encounters between a king and his scribe-with-benefits.)

Endless thank-yous are owed to the 2022 Debut Stars, aka Strap In Patricia, who eased my entry into the world of publishing and put up with a great deal of unrelated complaining. In particular, I must thank Ann Sei Lin, because it was at the book launch for *Rebel Skies* that I first met Bethan. Without that chance meeting, this book would not be in your hands. Likewise, I will never not be glad of Write Club, for years of encouragement, sprints, and snippets.

Further group chat thanks are owed to the Muddle Ages, my favourite medievalist meme goblins who inspire my creativity and aid my research; Gasbags & Gondolas; the Celtic Tearooms; and the Virtual London Tea Rooms. Thank you likewise to all the readers, booksellers and librarians who read and championed *The Butterfly Assassin* trilogy, and to everybody who has been putting up with me on social media or in person for the last however many years. I am particularly grateful to my Tumblr followers for their enthusiasm and their willingness to tolerate incredibly niche info-dumping about my research. I know many of you have been waiting for my Bisclavret novel for years, and now here we are.

And to my family, for all their support over the years. Finally, Mum, I've written one that you're allowed to read! Though if you could skip the sex scenes, that would be great.

Credits

Finn Longman and Gollancz would like to thank everyone at Orion who worked on the publication of *The Wolf and His King*.

Editorial
Bethan Morgan
Zakirah Alam

Copy-editor
Andy Ryan

Proofreader
Jamie Groves

Editorial Management
Jane Hughes
Charlie Panayiotou
Lucy Bilton

Audio
Paul Stark
Louise Richardson
Georgina Cutler

Contracts
Dan Herron
Ellie Bowker
Oliver Chacón

Design
Nick Shah
Rachel Lancaster
Deborah Francois
Helen Ewing

Finance
Nick Gibson
Jasdip Nandra
Sue Baker
Tom Costello

Marketing
Ellie Nightingale

Inventory
Jo Jacobs
Dan Stevens

Production
Paul Hussey
Katie Horrocks

Publicity
Jenna Petts

Sales
David Murphy
Victoria Laws
Esther Waters
Karin Burnik

Anne-Katrine Buch
Frances Doyle
Group Sales teams across
    Digital, Field, International
    and Non-Trade

Operations
Group Sales Operations team

Rights
Rebecca Folland
Tara Hiatt
Ben Fowler
Alice Cottrell
Ruth Blakemore
Marie Henckel

BRINGING NEWS FROM OUR WORLDS TO YOURS . . .

Want hot-off-the-press info about the latest and greatest SFF releases?

Look no further than the Gollancz newsletter! Your one-stop shop for news, updates, discounts and exclusive giveaways.

Sign up now:

@gollancz